VERA AT THE BALLROOM
HISTORICAL REGENCY ROMANCE NOVEL

BELLES OF THE BALL
BOOK ONE

ABBY AYLES

This is a work of fiction.

Names, characters, organizations, places, events, and incidents are either products of the author's imagination or are used fictitiously. Any resemblance to actual person, living or dead, or actual events is purely coincidental.

Copyright © 2023 by Abby Ayles

All rights reserved.

No part of this book may be reproduced in any form or by any electronic or mechanical means, including information storage and retrieval systems, without written permission from the author, except for the use of brief quotations in a book review.

PRAISE FOR ABBY AYLES

Abby Ayles has been such an inspiration for me! I haven't missed any of her novels and she has never failed my expectations!

-Edith Byrd

The characters in this novel have surely touched my heart.

Linda C - "Melting a Duke's Winter Heart" 5.0 out of 5 stars Reviewed in the United States on December 21, 2019

This book kept me on the edge of my seat and I could not put it down.

Wendy Ferreira - "The Odd Mystery of the Cursed Duke" 5.0 out of 5 stars Reviewed in the United States on April 13, 2019

Oh this was a wonderful story and Abby has done it again! This storyline was perfect and the characters were developed and just had you reading to see if they get their happily ever after!

- Marilyn Smith - "Inconveniently Betrothed to an Earl" 5.0 out of 5 stars Reviewed in the United States on April 8, 2020

The sweetest story, with we rest abounding! I especially liked the bonus scene - totally unexpected engagements. Well written with realistic characters. Thank you!

Janet Tonole - "The Lady Of the Lighthouse" 5.0 out of 5 stars Reviewed in the United States on December 27, 2022

I just finished reading Abby Ayles' The Lady's Gamble and its bonus scene, and I wanted to tell other readers about this great story. I love regency romances and I believe Abby is one of the best regency writers out there!

Carolynn Padgett - "The Lady's Gamble" 5.0 out of 5 stars Reviewed in the United States on March 16, 2018

Such a great Book! So enjoyed the characters….they felt so " real"….and loved the " deleted" scene. Thanks Abby, for your gift of writing the best stories!

Marcia Reckard - "Entangled with the Duke" 5.0 out of 5 stars Reviewed in the United States on May 22, 2021

I loved this story. It took you through all of the exciting ups and downs. The characters were so honest. I could read it again and again.

Peggy Murphy - "The Duke's Rebellious Daughter" 5.0 out of 5 starsReviewed in the United States on December 3, 2022

I am never disappointed when reading one of Ms. Ayles stories. They have strong characters, engaging storylines, and all-around wonderful stories.

Donna L - "A Loving Duke for the Shy Duchess" 5.0 out of 5 stars Reviewed in the United States on December 23, 2019

A thoroughly enjoyable read! Love the complexity of the intelligent characters! They have the ability to feel emotions deeply! Their backstories help to explain why they behave as they do! The subplots and various interactions between characters add to the wonderful richness of the story! Well done!

Terry Rose Bailey - "A Cinderella for the Duke" 5.0 out of 5 stars Reviewed in the United States on October 8, 2022

Vera at the Ballroom

PROLOGUE

The corridors of Welwick Hall, on the Bodmin Estate, were long and winding, as well as cold and damp for some of the lesser unused ones. If one didn't know where one was going, one might happen to lose oneself. But the three children sneaking along its passageways knew exactly where they were heading: the library.

Oscar led the way and had insisted that Vera stay in the middle, between the boys, as they tread with great care not to be heard. It meant that Vera's twin brother, Silas, was at the rear. She had to admit that she liked Oscar's idea of putting her in the middle, in between two people who she loved most dearly.

All three children were ten years old, all born in the same year, all born at Welwick Hall. But the twins were born in a small room in the large attic. This was where the residency of the servants was situated, of which there were many for such a large manor house. For Oscar, Vera knew that he had been born in a huge four-poster bed, because he had shown them it several times.

Nothing excited the children more than evading the adults who scolded the twins for daring to play with His Grace's son. Vera was well aware of what Oscar's father, the Duke of Cornwall, thought of his son playing with the servant's children. Yet this never stopped Oscar from seeking them out.

He was like another brother to her, and she'd feel sad if they didn't play together. In fact, Oscar was the one who came up with places for them to meet up because he usually knew the whereabouts of his father. They did everything they could to remain undetected. Not that Oscar's mother minded; all she wanted was for her son to be happy.

As they arrived at the huge double doors that opened up into the enormous library, Silas called out from the back.

"It's a bit of a risk considering your father's home, Oscar," he said in a low voice as the children huddled together in the hallway.

"He'd never think to find us here," Oscar said, determined to get into the library, for he knew that it was Vera's favourite room. "He has no idea that I have taught you both to read and write, he thinks you ignorant, remember?"

"Yes, but if we are caught, it will be Vera and me that will get the punishment dished out," Silas reminded him. "The last time he locked us in our room for a whole day."

"Stop being so soft," Vera said, poking her brother's arm with her finger, teasingly.

"Ouch! Stop doing that," Silas growled. Vera knew that he wouldn't poke her back because he never did anything to hurt her. Considering he was a boy, she was far tougher than him, and always happy to take risks, if it meant having fun with Oscar.

"Then stop acting like a baby," she teased again. "I want to see the books; I love books and well you know it."

Oscar opened one of the doors, and turned to Silas, "I promise if we are caught, I will make sure that Father does not punish you harshly.

Silas mumbled to himself, still carrying a look of worry on his face, but Vera pushed him through the door. When it came to books, she would risk anything because a good book was always worth the risk.

Oscar was the first to grab a book from a shelf at random because that was how they played their game. Whatever book was chosen at random, was the book they would read together. Silas and Vera went to hide underneath one of three long tables set up in the library. It was where they always hid when they managed to sneak into the library.

When Oscar joined them under the table, Vera was the first to speak, "What book is it?" she asked, keen to know if it was going to be a good one. Not that there was a book in the world that she wouldn't enjoy.

"It's called *Twelfth Night*, by William Shakespeare," Oscar read the title as he tilted the book. "Ah…it's a play."

"I love Shakespeare," Vera said, wondering if Oscar knew that the shelf held all the Shakespeare books and so had chosen it on purpose. "Let's get started…and stop fidgeting Silas, I want to listen to Oscar reading."

Silas moved around, peeking out from under the table to check the door.

"I know this story, we have read it before," Vera shared. "It is about a woman who dresses up as a man. The odd thing is that another woman falls in love with her."

Even Silas giggled at that because it was such a funny story, all three children were tickled by the concept.

Oscar began. "*O, when mine eyes did see Olive first, me thought she purged the air of pestilence! That instant was I turned into a hart—*"

"Wait, wait…" Vera interrupted him by taking hold of the arm that held the book. "As it's a play, we can all read different parts. But I must be Viola, and Silas can play my brother, Sebastian."

"I don't want to read out loud, we will be heard," Silas snapped, for he could not stop his worrying. "Our mother will be in trouble too, and she can't afford for the Duke to send us all away."

Vera turned to her brother, "Don't be silly, who will cook for the Duke if they send Mother away?"

"If Silas is so worried then we should leave," Oscar suggested, looking at her brother. He could see from his expression that poor Silas was fretting.

"Then you will get to miss playing Duke Orsino's part, and you know that's a great part to play," Vera said, attempting to entice Oscar onto her side of thinking.

"That means I get to marry you," Oscar said with a big, cheeky grin.

Vera nodded with the excitement that she had at least won Oscar over, now she needed to work on her brother. "I tell you what, let's skip to scene 4, where Viola is disguised as a man and the Duke believes her masquerade."

"I suppose it will cut our time in the library short," Silas nodded as he agreed.

"Now then, don't be laughing at me because I'm going to read with a deep voice, and that's because I'm pretending to be a man," she said, looking at the two boys with a perfectly serious glare. *"I'll do my best to woo your lady—"*

Without warning, the library door burst open, "Come out from under there, all three of you!" the Duke's voice boomed.

They looked at one another with growing dread, Silas seemed the worst, with a terrible fear etched on his face.

"Don't worry so," Oscar assured him, and he made to climb from under the table first. The twins followed close behind him.

"How dare you, Oscar?" his father said to his son, throwing his arms up in the air. "I do not want you associating yourself with the children of the servants. Now go to your room until dinner is served." The Duke turned to the twins, "You two do not belong in this part of the house. Ah, Barker, there you are," he said as he looked over at the house butler.

Vera watched as the stuffy butler came toward them. She turned her face to her brother, rolling her eyes at the butler's presence. His face was red with fury but that didn't frighten her, not one bit.

"Barker, return these children to the kitchen. Ask their mother to find them some work to keep them occupied," the Duke ordered, turned, and marched away.

Both children knew what was coming next. Barker grabbed hold of their ears and twisted them in his fingers. Silas yelped but Vera made no sound at all. She would never let the butler know that he had hurt her, it would give him too much pleasure. He then let go of their ears and grabbed each one of their arms, dragging them as his fingers dug into their skin.

"I ought to give the pair of you a good hiding," he told them in a stern voice. "You never do as you're told. You're a pair of scoundrels, that's what you are. Wait until I see your mother."

Somehow, he managed to keep his firm grip on their arms all the way through the large house, and down into the kitchens. There, he threw them to the cold floor, right in front of their shocked mother.

"I do not take kindly to finding your offspring on the loose about the house," he called out. "Give them some work of the hardest kind, immediately, or you will all find yourselves homeless!"

As he was leaving, Silas scowled at him, his anger finally stirring. "How dare he talk to you in that way, Mother? He's only a servant of the house too!"

"Sshh... I'll be having no cheek from the likes of you two. Now get out to the well and fetch me six buckets of water. I need to get it on the boil," she instructed them.

"But the buckets are too heavy for Vera," Silas complained.

"Nonsense, it serves her right," his mother said, pursing her lips. "If I know my daughter, she's likely the one who got you into trouble in the first place."

With miserable-looking faces, the twins turned to leave

through the back door, heading for the well. Fetching water was usually a job for one of the bigger boys.

"You can fill the buckets in the well, and I'll carry them back to the kitchen," Silas suggested to his sister, so that she didn't have to carry them.

"I might be a girl, but I can manage the buckets just as well as you can," she scolded "Oh dear, I... I'm sorry Silas, I didn't mean to shout. But I can carry my share and Mother was right, it was my fault. In the future, I'm going to listen to you more often."

"In the future, I'll be big and strong, and I'll protect you better from the likes of Barker," Silas promised her.

"Nah... He's harmless enough. He can be kind to us when he wants to be. Remember at Christmas, when he always gets a gift for us?" she grinned. "But he's the head of the household so he has to tell us off. If you ask me, I do believe that he likes us really."

With that proclamation, the twins got on with their task, between them they made a vow never to get caught again.

CHAPTER 1

15 YEARS LATER...

The new Duke of Cornwall walked the corridors of Welwick Hall as he approached the library. It was a corridor that held many memories for him, but the library held even more, and most of them were good ones. How he missed his childhood. With all the new responsibilities of running the Bodmin Estate, he carried a heavy load on his shoulders.

Oscar opened one of the double doors and entered the library, making straight for the shelves that held tutorial books on business. It was his hope that if he studied hard enough, he might be able to run the estate as well as his father had before him. As he stood in front of the shelves that towered to the ceiling, he felt a tinge of pride. Before him were all the books that his father had collected over a lifetime. Reaching out his hand, he took hold of a black leather-bound volume.

Sitting at one of the large, oak tables, he stared back at the shelves. They held an array of red leather-bound books. Many boasting golden letters with grand titles of Greek mythology, and philosophers from ancient times. It was a magnificent collection, and they were now his responsibility.

A flash of a distant memory came to mind, of a little girl's smiling face. In his mind, he pictured the cheery features of his dear childhood friend, Vera. They had often sneaked into the library, and every time her eyes would light up with anticipation. She would look upon shelves that held the novels and boast about all the adventures contained within their pages. How she had loved this room.

But then he reminded himself that was so long ago, time had moved on and he was no longer that little boy. Now he was the master of his family's estate. His parents had been taken from him so suddenly, and much too soon. The whole affair was all too recent and still wrenched at his heart.

How they must have suffered that night. *Mother, you must have been terrified, you could not even swim,* he pondered on their fate over and over in his mind.

The night was late. Far too late to be wandering around corridors and seeking books relating to business, but sleep would not come to him. Every time he closed his eyes he saw the image of a ship out at sea, on a dark and stormy night. His parents were standing upon a leaning deck as the ship sank into the enormous waves that swallowed all traces of them and the ship. It vanished into the cold, dark depths of the ocean.

Oscar rubbed his face with both hands as if the action might wipe away the image. But it was an impression that he could not rid his mind of. It was a recurring nightmare he had suffered every single night, ever since he had been told that his parents had drowned at sea.

His loving mother's face smiled back at him in his mind, how he missed her. Never again would he see her happy smile or hear his father's deep, baritone voice. His father was a man he had looked up to; he had been strict, but fair. For all that he had shown his son a severe hand, he had also shown his love.

Oscar jumped up from the chair and paced the room, growling to himself in frustration.

Why? Why? He mused, wishing the accident away. *There was no rhyme or reason for their deaths.*

He recalled how, on the day of their departure, he had waved them from the docks as they headed to France feeling happy with life.

And now, I am never able to see you, ever again.

Life felt so unfair!

How am I to run the estate on my own?

Becoming the Duke of Cornwall was a huge responsibility. One that he had not expected to shoulder for at least another ten years or so.

As he paced the dark, parquet library floor, he happened upon the Shakespeare shelf, and it caused him to pause. In front of his eyes, as if someone had pulled the book out a little for his attention, was the Twelfth Night.

"Ahhh...how many times have we enacted this play," he said aloud as a wave of nostalgia swept over him, followed by a feeling of deep fondness at the title. "And how many times have I married you, Vera?" he chuckled. "How many times did Father find us playing together? Oh, Father, why did you have a problem with me playing with the servant's children?"

He realised that he was talking to himself, but if the servants should hear him, he was sure they would understand. They all knew that his grieving process was difficult and painful for him.

He went to sit at the table again, holding the book open to read its pages. The words gave him a warming sensation. They were words that he and his two best friends had read over and over again. The twins' faces came to his mind as he read, and he didn't notice the library door opening.

"Y... Your Grace?" a light voice questioned.

He looked up to see Vera standing in the open doorway as she held a tray, and he knew that she had to be wondering what he was laughing at.

"Come in, Vera, come on in," he waved an arm to welcome her. "You are free to use the library whenever you like now," he called over to her. "Mind you, I know that you have most likely read most of the novels in this collection," he said as he watched her carry the tray. "But fear not, we will add to the collections. Anyway, what are you doing up at this late hour?" he added as an afterthought.

"I could ask you the same question Oscar, I... I mean, Y... Your Grace," she stuttered, remembering her place.

"I do wish people would not call me that," Oscar said, putting down the book. "It is going to take some getting used to, on my part."

"I've brought you a hot mug of milky coco," she told him as she put down the tray. "I see that you're reading the Twelfth Night," she said, staring at the book.

"Sit with me awhile, Vera, please," Oscar said, patting the seat by his side. "Let us reminisce upon all the times we re-enacted the Shakespeare plays."

Vera smiled as she looked at Oscar's sky-blue eyes, "You look tired. Perhaps you should drink your hot milk and then try returning to your bed."

"My dear Vera, always mothering me," Oscar smiled back at Vera's petite frame. Her rosy cheeks seemed to be a permanent feature and had always warmed his heart. But his favourite part of her pretty face had to be her almond-shaped, deep brown eyes, lending her an almost oriental appearance. "I thank you for your concern, but my nightmares make sleep difficult."

"I know it's a wearisome time for you," Vera sympathised. "But if you don't get some rest, you'll make yourself ill."

"You are right, as always, but I was about to read the shipwreck scene in the Twelfth Night," he said, thinking he could read the tragedy better with Vera by his side.

"That's not a good idea, Oscar," she warned. "It would do you better to push such thoughts from your mind for now."

"I much prefer it when you call me by my name than my title," he told her, watching her closely. "Promise me that when we are alone, you will always do that."

"It would give your father a terrible fright if he were to hear me calling you by your name," Vera chortled.

"Ha...yes, it would indeed," Oscar agreed, enjoying sharing such memories with his friend. "It was right underneath this very table where he found the three of us, the first time we came across this book."

"I remember it well too. We were about to start the scene where I was dressed as a man, when his booming voice demanded we all get from under the table," Vera added. Though it gave her a shiver recollecting the Duke's strict ways.

"Yes, when you're only ten years old, his voice could be very scary," Oscar agreed, feeling more relaxed now, in Vera's company. "I am grateful that the three of us managed to remain good friends over the years. Even if Father did not approve."

"I am too. And I know that my brother treasures your friendship," Vera agreed. But then a cold chill caused her to shiver. She noticed, in her peripheral view, that a figure was standing in the open doorway.

A tall silhouette filled the open space, making her body jolt at the sudden sight.

"What is it, Vera?" Oscar asked upon seeing her body jerk in her chair. Almost simultaneously, he spotted the figure too.

"It is not appropriate for you to be alone with His Grace," Barker's voice filled the air with disdain. "My apologies, Your Grace," he added in a softer tone. "The servants should know their places. Please, Atkins, go to your room."

Vera said nothing, but she knew the butler was right, it was inappropriate to be alone with Oscar, even though they were lifelong friends. She stood up and went to exit the room, under Barker's cold glare. He had left her only a small gap in the doorway, but she was petite enough to squeeze by him.

"Careful, Barker, you might have steam coming from your ears soon," she teased, knowing her comment would rile him even further.

Oscar smiled to himself; Vera was as defiant as ever, and he covered his mouth with a hand to hide his smile from the butler.

As she disappeared, he remarked, "Barker, it is not a good idea to be scolding our cook. You should soften your mood a little in your old age."

"Your father would disapprove of your being alone with a female, let alone a female servant, if I may advise Your Grace," Barker reminded him. "Certain servants will always try to act above their station, and it is my job to remind them of their place."

With that, Barker bowed and then turned to walk away from the doorway, leaving Oscar alone once again. The incident served to remind Oscar of his deep responsibilities. It was a role forced upon him, and a role whereby he should be the one putting the servants in their places too.

That's what I should have done with Barker, yet it felt so wrong. The butler was a man who'd always reminded him of his father. It simply didn't seem right to order his butler around. They had never shared a close relationship, but he was very fond of Barker. Then again, he had always been the one to punish the twins whenever they had been caught playing together.

Yet, he sighed, *it was indeed all so long ago, even though it feels like only yesterday.*

Much had happened in the years since then. The twin's mother had passed away with a deadly fever. Vera had become the head cook of the manor house, and Silas was now his valet. Although he no longer spent leisure time with his childhood friends, they were still ever-present in his life. He sought Silas's advice many a day and enjoyed Vera's cooking expertise daily. She was every bit as talented as her mother when it came to good food, her mother had taught her well.

Looking back at the book, he opened the contents page to scan the scenes. Fingering the pages, he searched for the scene where Orsino and Viola agree to marry. The words stirred his emotions, yet again. He had often fantasised about marrying Vera as they had acted out the scene. Imagine if his father had known his little secret, but then again, they were only children after all.

CHAPTER 2

The former Countess of Gosmore, Lady Olive Brent, had moved out of the Gosmore estate after the death of her husband over a year ago. The earldom had passed on to his oldest son and heir, a son from a previous marriage of his. She felt it appropriate to move out of the Gosmore estate to allow him and his family to move in. Her husband had left her a generous property known as Silsbury Manor. He had also left her a lump sum which worked out as an average income for many years to come. In her mind, it had been generous of him considering they had only been married for three months.

But it had never been enough for her mother. Lady Adelia Smith was always pushing her daughter to marry for more wealth. Olive had thought the battle with her mother had been won when she married Lord Jonathan Brent, the Earl of Gosmore. Though he had been quite old when they wed. And now that he was gone, her mother was pushing her to find a new, wealthy husband again.

It was quite late in the evening, and Olive was sitting brushing her long blonde locks as she stared into her own green eyes in the mirror. She had drifted off into a blissful daze, contemplating her situation as she recalled the day of the funeral.

She had been peering out of the window of the black funeral carriage. It had been a dull, grey day and the cold rain had lashed against the pain of glass.

"It is most inconvenient to hold a funeral on such a wet day," her mother had complained, seated by her side. "One supposes that the new Earl will be glad of his father's death. Goodness knows, he's inherited enough of the old man's wealth, and hardly a farthing for you, his wife."

"Mother, please," Olive had spoken up. "Is it not enough that you at least have a roof over your head? And my late husband left me a comfortable income, so you should be more respectful."

The carriage had rocked from side to side as it hit a bump, juddering Olive's nerves. Or perhaps she had been growling with contempt at her mother's attitude.

"He has left you an income that will not sustain what you have grown used to," her mother had snapped in her usual manner. "I will catch my death in this weather. I should have remained in the carriage instead of getting soaked for the likes of a husband who has all but abandoned my daughter."

"Might I remind you, Mother, that you were the one who pressured me into marrying the Earl," Olive had raised the issue. "He was already an old man and suffering from ailments of ageing. We had only been married but three months."

"You devoted every moment of your marriage to his comforts," her mother had insisted. "Never taking any time for yourself. And this is the thanks he gives you."

"Silsbury Manor is a beautiful house," Olive had stated, annoyed at her mother's persistent moaning. "As far as I am concerned, £700 per annum is more than enough for us both to live in comfort."

"We can barely keep a carriage with that income," her mother had whined, relentless in her discontent. "You were entitled to far more than they gave you, and you know it."

"I do not care, Mother!" Olive had called out yet again; her voice raised in frustration.

"Don't you shout at your mother!" her mother had snapped back.

"Then can we not have some silence for the rest of the journey home, Mother?" Olive had pleaded. "I have only this day buried my husband; can you not allow me some time to grieve?"

Her request seemed to have worked as her mother simply tutted at her, but she did remain silent from that point.

It had always niggled Olive because she had felt little, if any, sadness whatsoever over the death of her husband. This was still causing her a great deal of guilt. She had been lucky that her kind husband had left her anything at all.

He had been a kind soul, having lived alone since his first wife passed away twenty years ago. They had been introduced at a ball and he took a liking to her straight away. Of course, the introduction was all her mother's doing. Olive had liked the Earl, he had a sense of humour, for his age, though little in the way of energy. Most of the time she had spent with him, he had slept. Nor had he ever eaten much. She supposed he was already suffering an illness that he did not tell her about.

She read to him every night before bed. She took soup to him when he felt ill and entertained him with music when he was up and awake. Her mother had been right with that, she had spent a lot of time with him, but then he had not been awake that much.

Olive was fond of the house he had left her, Silsbury Manor. It wasn't a huge manor house, with only four bedrooms. But now they had fewer servants so they did not need as many rooms. They had a cook, who lived in the local village. They also had a couple of housemaids, who lived in the attic rooms of the house. And a groom for the small carriage they owned, who lived in the generous stable. Then there was the part-time gardener, who also lived elsewhere.

It didn't bother Olive that they had fewer servants, there were enough to do all that was required for two people. She would be happy with even less if it became necessary, but her mother constantly wanted more. Heaven forbid if they had to get rid of the carriage and horse, her mother would be mortified.

Snapping out of reverie, she looked at the light supper the maid had brought up to her room, recalling how annoyed her mother was with her for not attending dinner.

Her mother had immediately complained when she ordered a light supper in her room. She had insisted that the cook still prepare a full dinner for her, and she would eat in the dining room as *normal* people did.

Olive enjoyed the peaceful moments in her own room away from her mother. But when her mother entered her bedchamber, she sighed to herself, she was in no mood for her mother's ramblings. Getting up from the stool, she walked over to her bed, hoping her mother would take the hint that she was tired.

Getting into bed, she pulled up the blankets and sat up to read. Her mother surprised her when she approached the bed and started to tuck in Olive's blankets. She then proceeded to pull up a chair, to the side of the bed, and talk to her.

"A respectful period of a whole year's mourning has now passed us by. This is a good time to begin thinking about the need to remarry," she began.

"Mother, I am in no mood to discuss this. Nor do I desire another husband," Olive said, trying her best to remain calm and be kind to her mother. "Why do you worry so?"

"Hear me out, if you will," her mother continued, wagging her finger at her daughter to stop her from interrupting. "I have heard, along the way, that the Duke of Cornwall, Lord Oscar Wald, will be seeking a wife. He has now taken over the dukedom after his parents died at sea, oh, and he is young, handsome, and rich. What do you think of that then, my girl?"

"You want to know my true thoughts, Mother?" Olive asked with raised brows. "I feel very sorry for the Duke, that he is grieving his losses and I hope that you leave the poor man alone."

"Exactly my point," her mother squealed with delight. "It means that you both have a lot in common."

"I fail to see how you know if we have shared interests, Mother. We have never even met the man," Olive retorted, wishing her mother would give up and leave her in peace.

"You both understand the nature of grief," her mother explained. "That is enough to start a conversation. Think of it, Olive, marriage to a handsome, young man would be very pleasing, would it not?"

"I have no appetite for another husband," Olive tried again. "Let me get my strength back first before you go organising my life."

"There is little time to waste," her mother pushed, unwilling to accept defeat. "All the women of the ton will be chasing him. But none of them have your fortune in looks, and grace in demeanour. All the many talents that you possess impressed the Earl, so they will do so for a duke."

"I am very tired, Mother. Can we not discuss this another day?" she asked, and she knew that she looked pale as she had seen her dull reflection in the mirror.

"Yes, you do look a little peaky, but fear not, you will come around to my way of thinking, I know you will," her mother told her as she stood up to leave. "Get your beauty sleep for now. I want you to eat a full breakfast in the morning. You must keep up your strength for there is much work to be done. Leave it with me and I will sort out all the details of future meetings with the Duke."

Olive watched her mother leave and pitied the Duke if her mother was to get her claws into him. She was a tenacious little woman, petite, yet strong in willpower.

Sighing, she opened a poetry book to read by candlelight. Poems gave her so much solace with their arrangement of soothing words. She wanted to imagine running through a sunny meadow, not putting all her efforts into impressing some gentleman she had never met.

Opening a page with the named poet Charles Lamb, she read. *If you told me the world will be at an end tomorrow, I should just say, 'Will it?'* This was a poet who often made her chuckle, and she read on. *I have not volition enough left to dot my i's, much less to comb my eyebrows...*

The poem wasn't necessarily a cheery one, but the eloquence of Lamb's prose was unusual. It helped to take her mind away from other things. Soon her eyes felt heavy, and she was ready to lay her head on her soft pillow and enter the world of dreams. At least there, her mother hopefully would not haunt her.

CHAPTER 3

Silas was sitting with the other servants enjoying his breakfast, when his twin sister, Vera, came to sit by his side. He shuffled along the wooden bench to make room for her to squeeze between him and Lucy, one of the upstairs maids.

"Thank you, Lucy," she said to the maid. "I find myself in need of having a few words with my brother."

Silas was aware that Lucy had a crush on him, and she would not give up her seat lightly, that was why he'd been the one to move along.

Vera turned to talk in a quiet voice, which wasn't easy with all the chatter going on around them. Servant mealtimes were a welcome time in Welwick Hall, one of the few times that they got together to enjoy each other's company. Much of their chatter would be gossip, informing each other what they had heard upstairs, or from other servants on other estates.

"Listen, Silas," Vera began as he leaned into her to keep their conversation to themselves. "I'm worried about Oscar; he's suffering terrible nightmares and not getting much sleep. Have you noticed anything odd about his behaviour?"

"He's hurting bad, from his sudden losses, I can tell you that much," Silas nodded, though he didn't feel over concerned. "But I wouldn't call that odd. I do try to cheer him, but I remember how we felt when Ma died, and it wasn't good."

Vera nodded her agreement, "I'm more worried about his health due to lack of sleep. I heard him stir in the early hours of the morning when I was on bread duty in the kitchens. I guessed where he'd gone to and I was right, he was in the library."

"Yes, so I've heard," Silas smiled. "Word soon spread that Barker caught you both alone."

"Oh, for goodness' sake! I was taking him some hot milk to help him sleep is all," Vera sighed, glancing down the long table at the other servants. Gossip was always ripe among them, "You'd think they'd have better things to talk about," she added.

"You know what, Sis, it's my opinion that we shouldn't tiptoe around Oscar," Silas said. "Otherwise, he'll never get back to being normal. I mean, we should give him his space, and allow time to grieve and be sad, but not pity him. That's the last thing he needs."

His sister looked at him a little surprised as she flashed him a scowl, "We must pity him, Silas. Poor Oscar will be feeling all alone in the world, and he isn't. He has us, and I want you to tell him that, do you hear?"

Silas didn't feel like a lecture from his sister and jumped up from the bench. With one leg on either side of it, he reached over to the bread bowl and took out a fresh bread roll. "I thought this morning's bread was Isabelle's doing, it always tastes nicer than yours," he joked to rile her up.

"You cheeky…where do you think you are going?" his sister asked, looking up at him as he pulled out his other leg to climb off the bench. "We haven't finished yet."

"I'm escaping before you give me any more sermons," he smiled. Turning around he hopped away and marched out of the kitchen towards the servant's stairway.

Once at the top of the back stairway, Silas headed towards the reception hall. He always went there first to collect any letters for his master, where Barker would leave them. Today though, the butler was still around, sifting through the post.

When Silas was younger, the old butler used to frighten him silly. All the younger servants were still afraid of him. For many years though, he had held no fear for the man. Barker was one of those old men whose bark was worse than his bite, and what others didn't seem to see was how kind he could be too.

"Ah, Atkins, I want you to stress to that sister of yours how it is not right and proper to be alone with His Grace, do you hear?" Barker said with a sharpness to his tone.

"I am sure that your reprimand, when you caught her, should have been more than enough to make it clear," Silas replied, taking Oscar's post out of his hand.

"You know that she threatens her position in the household when she cannot follow simple rules," Barker tried again.

"If you say so," Silas sang out as he walked away from the grumpy butler of the house.

Silas had every respect for Barker, but when it came to his usual threats, he tended to ignore the old man. Oscar would never allow him to dismiss Vera, so Barker was fooling no one when he threatened her job.

He climbed the huge, grand staircase that rose in the centre of the large hall and headed towards Oscar's chambers. Oscar had remained in his old suite of rooms, not wanting to move into his parent's larger rooms after their deaths.

Silas reflected on how Oscar should be awake by now, Lucy having delivered his breakfast tray over an hour ago. Yet, when he opened the door, the heavy drapes were still drawn and kept the room in darkness.

Marching over to the windows to open the curtains, he called out in a cheerful voice, "Good Morning, Your Grace."

As he turned towards the bed where Oscar lay, he noticed how rough his friend, and master, looked.

"You haven't touched any breakfast," Silas pointed out. "Vera will be most insulted if you don't eat her food," he joked as he picked up the tray. "I'm going to get you some warm water to wash, Your Grace," he said before leaving the room.

Heading back down to the kitchen, he swapped the tray for a jug of hot water, as he did every morning. But when he returned to Oscar's room, he was still in bed.

"Your Grace, are we not to begin this wonderful day?" Silas sang out again, pouring the hot water into a large, blue decorative ceramic bowl.

"Do not start with any lectures, Silas, you sound like your sister," Oscar groaned. "And stop calling me by my title when we are alone. I don't wish to get up today."

"Nay, I must call you by your title now that you are the duke of the estate," Silas told him, pulling his covers down to his waist. "Come now, Your Grace, let's begin your day, for the world awaits your presence."

"When I am awake, I do nothing but think of my parents," Oscar told him, making the effort to get his legs out of the bed. "Why can't you simply leave me to my sleep? It took me long enough to drift off."

Silas was busy laying out Oscar's outfit for the day, pretending to ignore him, but he was pleased to see that he was making the effort to get out of his bed.

As Oscar started to splash water over his face, Silas passed him a thick towel to dry with. Within half an hour, Silas was performing his duties as a valet and ensuring that his master looked the part of a duke for the day.

Oscar stood in front of the long mirror while he allowed Silas to brush down his outfit, and Silas could see that his master was deep in thought. At that point, he stepped aside and went to get the silver tray that held the letters, handing the tray to his master.

"Heaven forbid that they are even more condolences," Oscar complained, breaking the seal from one of the folded pieces of paper. "Drat it! This is the last thing I need," Oscar declared as he read the letter.

"Is it bad news, Your Grace?" Silas asked, continuing to address his friend by his official title, as was only fitting.

"No, darn it, it's worse. It's an invitation to a garden party. Why can't they leave me alone? I would much prefer it that way," Oscar complained.

"Will you be attending, Your Grace?" Silas asked.

"No, I will not," Oscar replied with a sharp tone in his voice.

"The people who invite you are your friends, and they only wish to help you return some normality in your life," Silas said, putting on a brave face. "It would do you good to attend some social events, rather than sitting around Welwick Hall all alone, Your Grace."

"Has Vera asked you to say that to me?" Oscar asked, looking at Silas in amusement.

"She has spoken with me of her concerns for you, yes, Your Grace," Silas admitted. Though only because he wanted his friend to know that he and his sister still supported him. "And we have agreed that you should not drown in your sorrows alone. You are allowed to have some fun in your life, Your Grace. There will be many pretty ladies at a garden party, all of whom will want to pay you their attention, given your circumstances."

"Did you know that you and your sister have something particularly annoying in common?" Oscar said, straightening his jacket sleeve in the mirror. "You are both bossy."

"My apologies, Your Grace, but we only share our concerns for his lordship," Silas replied.

"No, no, Silas, it is me who should be apologising to you," Oscar came back at him. "You went through much the same when your mother passed away. I recall how the sadness tugged at both your hearts."

"Does that mean that you will listen to my advice?" Silas asked, hopeful.

"I suppose so, but I would hardly call a garden party fun though," Oscar grumbled back at him. "And the people who invite me are not my friends, not like our friendship of many years anyway. They merely wish to gawp at the new Duke of Cornwall."

"Perhaps not, but it will force you to mingle once again, Your Grace," Silas tried. "It will do you good to speak to others about your experiences. People are going to want to bring up the sadness in your life."

"You are quite right, Silas," Oscar said, softening to his friend's advice. "Though a good night's sleep before then would not go amiss."

"Yes, the whole house is abuzz at my sister bringing you hot milk in the library in the early hours of the morning," Silas informed his master.

"Is it? She won't like that, not if I know Vera," Oscar said, looking worried. "Is she terribly angry?"

"No, Your Grace, she is only concerned for your health," Silas said, giving his sister credit as it was the truth. He started to walk towards the door to open it for his master to leave.

"Will you join me on a stroll in the garden, Silas?" Oscar requested. "I could do with your companionship away from the ears of servants. I know that you are right, and I must stop being alone so much."

"Of course, Your Grace. It will be my pleasure," Silas replied, pleased that his friend was admitting that it was time to start socialising once again. He hoped that Oscar would accept the invitation to the garden party, and on his part, he would do all he could to ensure that he did.

CHAPTER 4

Vera could not believe the cheek of her brother. When she found him again, she would give him a piece of her mind. She felt it important for them to stick together in helping Oscar get through the difficult times and overcome his grief. He might be their master, but their friendship went much deeper than that.

Grief was something both she and her twin brother were familiar with. When they lost their mother to a fever a year ago, it had been a heart wrenching experience. She recalled how Barker had also been upset, for all the butler's airs and graces, he was a bit of a softie at heart.

For now, though, she was busy preparing the main meal of the day. There wasn't much cooking for upstairs, as there was only the Duke living there at present. There were still all twenty servants to feed though. She hoped that Oscar would not dismiss any of the servants. Welwick Hall was a large manor house and took a lot of care and attention to keep it spick and span.

Although she delegated many of the day-to-day tasks in the kitchen, she never trusted anyone with her sauces. Her mother had taught her that a sauce is the making of any meal, and she continued to practice that philosophy. Whilst stirring a meaty gravy, she noticed Barker entering her domain.

"Atkins, I must reiterate that you should never be alone with His Grace," he rumbled as he came to stand by her side.

Taking a small spoon, she scooped up a little gravy and handed it to him to taste. Barker did so, promptly shouting out as he burned his tongue.

"Ouch! I shan't be able to taste for a week now," he complained, handing her the spoon back again.

"Didn't your mother ever teach you to blow on hot food?" she teased, as she had done it intentionally, to shut him up.

"Stop your trickery and listen to me, will you," he said in a quieter voice, following her around her kitchen as she went off to do various tasks. "I know it's not particularly a rule for commoners, but for the nobility, it is considered a scandal if a lady is alone with a gentleman."

"Like you said, I'm a commoner so it doesn't apply to me," she sang out, walking away from him.

But he would not relent, and he continued to shadow her in the kitchen. "I know that you don't want His Grace involved in any gossip, equally as much I don't. You cannot communicate with him as if he were one of your own. He is a duke, and you must accept that and understand your role, as well as his."

"Well…you know what you can do with your orders, Barker," she retorted. "He is my friend, and he is all alone with his grief. I will continue to help him while ever I see him suffering."

"Don't go around saying that the Duke of Cornwall is your friend," Barker retorted back to her.

"Get out of my kitchen, Barker," she called out loud enough for everyone in the kitchen to hear. Many faces turned their way at the raised voices. "You have no role in my kitchen."

As she went to get something from the cold pantry, she was pleased to see the back of him as he marched off grumbling to himself.

"Cranky old man," she said to Frances, the scullery maid. Frances was a small, skinny, little shy thing, but she giggled at the comment.

"Is it safe to come out yet?" she called out to the kitchen maids, and they all laughed as the two of them exited the pantry. "Alright, let's be getting our dishes cooked. We don't stop for no man."

Although she got on with her tasks of the day, she couldn't stop worrying about Oscar. Becoming the duke would have huge implications for him. He had been in the process of learning how to run the estate, but it was a lot of responsibility on top of his grief. She knew the estate manager, Connor McIntyre was a good man, and good at his job too and he would be a godsend for Oscar. Connor had worked on the estate for fifty-odd years, if anyone knew about the running of the estate, it would be him.

She would get Silas to speak with Connor because he was a bit of a recluse. He needed to be advising Oscar at the earliest opportunity because her friend wasn't thinking straight. Again, she recalled the death of her mother and how she was inconsolable for such a long time. Losing someone you love was very painful, and poor Oscar had lost two people with whom he had been very close.

∽

At last, the working day was almost over, and it was time for the servants to have their dinner. Leaving the serving of the food to lesser maids in the kitchen, she went to join her brother at the long table.

She said nothing to him when he looked at her suspiciously, allowing him to enjoy his dinner first. But as the other servants started to leave the table, she asked him to stay on.

"How has Oscar been today?" she asked, once they were alone.

"I'd say he's had a good day," Silas nodded thoughtfully. "He asked me to spend most of it with him. We went riding, which always eases a man's soul."

"So, you think he's coming to terms with his grief?" she pushed for better answers.

"At times I found him a bit withdrawn," Silas said, being honest with his sister. It wasn't worth lying to her because she could always tell when he did that. "I don't think it's all about the grief that's a problem, he's more worried about running the estate by himself."

To this remark Vera huffed, "He's more than capable of doing it, but I suppose he's lost some of his cocky confidence. I want you to get Connor to speak with him."

"That's a good idea, Sis, I'll do that. Don't know why none of us thought of it earlier," Silas agreed. "I also talked him into going to a social event. You know…so that he'll start mixing with his own kind again."

"And has he agreed to go?" she asked, half-expecting him to say no.

"Aye, well…he doesn't want to, but I've badgered him all day about it. He finally seemed to agree" Silas said, looking pleased with himself.

Vera breathed a sigh of relief as she leaned her elbows on the table and put her head in her hands. Rubbing at her hair dark, brunette head of curls, she moved a few strands of hair fell that from the tight bun she wore when working. She then blew them off her smooth face.

"Thank the gods that you're his valet," she remarked. "It gives us a way to be close so we can keep an eye on him. That is until he gets back to normal again."

"Remind me if I've got this wrong," Silas said as she looked curiously at his sister. "But you're not still head over heels in love with Oscar, are you?"

"Do you want a slap?" she threatened as she shifted uncomfortably in her seat.

"I know that Mother always kept you in your place. She made sure you didn't get ideas above your station," he dared to suggest as she looked at him with a wide-eyed stare of shock. "But she isn't around anymore, so I wondered how you felt about him these days?"

"Would you like some more of that cake to take up to your room?" she asked, making to leave the table. "It's your favourite carrot cake."

"You would do that for me?" he asked in delight, not realising how she'd ignored his question.

"Of course," she replied with a cheeky smile, knowing her trick had worked. "I'll get Lucy to bring over another piece for you."

"But she doesn't work in the kitchen," he said. "Are you tricking me?"

"Lucy will be glad to bring you a piece of cake, she's over there look, chatting with Frances," Vera pointed her finger. "You wait there, and I'll go give it to her."

Vera knew that she'd had a close escape with her brother's prying question. Fortunately, she knew how to distract him, and it had worked. She could see him watching her as she approached Lucy, asking her to take some cake over to him, and give him an extra wicked smile while she was at it. Lucy was more than happy to oblige.

It wasn't until she was alone in her tiny office, doing her end-of-day paperwork, that she finally gave Silas' question some thought.

As a young girl she had believed herself to be in love with Oscar, and he with her. After all, they always re-enacted plays that led to them marrying. How many times had they married over the years of their young lives?

Tapping her feather pen on the blotting paper, she smiled to herself at the happy memories. Her mind was far away, recalling distant years gone by. For many years the three friends had been inseparable. Of course, the adults did all they could to stop the servant's children from playing with the lord's only son, but they were far too clever for them. They continued to sneak off together to so many places, to have their childhood adventures.

Her mother had once told her that she had a childhood infatuation with the boy. Then, as they all grew up, the twins grew apart from Oscar. They were starting to understand how they were breaking the social rules of mixing. By the time they reached their teens, they no longer sought out each other's company, and they didn't see Oscar every day. But knowing that he was always around had been enough for Vera.

Even now, every time she was in his company her body felt weak, and her stomach did so many flips she felt almost sick with it. As for her chest, that felt as if something might burst out of there it beat so fast, like a loud drum.

Do I love you, Oscar? She pondered on that question in her office.

A knock on the door brought Mary, the housekeeper, in. Soon enough she was discussing house business and menu planning. At least it took Oscar from her thoughts, but not for too long.

CHAPTER 5

"It seems I am to outlive your father, and my very good friend," the Earl of Devon remarked rather insensitively. He and Oscar were sitting together in one of the parlours of Welwick Hall, after he had turned up unannounced. "Sorry, old chap, I don't mean to sound heartless, but your father and I worked close together on many a business deal. A role that I hope you will also fulfil?"

"Once I have my head around the running of the Bodmin Estate, you have my word, Lord Pierce," Oscar assured the Earl. "I will get around to calling all father's business partners together soon enough."

"I do understand, Oscar. I am an old man with a few tricks up my sleeve so consider me at your service when you get your business head on," the Earl offered. "I have known your father for longer than you have been alive. I only have your best interests at heart, I can promise you that much."

"It is a relief to know I have someone I can trust and has such solid experience to call upon. Although I most likely understand business dealings better than I do the running this estate," Oscar told the old Earl. He had seen the gentleman around on occasion when his father had been meeting with associates in his study. Though he didn't know the earl too well, he gathered that would change soon enough. Oscar was not too proud to ask for help and would call upon the earl once he felt ready to pick up his father's business dealings.

"Another piece of advice for you, young fellow," the Earl said as he wiped at his brow with a large handkerchief. "You should take a wife as soon as is convenient. I find a woman always runs the house of any estate most satisfactorily. That will leave you free to see to everything else. Plus, you need to start thinking about producing an heir. The Duke of Cornwall is an important role in this country and one you cannot take lightly. You will have much influence in parliament, and with the royal family too."

"I will bear that in mind, though I must say it is not at the top of my agenda. Thank you, Lord Pierce," Oscar said. "I must say it has, been a pleasure to meet you. I look forward to that dinner we talked about sometime in the near future. It will be an opportunity to meet your lovely wife," Oscar added, hoping the old man would take the hint and get ready to leave.

"Oh, and I have a granddaughter or two that you can meet as well," the Earl chirped up, making no effort to leave. "Pretty little things they are, and around the right age for marriage, so bear that in mind."

"Indeed, I will, Lord Pierce. You flatter me with your trust," Oscar replied, although he had no intention of considering marriage yet.

"I have another engagement in an hour, so I must make haste and ready myself," Oscar tried again. There was no other way to get the old man to leave. Since his arrival, he had made himself comfortable in a chair that he had announced he always sat in when visiting his father.

"It is good then, that you are managing to socialise once again," the Earl said, looking pleased. "It is important for the local peerage to become more acquainted with you. Where is it that you go this day?"

"I have a garden party to attend at Middleton Manor," Oscar informed him. "It is my first social event since my loss, so I do not wish to turn up late."

"Yes, quite right too," the Earl agreed. "I must be on my way then. I have a meeting this afternoon to discuss the Whiteworks mine near the hamlet of Princetown. Have you heard of it?"

"I have, and I will happily discuss the mines with you at our next meeting," Oscar prompted. Though in truth, he dreaded the discussions, for his mind was still in a whir of confusion.

"I hear that Lord Barton, the Marquess of Northampton, will be bending your ear soon enough," the Earl said, looking as if it was a warning. He's seeking to purchase land, but I have my concerns as it borders my own. Let me know when he comes knocking on your door, will you?"

"I am not in any position to dish out advice yet, so I doubt he will come to me—"

"Nonsense," the Earl interrupted as a servant assisted him with his overcoat. "They will all wish to seek you out now. As I say, yours is a prominent role and you will carry much influence in these quarters."

It was with some relief that he saw the Earl right to the front door, at least that way he could make sure he left. As they arrived in the main reception hallway, Oscar spotted Silas.

"Silas, would you see Lord Ashbourne to his carriage," Oscar instructed his valet. "Then I would see you in my study."

Without a word, Silas carried out the orders as Oscar marched off to his study. There, he sat at his large, oak desk and tapped his fingers upon it as he awaited his valet. Soon enough, Silas arrived, and Oscar asked him to close the study door.

"Is there no way we can stop all these visits?" he asked Silas, feeling vexed. "I am fed up with all the earls, marquesses, and God knows who else calling on me to lend them my ear."

"But the Earl of Devon was a good friend of your father's, Your Grace," Silas said, looking a little puzzled at his master.

"And stop calling me that," Oscar snapped.

"What? You mean *Your Grace*?" Silas asked. "I have no choice, that is your title now."

"Yes, I know, but not when we are alone," Oscar said between slightly clenched teeth. "This is the one time in our lives when I wish you and Vera were not servants. I could do with friends I can trust, right now. It seems that every member of the peerage wants to advise me on how to live my life."

"All the more reason to spend the afternoon with pretty ladies, if you ask me," Silas hinted. He was still unsure whether his master was going to attend the garden party or not.

"Must I go?" Oscar whined, and it felt for a moment as if they were still children and he was seeking Silas' advice.

"You do whatever you like, Oscar, you are now the Duke of Cornwall," Silas replied. "But it would be a mistake for your friends to stand by and let you become a recluse. The sooner you get out there, the easier this whole process is going to be."

"Not when you know that all and sundry are hoping that I could marry their daughters or granddaughters," Oscar complained.

Silas grinned, "There is nothing more calming than being surrounded by pretty ladies. And that's why you need to attend this garden party. I doubt there will be any talk of business."

"Hmmm... I suppose the company of ladies can be a rather pleasant distraction," Oscar considered. "I will attend then, but you must go with me. I mean, you can wait for me in the carriage with the driver. It would be a great favour to me to know you are there should I need support."

"As always, it is my pleasure," Silas said. "I'll go and order the carriage and then see you in your chambers so we can change your attire."

"Yes, yes, I suppose so," Oscar sighed. "You see what I mean? I can trust you to have everything in hand. Personally, I would prefer to go out riding the horses on the moors where there is no one around but us."

Silas smiled as he bowed his head to leave and make arrangements for the visit. Oscar was thankful that he had such good friends as the twins. Many times, over the years of them all growing up, he had fallen back on their company. And now he wished that he was a servant too, then life would be so less complicated.

"It is jolly good that you chose to use the barouche, Silas," Oscar praised his friend on the carriage ride to Middleton Manor. "The air is fresh, and the sun is even making an appearance."

"If you get too cool, we can pull up the roof, Your Grace," Silas said as he accompanied his master to the event. "But I thought the breeze would clear your head so you can concentrate on enjoying some time to relax."

"Hmmm...it seems to me that you do believe I will enjoy this, don't you?" Oscar asked with a scowl, as he really didn't wish to attend.

"I do, oh, and Vera said that I had to tell you to stop sighing every two minutes," Silas grinned.

"Your sister knows me all too well," Oscar smiled back. "Ah, here we are then," he added as the driver pulled up the carriage outside the main doors to the manor house.

Stewards were awaiting the arrival of the carriages. As Oscar clambered down from the barouche, he was promptly led through the house and into the drawing room. There, French doors stood open that led out to the garden party. Through the doors, he could see at least thirty people, and he felt overcome with a sudden dread. An urge to turn around and return to the carriage was almost overwhelming, but he knew he had to at least make the effort. He promised himself that he would not stay for long, and he found himself sighing. Straight away he thought of Vera's comment that Silas had passed on to him.

I wish you were with me, standing right by my side. It would make this so much easier if you were here, Vera.

The hostess came forward to greet him. With lots of cheery smiles, she went on to introduce him to many of her guests, all of whom insisted on giving him their condolences. Although Silas had been right in one thing, the young ladies were buzzing around him. Their kind words and sympathies were helping him to settle and relax a little.

That was until he heard a murmur in a small crowd of people standing close by him. Without any warning, they parted ways as an older lady with an overly powdered face appeared. It looked as though she had pushed everyone out of her way in her attempt to get closer to him. In her wake was a younger lady. She looked as if she did not want to be at the garden party either. He felt instant empathy with her, the poor young woman looked so very embarrassed at the older one's behaviour.

"Your Grace!" the woman called out for all to hear, waving her arm at him. "I must introduce myself to you. I am Lady Adelia Smith, and I would also like to introduce my daughter to you," she called out, panting from the exertion needed to force her way to his side.

"Good day to you, Lady Smith," Oscar said, bowing his head in respect.

"This is Lady Olive Brent, late wife to the Earl of Gosmore," Lady Smith said with a rather loud voice. "She has much in common with you, Your Grace. She too has been bereft of a loved one, her husband, you see. And now she is all alone in the world." She spoke defensively, tilting her head as if seeking his pity.

"Good day to you, Lady Brent," Oscar said, bowing his head to the younger woman. "I trust you are not quite alone, as you have your mother to accompany you to social events such as this one."

"My daughter is quite shy and demure," Lady Smith pushed in, not allowing her daughter to speak. "I take her along to social events, for she is in great need of good company, other than my own, of course. I would say someone such as yourself, Your Grace, would find her conversation most engaging."

Oscar turned to the young lady, and they enjoyed a secret smile with one another. Lady Brent was quite beautiful, and he felt sympathy for her having such a mother as Lady Smith. Yet he could understand her loneliness, that was if she had loved her late husband.

"How long is it since the departure of Lord Brent, my Lady?" he asked her.

"Oh, she has taken a whole year out to mourn his death," her mother replied before her daughter could say anything. "We should call on you at Welwick Hall, so we can become better acquainted."

"I will be sure to invite you both when I am receiving guests once again," Oscar said, with a bow of his head.

He could see how uncomfortable Lady Brent was because he felt much the same.

"For now, I must say farewell for I have another engagement," he told Lady Smith and turned to make his way back through the open doors of the large drawing room.

In his rush to get away, he forgot to seek out the hostess to thank her for the invitation. Once out of the front door, he marched to his carriage, telling the driver to take him home at once.

CHAPTER 6

"Are you going to tell me why you left the gathering as though the devil was on your heels?" Silas dared himself to ask his master who had a look of fury on his face.

"Because every elderly female assumes I wish to marry their daughter, or niece, or whichever other female they happen to be related to!" Oscar barked back. "What's more, you were the one who pushed me into attending in the first place, so I am also angry with you. There! Now you have it, are you satisfied?"

"No, Your Grace, I am not satisfied," Silas said, nodding his head in response. "I pushed you to attend as your friend. You know, as well as I do, that you cannot hide away for much longer. Tell me that you can you see that?"

Oscar did not respond because he knew deep down that Silas was right. But that infuriating woman had pushed his anger to the edge of his limits, and he had to take it out on someone. Infuriating him further, the carriage bounded along and at every pothole, the occupants were thrown about. Oscar told Silas to instruct the driver to slow down.

"The last thing we want is a broken chasse," Oscar grumbled, but more to himself. Though he knew it was his fault, he'd been the one to instruct the driver to move at speed.

Yet speed was not what he wanted in his life. In truth, he had no idea what he wanted. And now he had shouted at one of the very few true friends he had, Silas, and he knew that he needed to apologise.

"Now that my brain is not being rattled by the fast wheels, I can think," Oscar said. "And I wish to apologise to you, Silas. I know that you mean well."

"I do, Your Grace," Silas told him. "It saddens me to see you so lost. You have forgotten your strengths and it feels like I am watching you sink. Vera also worries for you, so I am not alone in this."

"Yes, it feels to me like the two of you are the only friends I have in this world," Oscar said to his friend. "You are the only people who do not want anything from me. Well... I mean, I know you push me to do things, but only for my own good. Yet everyone else I speak with seems to have an agenda of their own."

"The sooner you can be your old self again, the better," Silas said, and Oscar could see that he was making every attempt to try and not to be too outspoken.

"You have my permission to speak your thoughts, Silas," Oscar told him. "I value your judgement, and Vera's too."

Silas looked over at the driver before he spoke. "Vera is right, you are more than capable of running this estate and all your father's affairs."

"Did she say that?" Oscar asked, a big grin on his face as he looked proud of himself.

Silas nodded his head. "She did, and I agree with her. But you are not your old self and there lies the problem."

"As soon as these damn nightmares subside," Oscar said, running his fingers through long, dark hair. "Then I can get a good night's sleep and my old self will return."

"You loved your parents very much," Silas pointed out as he

coughed to clear his throat, looking a little unsure of himself. "You must allow yourself to think about them in your waking hours. That way you may find that you can accept what has happened to them, instead of trying to push those thoughts away."

"You are right, as always. I try not to think about them during the day. What would I do without you and your sister?" Oscar said, knowing how much he valued their friendship. "I am lucky to have you by my side all day long, Silas. Then at night, your sister brings me hot milk, and lends me her ear. I have to tell you, seeing Vera last thing at night helped soothe my thoughts."

"She will be pleased that she's able to help you," Silas smiled. He knew that Vera would be happy to hear how her night-time company was helping Oscar.

The rest of the journey passed in relative silence. Both the men mulled over their thoughts and before too long the carriage pulled into the driveway of Welwick Hall. Silas was the first to disembark, opening the door for Oscar to climb out. It was protocol and neither of them wanted to let the rules slip when others were around.

"You know, I met the most overbearing woman today," Oscar told Silas as his valet walked by his side to enter the house. "Surprisingly, she has a most beautiful daughter. Lady Olive Brent, I do believe her name was."

While Oscar gave his hat and gloves to Silas in the hallway, Silas recalled that he knew of her. "Yes, she was the wife of the late Earl of Gosmore. He's been gone for over a year now, as I understand it."

Silas followed Oscar to the parlour. He went to sit in one of the large armchairs. It pleased him that he felt less stressed, all thanks to Silas.

"She was a real beauty. Now there is someone I could consider marrying," Oscar said, right at the moment Vera entered the room. She coughed a little to announce her presence, as Oscar and her brother were deep in conversation. Silas was peering through the window, but Oscar was pleased to see her arrival.

"I thought you might like some fresh cake that has barely been out of the oven an hour," she announced, looking a little troubled.

Oscar regretted his words about marrying Lady Brent. It seemed clear that Vera had overheard him. Any talk of a stranger taking over the household would not go down well with anyone. But talking of another woman in front of Vera didn't seem right, and he wasn't exactly certain why.

"Ah, Vera," he said, hoping she might not have heard his words about the woman's beautiful daughter. "I was telling your brother how I met the most obnoxious woman at the garden party."

It didn't seem to work as he could see the hurt in her deep brown eyes. It was a look that he did not like, and he wished he could unsay the words she had overheard. Oscar stood up to take the tray from her hands, smiling as he made eye contact with her.

"No, Your Grace, you don't need to help me," she said sounding a little shocked that he had done so.

"I will always help you, Vera, you know that—"

He didn't get to finish what he wanted to say to her as she gasped and turned to rush out of the room.

"Oh dear, it looks like I have upset your sister," Oscar said, staring after her and unsure what to think.

"Hmmm…she is acting strange, isn't she?" Silas agreed. "But you know women, they can get moody for no reason whatsoever. Well, Your Grace, I'd best not dawdle, I have work to be done."

"Yes, yes, off you go then," Oscar said, not really listening to Silas' words. "And thank you, Silas, for accompanying me today."

His valet bowed his head as he left the parlour, leaving Oscar alone with his thoughts. Today had gone as he had expected. Now that he was the lord of the manor, every single societal female in the locality would be trying to catch his eye, in the hope of a marriage proposal. It was like an unwritten rule that he must take a wife now that he was the head of the family and the estate.

Marriage had not been at the top of his agenda, but now that he gave it some thought, something occurred to him. He wasn't sure why, but the thought of marrying anyone other than Vera just didn't seem right. It had to do with all the times they had married while reciting plays. Vera did hold a special place in his heart. In his childhood and his youth, the only girl he had ever been interested in was Vera. The fact that she was of a different social status, and out of his reach, had never mattered to him then.

But the more thought he gave to the matter, the more he had to admit the truth to himself. His lack of interest in other women, and thoughts of marriage with another woman, were something he could not imagine ever happening.

What is this? Am I in love with Vera?

Shaking the very notion from his head, he attempted to convince himself that it was only the nostalgic thoughts that had excited him. It all meant nothing.

Silas was right, women do get moody over things that men do not always understand. Vera works such long hours in that kitchen. I should cut down on the servants, then she would not be under so much pressure. After all, there is only me living here now. Then again, the Hall must be cared for.

A memory of his father came to mind.

"*We are the caretakers of Welwick Hall and the Bodmin Estate, my boy. It is our responsibility to take care of the lands and our temporary home. We must always put those things first so that we can pass them down our family line.*"

It truly was time that he started to look at the accounts for the estate and face up to his responsibilities. Yes, he would take Silas' advice and arrange for McIntyre to come and meet with him in the house. They would go over the estate's affairs. He would start by dismissing some of the servants to make Vera's workload easier. If she didn't have to work so hard, she might be a happier person.

CHAPTER 7

Silas had feigned disinterest when his sister had dashed out of the parlour after Oscar's comment. He knew, by the fact that she had brought the tray into the parlour so soon after they arrived home, it likely meant she'd been looking out for them. On top of that, he had a good idea why she was behaving so erratically.

You are still in love with Oscar, aren't you sis? He thought to himself as he marched his way through the corridors of Welwick Hall.

It worried him because it was going to cause her nothing but heartache. *You must know it can never come to anything*, he continued with his private thoughts, fretting over how much pain this was going to be for her.

Silas always had a close relationship with his sister, after all, they were twins and identical ones at that. He had been born six minutes before her and so always considered himself her older brother. Though his sister considered herself the one in charge between them. They both had fiery tempers, but Vera had always been the calmer of the two.

They were brought up close to Oscar, who had been born a

month before them. For Silas, Oscar was always looked upon as the older brother of him and his sister, or that's how it felt to him. For Vera though, it was fast becoming clear that she did not look upon Oscar as an older brother; she was in love with him.

What am I going to do to help you through this? Oscar must take a wife and you're going to have to accept it. His thoughts tumbled around in his head. "Oh Lord, Sis, this is going to hurt you so much," he added, mumbling under his breath.

Any pain that his sister felt, he would feel too. They were that close; she a part of him, and he a part of her. He would give his life to protect her, yet that would not be enough. This situation was going to break her to pieces.

As he turned to take a different corridor, he held his head down, deep in thought. Within moments in the new hallway, he almost knocked someone over. Jumping back at the shock of practically bowling someone over in his rush to the kitchens, he looked up to see Barker's face glaring at him.

"Good grief, Atkins, is there a fire somewhere?" the butler asked as he wavered to stay upright.

"I'm in a rush to see my sister," Silas replied, knowing that Barker would delay him if he could, the man always wanted to talk.

"Have you come from seeing His Grace?" Barker asked with a glint of curiosity firing in his eyes.

"I have, why do you ask?" Silas questioned, but regretted it straight away, it would only serve to delay him.

"I hear through the grapevine that His Grace was quite taken with Lady Olive Brent at the garden party, is it true?" Barker asked, looking rather smug at his revelation.

"That new driver needs dismissing," Silas answered. "He should not be listening into conversations that don't concern him."

"So, it is true then," Barker nodded, knowing the answer by Silas's bluster. "Actually, I heard it myself. As you both arrived in the hallway you were discussing it. But don't you see, Silas, this is good news. His Grace needs to take a suitable wife so life can return to some kind of normalcy at Welwick Hall."

"You are far too nosy," Silas snapped, making to get past the butler who had done his best to block his way.

Barker took hold of Silas's arm, leaning in to speak to him in a low voice. "I know you have a long-running friendship with His Grace, but you and I both know it must end. Since he's been alone, I've allowed it to go on, but it is unnatural. The sooner he begins to mix with people of his station, the better for everyone, including you and your sister."

Silas was in no mood for a lecture, and he shook off Barker's hand from his arm. As soon as the butler let go, Silas stormed away in the direction of the kitchen. If Barker had already heard the rumour, then Vera would know of it too. Damn people who can't keep their thoughts to themselves!

The kitchen was as busy as ever. Pans bubbled away, coals burned in the ovens, and the noise of clattering filled the air. At times like this, the kitchen servants had to speak in loud voices to hear each other.

Vera was nowhere to be seen, which was unusual. He approached Frances who was busy scrubbing pots in a huge sink.

"Where's my sister?" he asked her as she paused to look at him.

"She's locked herself in her office, thank the Lord," Frances told him. "She's in a foul mood, so I'd tread with care."

Silas nodded his head, heeding the warning that didn't surprise him one bit. This was not going to be an easy conversation with his sister.

Arriving at the closed office door, Silas didn't bother to knock because she'd only tell him to go away. Instead, he barged into the tiny room. His sister was seated at the office desk but she wasn't doing any paperwork. She held her head in her hands with her elbows on the desk and turned to look at him with a solemn expression. He sat down in the only other chair. It happened to be next to her, allowing him to take her hand in his as a show of concern.

"I couldn't help it, Silas," she admitted. "I had to get out of there because it felt odd when I heard Oscar talking about marrying this new lady in his life."

Silas looked into the eyes, the same eyes that he saw when he looked in a mirror, they were so alike. "We have always had a precarious position in this household, sister," he began. "And Oscar has never, in his entire life, turned away from us."

Vera nodded her agreement, her eyes glistening as she fought back tears.

"You and I have helped him all we can with his grieving, but it's time we stopped," he suggested. "He's under immense pressure from his peers to take a wife so that he can run this huge estate."

At this statement, Vera's eyes opened wide with horror, "Stop it, Silas, I don't wish to hear."

"No, Vera, you must listen to me. I'm telling you nothing but the truth," he continued, squeezing her hand in his. "If not this lady, then it would be another. We must accept it, Sister. You must accept it. He has no choice but to marry a lady of equal standing. You know he can never take you as his wife."

Vera began to sob out loud at his direct words, and he held her in a firm embrace to try and ease her sadness. "We are lucky to have such a faithful friendship from him, we could never expect more."

Without warning, Vera pushed him away and jumped up from her chair. Wiping her face with the bottom of her pinafore, she said nothing to him as she opened the door. Storming out of the office she left him alone, and in a little shock at her sudden movements. He could hear her shouting orders at the kitchen servants. With a big sigh, he followed in her tracks, hoping to speak calming words to her.

"Vera," he said, approaching her as she picked up a pan of boiling water. "Please, you must take some time to think—"

"Out of my kitchen!" She yelled back at him as she banged the pan onto a surface, hot water splashing out through the sides of the pan lid.

He was relieved to see that no hot liquid touched her, but he knew when Vera was serious. This was not a time she would see reason; she was using her energy to push away the hurtful thoughts. Silas knew it would be better to leave her to her work. She wasn't thinking straight at the moment, so he would not waste his time trying to reason with her. He'd return later.

As he turned to exit the kitchen, Barker showed his face again.

"Put her in her place, have you?" the butler spouted his mouth. "About time too, that someone told her the truth. Getting ideas above her station."

Vera had often lectured him about how Barker was a kind, old man. She thought that the butler forgot his true nature due to his responsibilities in the household. Silas had tried to like the man, but somehow, he always managed to rub him up the wrong way. And now he was doing it again.

Silas looked Barker in the face and pushed at the odious man's chest. It surprised him how weak the butler was, as he almost wavered to fall on the hard ground. Silas didn't hang around to see if he was hurt, he was too angry with him. As he left, he heard lots of hullabaloo behind him, as others ran to Barker's aid. He didn't bother to look back.

Serves him right, he convinced himself, but he knew he shouldn't have treated the old man like that. He was taking his frustrations out on him, and it was wrong.

It wasn't the butler's fault that his sister was in love with their master. God knows, Barker had done all he could over the years to separate the twins from the Duke's son. But Silas wished that Barker had tried harder. He wished that everyone had forced them apart, then Vera would not have fallen in love with Oscar. His mother knew about it, and she had warned them off so many times.

For the first time in ages, he thought of his mother.

If only you were here to talk some sense into her, Ma, because she won't listen to me.

"How am I going to help you?" He called the words out loud.

Silas headed outside and continued his march as he headed into the grounds of the Bodmin Estate. He would take a brisk walk around the gardens to cool off. No doubt when he returned, he would be in big trouble. Poor Barker happened to be in the wrong place, just as his fury was peaking. He never meant to mistreat the old man, but he was always spouting off spiteful words.

No, this wasn't about Barker, or even about him, it was about his poor sister. She was never going to be able to stay on at Welwick Hall once Oscar married. But wherever she went, he would be right by her side. Her pain would be his too and would never leave her to face anything alone.

CHAPTER 8

At the best of times, Vera had little patience for Barker's interference, and she had even less today. But seeing as her brother had almost knocked the poor man onto the kitchen floor, the least she could do was make sure he was not hurt.

"Lucas, come over here and me steady Barker, will you," she called over to one of the stewards who happened to be in the kitchen. "Are you hurt?" she asked as Lucas assisted the man as he leaned on the kitchen wall to steady himself.

"You and your brother are the bane of my life," Barker mumbled. "Neither of you will ever see reason—"

"Unless you have something useful to say, Barker," Vera interrupted him. "Then get out of my kitchen. What is it with the men of Welwick Hall, always harassing me? Don't you know that I have better things to do than pamper to you lot?"

She was aware that she was being unreasonable as she snapped at him, but he was the least of her worries. And Barker knew better than to hang around when Vera was in this mood. It had got him nowhere in the past, and would serve him no purpose this day either. She stared at him as he turned and marched away and up the servants' stairs.

"Back to work, the lot of you," she yelled to those who worked in the kitchen alongside her every day. Unable to stop herself from being snappy, she tried instead to say nothing. Everyone knew their role in her kitchen, and they didn't need her to intervene in their tasks, so she let them be.

I can't help it, the thought of Oscar marrying someone else seemed so odd, she thought as she started to weigh out the ingredients for a fruit cake.

One thing that her mother prided herself on was that Welwick Hall had a constant supply of fruit cake available in its kitchen. It had been one of those comforts of their childhood; a slice of fruitcake with a chunky slice of homemade cheese. Cheese that her mother made from the cows that were milked on the estate.

She too had carried on with those traditions. It was almost as comforting to make the cake as it was to eat it. The warm smell of cinnamon, in contrast with the sharpness of the juice from fresh oranges. At Christmas, she would add some dark rum to it and give the cake a real lift.

But today, the currants and raisins tumbled out of the bowl that she was weighing them in, and they crashed onto the tabletop. Not that she needed to weigh out the fruits, she knew the amounts by sight because she'd made that many fruit cakes. But her mind was a muddle and as she knocked the bowl from the weighing machine, she cried out in frustration.

"Frances!" she shouted out for her scullery maid. "Clean this mess up."

The poor girl looked terrified and was reluctant to approach the table until Vera had stepped away. Vera felt guilty about scaring her and thought it best to make herself scarce while she calmed down.

"I'll be in my office if I'm needed!" she said in a quieter tone, shocked as she noticed the look of relief on the faces of her friends in the kitchen.

Was she acting so dreadful that they were content with her absence? *Am I so bad*? she thought as she arrived in her tiny office once again. She slammed the door closed behind her. A hot sweat ran around the hairline of her face and on her neck. Vera knew that she needed to calm down and she dropped back into her office chair. Within seconds, tears streamed down her cheeks, and she wept uncontrollably.

"What is wrong with me?" she called out, pulling up her apron to wipe her face dry.

Her body shook from the sobs that wracked her; all from the sadness that she held in her heart.

"I can't bear it," she sobbed. "Oh, Oscar, I can never be yours and I have to accept it. I don't know how will I bear to see you loving another woman?"

Trying to keep the noise of her sobs quiet, she took a deep breath in, just as the door burst open. Standing in the doorway was Oscar, and she jumped up from her chair in a fluster.

"Your Grace, I... I'm sorry—"

She felt helpless. All she could do was watch as he stepped into the room and closed the door behind himself. They were alone and together, and something in the back of her mind niggled that it wasn't right, but she didn't care.

His handsome face looked so worrisome, that all she wanted to do was run into his arms. Yet, she held back, she knew that was the wrong thing to do. She was no longer a young girl in need of her friend's embrace, she was an adult and perfectly aware of all the rules of etiquette.

"No, Vera, please don't apologise to me," he said in a gentle voice. "You must sit down while we talk," he added. As she took her seat again, he took the spare chair by her side.

At least she had stopped her caterwauling, but she knew that she had to look a terrible mess. Oscar catching her crying had caused her to hang her head so he couldn't see her shameful face.

"I...we...we need to speak, you and I," he said, breaking the silence. "I want to talk to you about...about all the conflicting emotions I know that you must be suffering. Most especially as I begin to attend social events once again."

Does he know of my love for him? she wondered as he paused. *But I've never declared it. Has he come to tell me how he feels the same for me?* Her thoughts caused her cheeks to flush as she prayed hard that he was going to find a way for them to be together.

He took hold of one of her hands, another inappropriate act, poor Barker would have a fit if he saw them together.

Is he fighting all the rules to declare his love for me?

She looked up into his sky-blue eyes, unafraid, for she had looked into them so many times as a youngster.

"When we were younger, you dreamed of attending balls and garden parties. I recall it all so well because I dreamed of taking you to them," he told her. "And now, here I am, able to go to as many as I like, and here you are, stuck in your role as a servant. And you work far too hard."

Again, he paused as he too glared back into her deep brown eyes. *What is he seeing in my eyes? Is he reading of my love for him?*

"We have done so many fun things together in our early days," he continued. "I do feel selfish, having all the fun to myself while my friends...you and Silas...slave away as servants."

"It is our role, Your Grace, you can do nothing about that—"

"Sshh..." he said to her as he touched her locks with his fingers and moved the straggling hair away from her face. "I can, and I must do something about it," he added.

She wanted to ask him what he meant, but she didn't want him to delay his declaration of his love for her, so she remained silent.

"I love you and your brother so very dearly." He spoke again. "I promise that I will create situations whereby we can all be together again. We will begin to enjoy some time in one another's company. I intend to improve your lives and make it so that we can have picnics and outings together. I don't care if Barker disapproves, he always has anyway so it will nothing different for any of us. What say you, my dear Vera?"

Vera found herself speechless, this was not what she had expected, or hoped for.

He let go of her hand, smiling at her. "I mean, Father is no longer around to stop us from continuing our friendship. You are two people who I want in my life forever, and I hope that you both feel the same way. Yet you look disappointed, are you?"

She managed a half-smile but couldn't hide her disappointment. What a fool she had been, expecting him to declare his love for her. Whilst he had declared his feelings, they were not quite what she had hoped for.

"But Your Grace—"

"Vera, do not call me that when we are alone, please," he begged. "You, Silas, and me, we are all equals, we are friends together, sharing a bond that is stronger than any societal rules."

She nodded, willing herself to look pleased with his announcement. She must have succeeded because he seemed content with her response.

"That is it then," he clapped his hands together in delight at her acceptance. "We shall organise a day out together. Even better, we will go and visit the sea and find a spot where no prying eyes can bother us. Do you like the sound of a trip together?"

"I do, Your G... Oscar," she nodded, as he got up from his chair.

"And so it shall be done," he said as his hand reached out for the door handle. "I will leave you to your day for now. When next we meet, we can discuss the future of this estate, for I value you and your brother's opinions greatly."

She watched with a broken heart as Oscar left the office,

leaving the door open. It was not what she had wanted to hear, and she felt complete and utter misery. He had not declared his love for her as a woman, only as a friend.

"What did I expect!" she shouted out before quickly placing a hand over her mouth, realising the door was still open.

Staying in her chair, she was spellbound with disappointment, and now guilt was setting in too.

I can't expect him to give up his entire life, for that's what it would amount to, she pondered. *Who do I think I am, to suppose a duke would be interested in loving one of his servants? What am I to do?*

She hung her head in her hands and rubbed at her eyes.

A light knock came at the door.

"Ma'am, there be a delivery at the back door," Jess, one of her assistants informed her. "I know how you like to deal with the larger deliveries, or would you prefer that I do it?"

"No, it's fine, Jess, I will be along in a minute," she said with a spring in her voice. "Is it the butcher?"

"Yes, Ma'am," Jess replied, hovering in the doorway.

"Offer Jacob a cup of tea and a slice of cake in the servant's dining room," she suggested. "All him I will check his order and join him shortly.

Jess gave a small bow of her head at her instructions and dashed away, leaving the door open.

Vera wiped her face with her apron again, and straightened the pins in her head, tucking away any straggling hairs. Soon, she was back out in the kitchen and checking the delivery of meat for the month. She'd get someone to salt the beef, and then she looked over the skinned rabbits. It was good of Jacob to skin them for her, but she must remind him that he didn't need to do that.

The problem was that Jacob had a soft spot for her, and she was aware of it because he had told her so. He had hinted so many times about enjoying a picnic with her. And so many times she had refused his offers.

He was a good-looking man with a good trade, and many of the local female commoners would jump at the chance of a picnic with him, but not her. Vera only ever had her eyes on one man. And that man had captured her love forever. There was no other man in existence who could ever take Oscar's place in her heart.

CHAPTER 9

"It is imperative that you look your very best, my dear," Olive's mother fussed in her usual manner.

As usual, Olive only half listened. It wasn't that she didn't love or respect her mother. But she was used to her. Olive had learned over the years how to cope with her and live a peaceful life.

They were in the carriage on their way to Falmouth to visit a specific dressmaker whom her mother preferred. It seemed a long way to go for a dress fitting, but she knew better than to complain, ever the dutiful daughter doing as her mother wished. Her mother insisted that the local dressmaker wasn't good enough, and so here they were, travelling all for the sake of vanity.

"We must impress the new Duke of Cornwall. He is a most handsome man and I mean to have him for your husband," her mother rambled. "You should be grateful that I push you to improve your lot. I want only the best for you, my dear."

Olive's mind wandered as she watched the outside scenery pass them by. The road was a rough one and hardly worth a new dress, but it was easier to put up with the journey than it was to refuse to go.

After a three-hour journey, the driver finally dropped them off as close to the dressmaker's house as possible. They still had a short walk on the muddy wooden walkway, but at least the mud here was mostly sand.

"Come back in two hours, do you hear me?" her mother ordered their driver, who tipped his hat to her in acknowledgment.

All Olive could think was they had another three-hour journey to return home, this was going to be a long, dreary day. She glanced out to peek at the grey ocean waves, but it made her shiver as she recalled how the Duke's parents had died. The sea air was chilly at this time of year, and she would be glad to get indoors.

As she turned around, her mother had set off towards the shop without her. Looking up the street, she spotted her mother speaking with a gentleman. It wasn't until she got nearer that she recognised it to be the new Duke of Cornwall himself.

"Come, come, my dear," her mother made a gesture with her arm as she wore a huge smile on her white powdered face. "Look who I have bumped into. I was just telling the Duke here, that we were discussing him."

Olive curtsied, "Your Grace," she said, but not a word more than was needed. Her mother would have plenty to say, and it was always a good excuse for her to say nothing, exactly how she liked it.

"It must be fate that keeps bringing us together, Your Grace," her mother suggested. "We are visiting the most experienced dressmaker that money can buy, so what brings you this far?"

Trust Mother to be so forward, and why is she admitting to him that we were discussing him? Olive wondered as she stood next to the Duke.

"It is time I put my head to some business dealings," the Duke replied, revealing as little as possible without appearing too rude.

Olive thought that her mother might take the hint by the Duke's short reply, but she soon realised the error of her ways. On the contrary, her mother would keep digging until she knew the truth of things. Olive, however, could see that the Duke was ill at ease.

"Mother, we should get indoors where—"

"We could not discuss matters at the garden party," her mother continued, ignoring her. "Too many ears listening, do you not agree? But my daughter understands how you must be feeling, having suffered so much grief herself. However, she has pulled through a whole year of mourning for her late husband. Is that not a true commitment and fine quality for a future wife? My Olive is a fine lady of standing. She has many talents and was, indeed, a most loyal wife to the late Earl of Gosmore."

"Once again, you have my condolences, Lady Brent," the Duke bowed his head at Olive, giving her a half smile.

"Thank you, Your Grace," was all Olive said. Like him, she had no desire for long conversations.

Her mother though was intent on delaying the Duke from going about his business. It caused Olive to squirm with embarrassment, and she tried again.

"I am sure that His Grace has places to go, Mother, and it is chilly—"

"And now my daughter suffers from terrible loneliness," her mother spoke over her protestations yet again. "The present Earl of Gosmore plays no role in her life, shunning her into seclusion. It is a sad day when a lady of nobility is ignored, do you not agree, Your Grace?"

"It was a blessing then, that you had an invitation to the garden party—"

"Yes, that was more or less the first social event we had attended," her mother continued, daring to cut off the Duke's words.

As Olive switched off her ears to her mother's discourse, she observed the Lord before her. He was most certainly young and handsome, with strong features, thick brows, and a full nose set against strong cheekbones, with a square jaw. His long, thick, dark hair was tied at the back, but she could see that he had unruly waves. She wondered at the colour of his eyes and attempted to study them when she became aware that she was staring at him.

"What she needs is the strength of a good husband behind her," her mother's words came to her ears. "A loving husband who will care for her and bless her with children. I would make the most perfect grandmother; do you not agree, Your Grace?"

It seemed that the Duke was learning fast, and he did not attempt a reply, instead, he smiled and bowed his head in response. Olive though had never felt so uncomfortable at her mother's attempt to delay the Duke. The whole situation was awkward with her mother openly discussing things she had no right to say in public, let alone to such a gentleman of nobility.

"You must come to dinner at Silsbury Manor," her mother declared. "It is a cosy place and serves our needs for now, but I insist that you join us sometime. My daughter would be most honoured to have such a distinguished guest over for dinner."

Olive was frozen on the spot, shocked at her mother inviting the Duke to dinner.

"Why I..." the Duke stuttered but soon saved himself. "The honour would be all mine, Lady Smith."

"Excellent, we shall expect you tomorrow," her mother pushed.

Olive wanted to step in and save the Duke, but she didn't want to insult either her mother or him, so she said nothing, playing it safe. The poor man could hardly refuse, so it was better that she too accepted the situation forced upon them.

"Good day to you, Your Grace, we must be getting along now," her mother announced as if he was the one holding them up.

"It has been a pleasure to meet with you, Your Grace," Olive added, if only for an excuse to show him a friendly smile.

He bowed and said his farewell before they parted ways. Olive felt annoyed with her mother's presumptuous behaviour. They arrived at the dressmaker's house and met with two other ladies who were just leaving, after a fitting of their own. Olive watched on as her mother did what she did best...

"Oh my, it is good that you have finished. My daughter is in great need of a new dress now that the Duke of Cornwall is dining with us," her mother said to the ladies. She was blocking the outer door and thus stopping them from leaving. "I do hope that the seamstress has the finest of fabrics available, for we will be needing nothing but the best."

Whilst the ladies smiled at her mother, they said nothing, and Olive felt uncomfortable once again.

"Do you have any dresses on your racks, Beacham?" her mother called out to the dressmaker in a loud voice, as she forced her way into the front room of the house. "We are in dire need of a dress this very day. My daughter must look her best for the dinner on the morrow with the Duke. Your reputation depends on it."

Olive was sure that the ladies saw this moment as an opportunity to escape. They quickly dashed out of the front door that had remained open. Olive followed her mother into the room where the dressmaker greeted them.

"I have many exquisite dresses, Lady Smith, please come in," Beacham said with a false-looking smile.

"We still require a fitting for a ball gown," her mother continued. "The Duke, I am sure, will be inviting my daughter to endless balls."

Olive knew that she looked embarrassed at her mother's assumptions, but it wasn't worth trying to put her to rights. She wouldn't listen, and if anything, she'd be most likely to make her look a fool. As always, Olive left her mother to it; anything for a peaceful life.

"Congratulations, Lady Brent," Beacham said to her as if she had secured a marriage deal instead of a simple dinner invite.

"There is nothing to congratulate, Beacham," Olive said, doing what she could to undo her mother's exaggerations. "Mother magnifies things, as always."

"Nonsense, my dear!" her mother responded with a scowl. "His Grace is so keen on you, that he is coming for dinner tomorrow. It doesn't give us much notice, does it? But who are we to refuse a member of the nobility? It is just as well that we are at the dressmaker's today, is it not, Beacham?"

Olive merely tutted at her mother's response, ignoring how the dressmaker fussed over her. Meanwhile, she went over to the rack of handmade dresses and started to look through them. Accepting her fate, she knew that the only way to live peacefully with her mother was to make the best of every situation.

Who knows, perhaps a new dress and dinner with a handsome gentleman might cheer me after all.

CHAPTER 10

"She gave me very little in the way of choice over the matter," Oscar grumbled as Silas dressed him to go to dinner at Silsbury Manor. "God knows how I managed to bump into that woman in the middle of Falmouth. She seems to follow me around; I am sure of it. Anyway, I could hardly refuse because I did not wish to embarrass her daughter."

"It will do you good, Oscar," Silas remarked as he was attempting to puff up the neck ruffle underneath Oscar's chin. "Stand still, will you."

"And whilst I must put up with Lady Smith, I shall enjoy the more pleasant company of Lady Brent, do you not agree?"

"I do, Oscar, and it's only right that you put yourself about more," Silas replied. "What is that saying that my sister always quotes to us?"

"*A busy mind is a happy mind,*" the two friends announced the quote together, laughing in harmony.

"She keeps us in our places, do you not agree?" Oscar said, chuckling at how Vera kept him grounded, which for him was a good thing

A light knock came at the door and Oscar glanced through that the mirror he was standing in front of, to see who it was. Vera opened the door and stepped inside, looking a little confused. He hoped she hadn't heard them, or she might consider them making fun of her, which neither would ever do. Silas turned to see his sister entering Oscar's chambers, greeting her with an admission of sorts.

"Vera? Your ears must be burning because we were just discussing you?" Silas told her, and Oscar wondered if she would be annoyed at such a declaration.

"Yes, I heard you both mocking my words," she said, not breaking into a smile. "Making fun of me, were you?"

"Not at all… Vera and you know it," Oscar said, watching her through the mirror while Silas continued brushing down his dinner jacket. "Thank you for answering my request to call on me. As you can see, I am out for dinner this evening. I should have informed you earlier, but I had hoped they might send me a cancellation. This is not a dinner that I wish to attend."

"No, Oscar, don't think in such a way. You are doing the right thing by socialising more," Silas insisted as he finished arranging the neck scarf. He stood back to look at his master, "there now, you look the part of a proper duke."

"I agree with Silas on this one, Oscar," Vera said, smiling over at him. "You look very handsome, and it will do you good to relax in the company of others."

"Well, do not think for one moment that I have forgotten my promise to you, my dear Vera," Oscar said. He turned around to speak with her, just as Barker made an appearance behind Vera.

As if by some kind of instinctual response, the three friends tensed up the moment the butler appeared. Whenever the three were together, and Barker showed up, they always clamped up. It was as if they were still children, and he was still the enemy.

"Oh drat, Barker," Oscar said as he looked at the butler. "What have we all done now?" He chuckled as he finished speaking, causing Vera and Silas to laugh too.

"I don't see what's so funny," Barker said in his usual formal tone as he glared at Silas. "Especially when I have come to speak with His Grace on an important matter."

"Very well, the two of you had better leave us alone so Barker can divulge his secrets to me," Oscar said, knowing they wouldn't feel insulted at all. "You had better come in, Barker, and shut the door behind you."

Barker first watched the twins leave and Oscar watched Barker. He noted how the butler gave the twins a smug look along with a knowing smile. He must think he had got the better of them, but Oscar knew it was all a game and he ignored Barker's self-glorification.

"I haven't got long, Barker," Oscar said with a little sternness in his voice, so that the butler wouldn't dawdle with whatever he had to say.

"I wish to discuss an idea with you, Your Grace, that is of a delicate nature," Barker began, standing up straight as he attempted to appear as if his visit was official. "You see, I know that your father would wish for me to bring this up with you."

"Now you have my curiosity piqued, Barker," Oscar said, looking at his attire in the mirror. "Get on with it, man."

"It is of my opinion, Your Grace, that you should be considering hosting a ball," Barker said.

"Good grief, I don't feel ready for that yet," Oscar said, turning to glare at the butler. "Whatever has given you such a notion in that head of yours?"

"Please hear me out, Your Grace," Barker pushed. "I have heard from other butlers in the area that there is lots of curiosity among the ton about you. The lords and ladies are all keen to get to know the new young duke better."

"Well, they can jolly well wait until I am ready to meet with them," Oscar said, not feeling too pleased with his butler's suggestion.

Barker raised a finger in the air as if to make a point of what he was about to add. "Your father had a reputation of hosting some of the grandest balls throughout the winter months, Your Grace. It is an excellent way to re-introduce you back into society after your terrible loss."

"I suppose you have a good point there, Barker," Oscar admitted as he thought on his words. "Others are also advising me to socialise more. I will give the matter some serious consideration."

"That is all that I can ask of you, Your Grace," Barker bowed his head. "But a ball does take a lot of organising. The sooner you make your decision, the better. The household servants can then ready Welwick Hall to host a ball that both you and your father will be proud of."

"Quite so, but for now I am due to dine at Bilberry Manor, as you know," Oscar pointed out. "Have you arranged a carriage for me?"

"Yes, Your Grace, it is already at the front with a driver, both awaiting your arrival," Barker said.

"Then let us get down to the reception hallway so I can put on my overcoat," Oscar instructed as he opened the door and headed to the grand stairway. "The weather is changing quickly, and it is fast becoming quite chilly on an evening. I don't want to get caught out if rains too."

Barker followed in his master's wake. He would be the one to assist his master to put his coat on before he went outdoors. He would then offer him his hat and gloves before he left the manor house.

"I thank you, Your Grace, for taking my suggestion into consideration" Barker sang out as Oscar walked to the carriage that awaited him.

Again, his butler followed him, though that wasn't standard

practice. It annoyed Oscar that Barker was wanting to serve him so thoroughly.

"What is it now, Barker," he snapped as he turned to speak with the butler.

"I am to open the carriage door, Your Grace," Barker said, looking surprised. "My duty is to care for you, as I did your father."

"Forgive me, Barker," Oscar gave in. "I have not yet learned all the ways of a duke, but I assure you, I can manage the carriage door myself. Please, take yourself out of this rain."

"As you wish, Your Grace," Barker said with a bow of his head and a look of horror on his face.

"Damn the rules!" Oscar mumbled to himself, wondering if he would ever have his life to himself again.

He was never keen on travelling in the carriage at night, the roads were filled with muddy holes and often felled branches from trees. It had started to rain and the wind was picking up. Before getting into the carriage, he went to speak with the driver.

"I am in no rush to get there, Jenkins. Mind how the horses tread, I don't wish for any accidents to happen along the way," he instructed Jenkins who nodded his understanding.

Barker waved him off from the open doorway of the manor house. It seemed a little odd and Oscar ignored him, the butler was getting old and set in his ways. No doubt he perceived himself as some sort of paternal figure to Oscar since he'd lost his parents. He was fond of Barker because he had been around all of his life. Even though he could be a pain at times, especially when he was younger. If he ever caught him playing with the servants' children, he would inform his father. Not once, as far as he was aware anyway, did he let them get away with it.

Then again, childhood memories were selective. The more he thought of Barker, the more he realised that he had not always been as stern as he seemed to remember. For some reason, the kinder side of Barker were memories that had faded. Perhaps Barker was right to bring up the possibility of hosting a ball. Oscar had no intention of hosting as many balls as his father had. Rather, it had been his mother because she was the one who was fond of balls in the winter. She always said it kept dreary days at bay. Her laughter echoed in his head; how he missed them both.

At least he still had Oscar and Vera, and to some extent Barker too. They were like family to him, and he was ever grateful they were still in his life. Without them, he would be very lonely.

The journey passed by quickly and was all but done. They arrived at Silsbury Manor without incident, in fact, it had been a smooth ride and he thanked his driver. Lately, he had been thankful for so many small things that had made his life easier since the death of his parents. He observed the driver take the carriage towards the stable where he would await his master to return home.

Taking a deep breath, Oscar approached the front door to Silsbury Manor. He prepared himself for an evening of socialising that he really didn't want. Still, if he focused on the lovely Lady Brent, he should get through this without too much discomfort, or so he hoped.

CHAPTER 11

Olive and her mother stood in the small reception hallway as they waited to greet their dinner guest. One of the maids held the front door open and the rain was now lashing down and bouncing back up from the shiny, wet ground.

"Do come inside, Your Grace," her mother fussed. "Let us get you out of that cold rain."

Olive stood further back, watching as the handsome Duke entered her home. She had to admit that he was quite pleasant to the eyes, but still, she could see him as a potential husband. She thought of him as a very pleasing gentleman and would no doubt make some noble lady a fine husband, but not her because she was not ready.

In truth, she was tired of the whole charade of her mother pushing her to remarry someone she did not love. It might be her mother's way, but it wasn't hers. Putting her thoughts aside, for now, she too welcomed the Duke with a warm smile. She found herself looking forward to his company over dinner, that was if she could manage to get a word in, over her mother.

"Do come straight through to the dining room, Your Grace,"

her mother offered. "We have a lovely venison cooking, and plenty of other appetising delights too. I do hope you enjoy good food for our cook is most experienced."

It was Olive who led the duke to the head of the table, and both women sat at either side of him. The table already had a fine spread of rich foods, brightly coloured fruits, and freshly baked bread that were all laid out to whet the appetite.

"There is far too much food on the table already, just for the three of us, but I will do my best," Oscar smiled at his hostesses.

"One would have thought that you always ate such fare, Your Grace, and we did not want to disappoint," her mother told him.

What her mother didn't bother to say was that Olive had already said there was too much food set out on the table, but as usual, she wouldn't listen to her advice. Olive, as always, let her mother do as she wished; anything for a peaceful life.

A meaty soup was soon served, one of Olive's favourite courses. She often enjoyed a soup on its own, not having a large appetite. But tonight, she would attempt to sample from each course so that the Duke felt at ease. Then again, her mother's appetite was never small, so she at least would eat plenty.

"This is a hearty oxtail soup," the Duke said. "Exactly what one needs on a cold, winter's night.

"Yes, it is starting to get cold on an evening," Olive quickly interjected before her mother had the chance to reply.

"The servants have built up the fire in the hearth so that we do not feel any chill while we eat," her mother added because she had to say something, didn't she?

For a few moments, there was blissful silence as they all enjoyed the soup.

It was no surprise to Olive when her mother broke the peace, "Tell me, Your Grace, do you intend on hosting any winter balls, as your father often did?"

"As it happens, I have been considering holding a Christmastide ball," he replied. With a smile, he dabbed at his lips with the crisp, white cotton serviette.

Her mother clapped her hands together at the news, "Oh marvellous," she exclaimed. "You know that a ball will be the perfect occasion to find yourself a wife."

"Mother, I hardly think His Grace is hosting a ball to seek out a wife," Olive said, feeling embarrassed at her mother's forwardness.

Luckily the Duke took the remark in his stride and showed no offence. "The main aim of the ball, Lady Smith, is to celebrate Christmastide."

"My daughter and I love this time of year, don't we, my dear?" her mother chimed in.

Olive hated the dark, dreary winter months, so she wasn't sure why her mother should suggest such a thing, but she merely gave a half smile in response.

"We like to fashion many traditional greeneries with ivy and holly buds. And, of course, starting with Stir it up Sunday for the Christmastide pudding. It is a good season for inviting guests to our home, for we have been bereft of good company due to my daughter's lengthy mourning process," her mother continued. "But that is over now, and we look forward to the many invitations that are to come our way to dine with others at this time of year."

"I agree, my parents always invited in the mumpers on St Thomas Day," Oscar recalled with a fondness.

"Good grief, Your Grace, surely you will not allow those old hags into your beautiful home?" her mother said, looking shocked to the core.

It was most amusing as she and the Duke enjoyed a small smile at one another.

"Yes, Lady Smith, but not only the elderly ladies. They also invited anyone from the village who wished to come," Oscar continued. "We will have tea and cake, together and then give out the gifts of food. I have very fond memories of those days and will most certainly continue the tradition."

"Good for you, Your Grace," Olive added, delighted at her mother's shocked face.

"Thank you, Lady Brent," the Duke said to her, and she thought he looked pleased to be talking with her instead of her mother for once. "There is still the child in me that recalls all our Christmastide traditions. I will savour them all and wish to continue in my parent's footsteps now that I am the Duke."

"I…erm we… Well, we look forward to the ball, Your Grace," her mother said. "Ah, the venison is arriving…"

"It smells delicious Lady Smith, you do your house proud," the Duke remarked.

The servants went around the table serving various vegetables, potatoes, and meat to the lord and ladies. Though Olive did her best to keep the portions small. She hoped to empty her plate, but her mother had put on such a large feast, she knew it would be a struggle. As she glanced up, she could see the reason why her mother had gone so quiet, she was busy tucking into a huge plate of food. Olive took it as an opportunity to speak with the Duke herself.

"Mother tends to make rather large portions for so late in the evening," Olive pointed out. "Please do not feel that you must eat every morsel, Your Grace."

"Nonsense!" her mother called out between mouthfuls. "A man needs to have a good appetite, is that not right, Your Grace?"

"I have not had much of an appetite since my parents passed away, I am afraid," the Duke responded.

"Yes, Your Grace," Olive quickly replied before her mother spoke again and made some distasteful comment. "I do understand. When I was in mourning, food was the last thing I desired."

"That's because you eat like a tiny mouse," her mother remarked.

"Mother, it is nothing to do with what I eat. I am pointing out that we must show respect for His Grace's current predicament and make exceptions," Olive insisted. "This is a very difficult time for him."

She was glad to have pushed the point because the Duke looked at her and gave her an appealing smile. It seemed clear to Olive that he appreciated her comments.

"My daughter often misses the evening meal," her mother snapped back.

Is she trying to embarrass me even more? Olive wondered as she looked over at her mother with wide eyes, wondering what she would say next.

"It is true to say that men have hearty appetites for a dinner, while ladies prefer cake and tea," the Duke said.

Is he sticking up for me? She wondered if she had an ally in the Duke.

"You are quite correct, Your Grace," her mother called out, far too loud. "We ladies do have a rather sweet tooth. I hope you will stay for dessert?"

"Actually, I could not eat another mouthful, Lady Smith," the Duke said, putting his knife and fork neatly on his dinner plate. "And I am keen to return before it gets too late. I hate to risk the horses out in the darkness of night."

"Are you fond of horses, Your Grace?" Olive asked, knowing her mother knew nothing of horses, so it may be a topic she could not join in.

"I am indeed, and their safety is my main concern when travelling in the dark," the Duke replied.

"I enjoy riding too," Olive told him, liking him even more for his fondness of horses.

"Goodness, she rides far too much," her mother commented.

"You can never ride too much, Mother," Olive responded. "It is a pastime that can take you to a riverside, or up the topmost point of a hill. And there, you will find a wonderful peace while your horse grazes."

"That is very true, Lady Brent," the Duke said, giving her a most gracious smile that made her notice a dimple in his left cheek. "It seems we share a common pastime. We may well bump into one another while riding at some time."

"I do not allow my daughter to leave the grounds, Your Grace," her mother interrupted. "She insists on going alone and I insist on her safety. But perhaps His Grace would enjoy her company on one of his rides and call upon us?"

"Whilst that sounds very pleasant, I do not have the time to go out riding of late," the Duke replied, and Olive felt a little disappointed. "There is so much for me to learn about running Bodmin Estate and my father's business dealings."

"That is understandable, Your Grace, it must all be a little daunting for you at present" Olive remarked.

"Well, the offer still stands, Your Grace, should you find yourself with a moment to spare," her mother added.

Olive felt annoyed at her mother's insistence, but she said nothing as she had no desire to embarrass the Duke.

"Sometime in the future perhaps," the Duke replied. "For now, I must be on my way. It has been a delightful meal and my congratulations to the Lady of the House," he said, pushing out of his chair to make tracks.

"I will have one of the servants ready your driver," Olive said, raising her hand to one of the servers. "Browning, will you go and tell our groom that His Grace is almost ready to leave."

The servant nodded her head and left the room.

"It is disappointing you could not stay longer, Your Grace," her mother said as the Duke was standing up. "My daughter would like to have entertained you with her musical skills, which are most pleasant."

"My apologies, ladies, but I have an early start in the morning," the Duke replied most graciously. "Some other time perhaps," he said as he made his way out of the dining room.

Olive and her mother rose to follow him to say their farewells. Her mother was horrified when the Duke went to get his coat, hat, and gloves, and Olive chuckled behind her back. The Duke thought nothing of it, but Olive knew that one of the maids would get an earful for not being there to assist the Duke. The maids had enough to do without being chastised by her mother, so she would intervene when the time came.

As they said their farewells to the Duke, they watched as his carriage rode away. Olive was left with a very good impression of the Duke. There were not many men who sit through a dinner with her mother, and he had been the best that company could expect. Her opinion of him was rising, but still, she would not be led by her mother to marry anyone yet. Of this, she was quite determined. She put up with her mother's ways every day, but she was the one who was going to choose her next husband.

CHAPTER 12

"Well, that went rather well, don't you think?" Olive's mother announced as the maid rushed past them to close the door. "It seems that the Duke is keen to take a ride with you."

Olive glared after her mother who had already begun to make her way toward the smaller parlour. They preferred the smaller room to the larger drawing room as it was easier to keep warm. She followed her mother, determined to have her say on this matter.

"Mother, that is not what the Duke said, and well you know it," Olive said with firmness to her voice. "I do wish that you would stop trying to match me with the poor man."

"The Duke is most certainly not poor. Be honest, my dear, he has a fondness for you. I can see it clearly. You cannot blame me for that, it has nothing to do with me," her mother said haughtily as she took to the chair nearest the open fire. "Can I help it if he has fallen for your charms? I must say, you take after your mother in that way."

Olive bit her tongue. She didn't want to say the first thing that came into her head because she knew it wouldn't be a good thing.

Instead, she forced herself to calm down and took the chair opposite her mother. The maid approached them with a blanket for each of their knees, to keep out any drafts as they sat. Olive thanked the maid, whereas her mother said nothing.

"Mother, I rarely intervene in your plots and schemes, but I will this time. You know that refuse to make the same mistake of marrying a man I do not know," Olive said, staring at her mother, who was doing her best to avoid looking at her. "What's more, I will not marry out of your convenience either. Whoever I marry will court me for as long as I need, so that I can make up my mind whether I love them or not. Do you understand me, Mother? And that does not mean that I will marry for money or a title either. If I fall in love with a trader, then so be it."

"Heavens above, you have no idea what you speak of," her mother finally looked her way. Her eyes were steely, and it was obvious she was now ready for battle. "I realise that you do not have the guidance of a father figure, God rest his soul, but that does not mean that you can be loose with your ways."

"Loose?" Olive repeated the word as she raised her voice. "I am hardly being loose, Mother! On the contrary, you would have me marry anyone, all for the sake of money and a title. At least I would like to know the man that I am to marry first."

"A woman's commitment in life is to her family first and foremost. Your father would have made you see that," her mother replied. "I must take on that role and do the best I can to keep this family in the station it deserves."

"Father was not of noble birth, and you need to admit to yourself," Olive answered. She knew the words would hurt her mother, but she'd had enough of it all. "He was a baronet, mother, not even a baron, and not a peer."

"He was gentrified, and you know it," her mother laughed, with a slight hint of hysteria.

Olive did not counter-argue, for she had loved her father very much and did not wish to use his memory in this way. He had been a very successful merchant and they had owned a grand manor house. That was until his business fell into difficult times because of the wars with France. Her father had died as a result of the hardship they had endured after they lost their home. That was how she had met with her late husband, the Earl. He had taken pity on her and her mother because her father had been a good friend of his. In truth, she is sure he only married her out of pity, but he had left them very comfortable.

"The income you have will not be sustainable if we are to be kept in the comfort that we are accustomed to," her mother spoke her opinions again. "You know all too well that the first thing to go will be the carriage, and then the servants. We must fight for our rightful place in society."

"We will lose none of that, Mother, not if we are careful with the money we have," Olive argued. "We don't need to have fittings for new ball gowns, not when I have a wardrobe full of dresses."

"Oh, my dear, you are so naive. You will not know what has hit you once we are at the cruel mercy of the ton," her mother told her, taking out her lace tissue and dabbing at her eyes.

Olive knew that her mother had won this battle, for she would not continue when her mother was so upset. That was why most of the time she gave into her mother's drama.

"All I ask, my dear, is that you allow me to do what a parent should do, and arrange a suitable suitor for you," her mother said with a quieter tone. "Should you not re-marry we will be treated as two single ladies, and soon enough we will be considered as poor. It will be terrible when we go into a tearoom. We will no longer receive invitations to balls and soirees—"

"But that is my point, Mother," Olive couldn't listen to such nonsense anymore. "I care not what others think about us, even if you do. What do I care about balls and garden parties!"

"You cannot know what you say, Olive," her mother sobbed. "You need to marry to protect us both from the cruelty of the ton. And it will come to us if we do not find you a husband. I could not live through such disgrace. The Duke of Cornwall is such a kind and gentle man, he would protect us and care for us."

Olive said nothing in response, while her mother sobbed on. She was well-aware of her mother's fake sobbing sessions, but still, she pitied her that she relied so much on other people's opinions.

"I do like the Duke, Mother, but I do not want you throwing me at his feet," Olive explained as her mother's sobs lessened. "I must choose my husband and in my own time. It is time to bring love into our family and I will no longer live by your rule."

"I cannot believe that a daughter of mine would speak to me in such a way." Her mother began sobbing again.

Olive sat tapping her fingers on the chair arm, biting her lips and holding back on the words that she knew would only upset her mother further.

"I implore you to listen to my advice, Daughter," her mother began again, determined not to give in. "The Duke of Cornwall will be pressed into seeking a wife by those who care for him, in much the same way I press you to seek a husband. He'll need a good woman to help his business dealings run smoothly, and to produce an heir for the estate. What is wrong with that wife being you? He is taken by you, that much is obvious. He is a gentleman of nobility, and he is kind and considerate, as well as handsome and young. That, to me, is the perfect husband for you. Why can I not want what is best for my daughter?"

Olive had no answer because the situation was hopeless, her mother was never going to give up, with or without her blessing. This was why she so often refused to engage with her mother on this subject because the woman was such hard work. Feeling tired of the argument, one that she knew she could never win; she stood up to say her final words.

"I am not well, Mother," she said, holding her head. "My head aches and I must go and lay down in the dark, so I will take myself to my bed."

"I do not wish to cause you any discomfort, my dear," her mother interjected before her daughter left the room. "I want your life to be a happy one. You should be thinking of having a family and becoming a mother yourself."

Olive approached her mother's chair and leaned over to kiss her mother's forehead.

"I will say goodnight for now," she said, giving her mother a tired smile.

"Yes dear," her mother replied. "I too will turn in shortly, for it has been a fraught evening. Once you have slept on my words, you will soon come around to my way of thinking."

Without another word, Olive left the room and took herself to her bedroom chamber. She knew that she would soon go back to tagging along behind her mother and allowing her to drag her around soirees and balls. And that she would allow her mother her ways for now. But when it finally came to her seeking a husband, she was most certainly going to take the lead role. Olive was determined that she would love her next husband rather than being his personal nurse maid, as she had been with the Earl.

"There is a man out there for me somewhere," she said to herself as looked at her reflection in the dressing table mirror. She looked at the jewels she had taken from her ears. "We have plenty of jewellery to sell before we are in the poor house, so I will not be rushed by my mother."

Putting on her long, white, cotton night dress, Olive was soon glad to be under her heavy blankets. She thought of being a mother and wondered what it was going to be like, having children of her own. But they would be children of love, welcomed into the world by her and their father, who would be a man that she loved too.

CHAPTER 13

Oscar arrived home to a quiet house as the servants had already taken to their beds. That was with the usual exception of Barker. As Oscar arrived at the front door to Welwick Hall, the door opened and there stood the butler to greet him.

"You need not have stayed up until this late hour, Barker," Oscar told him as the butler helped him to take off his coat.

"I do not finish my day until the master of the house is settled, Your Grace," Barker informed him with a formality to his tone.

"Very well," Oscar said, walking away from him as he headed towards his study. "Who am I to break traditions?"

Not being in the mood for conversation, he left the butler behind and hoped he might go to his bed now that he was home. But Oscar knew that sleep, for him, would not come easy. He had started to sleep better at night now that the nightmares of his parents' deaths weren't so frequent. But he had a different reason to be anxious this evening.

Oscar knew that the pressure to marry was getting greater and that it was expected of him to find a wife soon. The Duke of Cornwall played an important role, in representing the royal family.

Meaning that he also needed to produce an heir too, so that added to the pressure all the more.

All the way home he had been thinking of Lady Brent. But then his thoughts had wandered to Vera. There was no hiding the fact that Lady Brent did not have Vera's gutsy charms. Lady Brent was gentle, and the kind of lady who would know all the social rules. No doubt they had been drummed into her head by her mother, Lady Smith. Vera though didn't care about societal rules. She was a breath of fresh air and would never be afraid to say what she thought.

I must stop comparing every lady I meet with my beautiful Vera. Why am I even comparing the Lady Brent with Vera? It's not as if I've known the lady for long. He contemplated. *It must be that my Vera is the only female I have really been close to in my life, other than Mother. I suppose I must be using her behaviour as an example of what I like in a woman. There's nothing about Vera that I dislike, but I cannot compare every lady I meet to her, can I?*

As he deliberated on his thoughts, he'd left the door open and could hear footsteps approaching his study room. The tapping of shoes echoed off the tiled floor of the grand reception hallway.

It didn't sound like Barker, he moved much slower. Nor did it sound like Vera, she was very light-footed, often appearing out of nowhere. Oscar looked over at the open doorway to see who was about to enter his study.

"Good evening, Your Grace," Silas's cheeky smile appeared, with the same slight slant in his eyes that his sister had. It was part of what made them both so unique.

He recalled the story from the twin's mother that the twins got their exotic looking eyes from a father who was a sailor from some far-off exquisite shores. But the man never returned from his last journey after they were born, and the twins never knew if he was dead or alive. All they had left of him were his eyes.

"What the blazes are you doing up at this hour, Silas?" Oscar questioned his friend.

"Doing my duty to my master and friend," Silas said in a strange voice.

"What you really mean is that you are here to assist me to my bedchamber," Oscar said sardonically. "Well, I am having a brandy first, would you care to join me?"

He got up to approach the spirit cupboard, reaching out for the brandy and two glasses, but Silas didn't reply. Turning around to ask Silas again if he wanted a drink, he noted that he still wore that lopsided grin.

"I would know that smile anywhere," Oscar laughed. "By Jove, Vera, it is you, is it not?"

"The night is young," she answered, mimicking her brother's voice. "And so are you, Your Grace. You should be having more fun in your life and stop all this brooding."

"Pray do tell me why you are dressed as your brother?" he asked, though it was very amusing and had lifted his spirits no end.

"Because some people around here," she said in a strained deep voice. "Some people are too miserable and far too serious."

The two friends laughed at her efforts to take on a man's voice. "But you look the part," Oscar remarked. "I thought you were Silas when first you arrived in my study."

"Some are born great, some achieve greatness, and some have greatness thrust upon 'em." Vera said, using Silas's voice.

"Twelfth Night, Act II, Scene 5," Oscar said, pointing his finger in the air as he recalled the scene. "Malvolio's letter, oh such a great scene. *I do not now fool myself, to let imagination jade me; for every reason excites to this, that my lady loves me.*"

Vera clapped her hands together, "Bravo, Your Grace," she giggled.

"She did commend my yellow stockings of late, she did praise my leg being cross-gartered," Oscar continued to recite the scene from Twelfth Night.

"Yet, it is all a wicked joke of love," Vera added. "Though my joke

on you was meant to cheer you. I assure you that I would play no wicked jokes on you, Your Grace."

"Oh, Vera, you are such a delight" Oscar replied "Your joke has indeed cheered me. You look so alike you and your brother, but your voice gave away the trick."

"I am meant to be my brother, giving you a lecture on how you should be enjoying life more," Vera admitted. "We both worry over you, going around with such a miserable face. I felt I needed to do something dramatic to make you smile."

"Am I not the one who promised you that I would provide you with more fun in your life, not the other way around?" Oscar smiled as she sat herself down.

Vera was about to answer when Silas came dashing into the study. "What's all the noise coming from this room?" he asked, looking at his master with worry on his face. "Vera? What?"

"I am not Vera, I am Silas," Vera said to her brother. She was attempting to use her faux male voice again, but the deep notes caused her to cough.

"Are you trying to mimic my voice?" her brother asked, looking shocked at her efforts. "Well, if that's the case, you're terrible at it."

"Aw come now, Silas, your sister looks the spitting image of you," Oscar said." You have to agree on that much?"

"You do, Vera, and I must say I am a very handsome devil, do you not agree?" Silas joked.

All three of them burst out into laughter. Silas closed the study room door so their raucous laughter would not awaken the entire household, or even worse, it might summon Barker.

As they all sat down their laughter settled down, "It feels like old times again," Oscar declared.

"It does, but I must insist on attending to you, Your Grace. I wouldn't want my sister helping you out of that formal wear," Silas pointed out with raised brows at the very thought.

"Yes, yes," Vera called out as she stood up to mimic her brother and repeat his words. "I must insist on attending to you, Your Grace, and helping you out of that formal wear."

"Stop that," Silas said. "You don't sound anything like me. All you do is make a mockery of my manliness."

This had Oscar and Vera hooting in laughter once again.

"My brother believes his masculinity is at stake by his sister's squeaky voice," Vera giggled behind her hand.

"Thank you, you have lifted my spirits no end, the both of you," Oscar admitted. "Of late, life seems so serious. But there is never a dull moment when you two are by my side."

"Good, I am pleased that you two have had your fun at my expense," Silas mumbled. "Vera, to your bed and take off my clothes. Oscar, let's go and ready you for your bed too. Should Barker get wind that we're enjoying each other's company, he might come and twist our ears."

"Now that is not funny, brother," Vera said, yawning, her tiredness getting the better of her. "I've been in hiding while I awaited Oscars return so I could play my joke on him. You looked utterly miserable when I first entered the room. I am only too glad that I helped to bring some cheer into your life. Even if it is at the cost of my brother's dignity."

"The trouble with you two is that neither of you ever grew up," Silas declared, looking stern at the pair of them. "Life is not one big play, and it is a serious matter that His Grace gets his sleep, finds a wife, and runs the estate."

"Oh, come now, Silas, Vera was not making fun of you," Oscar said, seeing how cross Silas was with his sister. "She looks adorable in your clothes. That is until she attempts to speak."

His remark caused another bout of laughter between Vera and Oscar, with Silas looking on bewildered.

"You will both know about it if Barker hears you," Silas warned.

"What's wrong with you, brother?" Vera asked. "We agreed to

do all we could to cheer Oscar. That was all I sought to do. Do you not see the connection with Twelfth Night?"

"I do sister, but did you have to choose me to dress up as?" Silas snapped. "If anyone should see you, I'd be a laughingstock."

"It is me they would laugh at, not you," Vera said, waiting for her brother to calm himself. "Besides, I made His Grace laugh, is that not an achievement in itself?"

"You did indeed," Oscar agreed. "Whatever would I do without my Vera in my life?"

"Have some peace and quiet for a start," Silas answered. "Now go, Vera, before anyone, and especially Barker, might see you dressed like that. You're far too skinny to be me anyway."

"I'll put socks in my sleeves next time," Vera chuckled, making her way to the door. "So, I look like I have your big muscles," she said, making a run for it before her brother could reply.

Silas was about to instruct Oscar that he needed to take his bed too, when Vera stuck her head back around the doorway.

"Goodnight, Oscar," she said in a deep voice, along with a giggle, and soon disappeared again.

"Your sister is the light in my life," Oscar said, as he waved to her. "But you, Silas, are becoming all too serious. You could dress as your sister if you want to get her back," he chuckled.

"I beg your pardon," Silas said, putting more depth in his voice. "Shall we go and hang up that formal attire, Your Grace, and get you in your bed where you belong?"

"Silas, be careful," Oscar said, leaving his study to go upstairs. He was starting to feel tired after his evening's entertainment. "You are starting to sound too much like Barker!"

Silas followed his master, saying nothing but thinking that Barker was the only sane one in this manor house.

CHAPTER 14

It was a brisk morning, and the winter sun was fierce, bringing out most of the autumn colours on the fallen leaves upon the grounds of the Bodmin Estate. As Oscar spotted the scenery through his bedroom window, he decided to sit on his balcony and eat breakfast outside. Whilst waiting for his breakfast to arrive, he read a newspaper. It was a good time to start catching up with all the business news, now that he felt almost ready to face the world.

It was Barker who arrived with his breakfast tray, which surprised Oscar somewhat.

"Where is the steward, erm... Millard is it?" Oscar asked as he folded up his newspaper. "I thought it was not your place to serve food, Barker?" He teased his butler because he knew how he was a stickler for protocol.

"I must say, Your Grace, I too am surprised," Barker replied. "Why are you out in the chilly air?"

"The sun is out, Barker, and the vista is wonderful," Oscar replied, lifting his arms to embrace the beautiful autumnal scenery. "We shall all be stuck indoors soon enough, once the winter sets in. Now then, are you going to answer my question? I thought we had rules to follow about which servant did which task."

Barker bowed his head as he started to pour the hot water into the teapot.

"That is quite correct, Your Grace," Barker said, showing little in the way of any expression on his face. "It is my task to see that everyone knows their place, but I wished to speak with you this morning before you go about your day."

"Get on with it then, man," Oscar said, annoyed that Barker was disturbing the tranquillity of his peaceful morning breakfast. "What is on your mind now?"

"I would like to ask if you have thought any further about my idea to organise a ball?" Barker asked as he stood up straight and awaited his answer.

Oscar began to eat his scrambled eggs before they became too cold. Vera knew exactly how he liked his morning eggs, and she went to great efforts to deliver them warm.

"Hmmm... I am thinking of a Christmastide ball, but I wish to speak with Cook before we begin the process."

As Oscar looked up and noted a break in Barker's dour face, was that a half smile?

"But I am the one who will organise everything, Your Grace, surely you would speak with me first?" Barker enquired.

"Oh, I see," Oscar said as he chewed on a piece of freshly baked bread. "So, you will do all the cooking of the food will you?"

"Well...no, of course, I will not," Barker mumbled as he faltered. "But I will be the one to discuss the menu with cook. We do not expect you to take on such a menial task, Your Grace."

"Ah...well, I do not consider it menial," Oscar said, buttering another piece of the delicious soft bread. "What I want you to do Barker, is to go to the kitchen directly and tell Cook to pack a picnic for three people. Then inform her that I wish her to attend said picnic so that we may discuss the Christmastide ball. Can you do that for me, Barker?"

"I...well...if Your Grace insists, but it's highly unusual. You will be the topic of the gossipers if you should be seen taking food with your servants," Barker stuttered. "Perhaps I should attend too, as I have much experience in the organisation of balls."

"No, I will have Silas and Vera accompany me, they will see to my needs," Oscar insisted. "At the same time, I will discuss the menu requirements with our cook. Now thank you, Barker. You are dismissed."

Oscar watched the butler through the corner of his eye and could see him acting quite flustered. Yes, it was even time to put his butler in his place too. Oscar was stronger every day and almost felt like his old self again. He had come through his experience an even sturdier man, ready to face battle.

"Your Grace, I must insist that there are far more suitable maids to serve your picnic than a cook," Barker tried his old ways of cajoling Oscar all he could. It worked fine when he was a boy, but not anymore.

"I have said my last word on this matter Barker, are you refusing to do my bidding?" Oscar teased, trying his best to hold back his smile.

Barker bowed, "No...no, of course not, Your Grace. I will see to it at once."

"Oh...and inform my valet that I wish to see him at once," Oscar called after Barker as he was leaving his room. "Tell him that I want a casual outfit for a day by the sea."

Barker stopped for a brief moment as if he was about to object, but he said nothing and went about his business.

Good, Oscar thought. A butler who finally knows his place.

He couldn't help but chuckle to himself at how the tables had turned. Gone were the days when the butler scared the living daylights out of him. He was no longer a mischievous boy trying to avoid Barker so he wouldn't get into trouble with his father. Leaning back in his chair, he looked out at the oranges and reds of the trees. Life felt good. Thanks to his friends, and especially Vera, he had come through the worst of his grief. Not that he didn't feel the sadness of his loss anymore, he did, but he felt ready to take up his father's mantle.

The bedchamber door soon opened again, and this time Silas stepped inside.

"What's this about you going on a trip to the sea?" Silas asked. "By the gods, it's chilly in here."

Oscar stood up and entered through the French doors into his bedchamber. "A bit of fresh air never did anyone any harm. You and your sister are to accompany me on a picnic by the sea this very day."

"What? A picnic in the autumn, Oscar, are you mad?" Silas expressed.

"You can wrap up in an overcoat, and I happen to know that your sister not only loves this time of year, but she loves the sea too," Oscar pointed out. "Now then, I would like something warm to wear, but casual. After a night in that dinner jacket, I wish to relax and enjoy some time with my friends."

It pleased him when he spotted a smile on Silas's face.

"So, you approve then, do you?" Oscar asked his valet.

"I know how much it will cheer my sister, and for that, I approve Your Grace," Silas answered with an exaggerated low bow.

"Stop your fooling around," Oscar said feigning annoyance. "You are being over dramatic as always. I want to spend some time with you both, it is that simple."

***

Silas drove the open-topped carriage for their trip. Oscar had requested the two-seater barouche, so they could open or close the roof of the carriage as the weather allowed. It also meant that Vera would be forced to sit by his side, which pleased him greatly. He was looking forward to enjoying Vera's company all to himself Something he had been missing as of late. The twins were everything to him and he was not going to allow their social differences to come between them.

"Did I not promise you fun?" Oscar said to Vera.

"I must admit, Oscar, this is wonderful," Vera replied, looking pleased.

"It's important to me that you both are by my side if I am to take on all the responsibilities of being the Duke," Oscar told her.

"No, Oscar, you need to distance yourself from us," Vera said, turning to stare at him, her brow furrowed with worry. "As much as it hurts me to say it, I know it to be true."

"This trip is the perfect excuse for us to be together. Should anyone see us, you can make that you are my maid, if you must stick to protocol," Oscar suggested. "I thought you would be pleased."

"I am pleased, but do tread with care," Vera said. "You have a great social standing now, Your Grace."

"Stop calling me that, Vera," Oscar said, his annoyance rising. "Where has your sense of adventure gone?"

"It's because we care for you, that my brother and I ask that you be careful."

Oscar couldn't help himself and he took hold of her hand in his. her response was unexpected as she instantly shook him off.

"No, Oscar, you cannot do such a thing," she said, looking shocked.

"But you and Silas are my only family," he complained. "Please, Vera, let's not spoil our time together."

She looked at him and gave him one of her most charming smiles.

"That's better," Oscar said. "Can we enjoy our day together at the very least?"

She nodded in agreement, "Of course, and thank you for including us, despite the risks."

"It is no risk," Oscar said. "I have no care what others think, Vera, you know that."

"I don't know what you two are arguing over back there," Silas's voice called out. "But I'm pulling up at that tree over there. There's grass for the horses and we can picnic on the dunes."

Oscar was pleased to see Vera's face relax, now that they had arrived.

"Can you smell it? I can hear the sea already," she said, looking out over the dunes. "Look, isn't it a magical wonder," she pointed out to the grey sea waves.

Silas saw to the horses and carriage, while Oscar and Vera began to set up the picnic together.

"You shouldn't be helping, Oscar, what if someone was to see?" Vera chastised him.

"Out here?" He questioned. "I asked Silas to bring us to a secluded spot and he has. We could likely stay here all week and not see another soul. Please, Vera, I want no airs and graces when we are all together. The only time I have real fun is when I am with my two best friends."

Vera soon gave in; poor Oscar had a lot on his shoulders, and she should help him unwind.

White fluffy clouds blew across the blue skies as they walked towards the seashore. Vera had insisted on taking off her shoes, so the menfolk followed her lead.

She dipped her toes into the water, "Brrr...it's cold," she announced, giggling.

They splashed each other by kicking up the seawater, the coldness of the sea soon forgotten. All this activity made them hungry, and they returned to the picnic area to eat.

Once back at the picnic spot, Vera began to serve the food.

"I am starving," Oscar said, accepting the offerings. "I even brought some wine so we could have a toast to our friendship."

Silas went to get the bottle of wine and glasses, as he returned, he boasted, "Did I not promise you that I knew of a good spot where other folks won't bother us."

"It feels like we have the whole world to ourselves," Vera said as she smiled up at Silas to accept a glass of ruby, red wine.

Once they had their fill of food, Oscar announced, "I have even brought the skittles from the garden so we can have a game. Silas, will retrieve them from the carriage storage?"

Vera helped to set them up and they all three had a turn in the sand. It wasn't an easy game to play with the shifting sands, but they had fun trying. After the game, all three lay on the picnic blankets and stared up at the clear blue autumn sky.

"Oh, that was fun," Vera said as she puffed out of breath from all the exertion of their games.

"Let us do another toast to our friendship," Oscar said, sitting up and holding up his glass for the second toast of their friendship.

"Wait a moment," Silas said, looking off into the distance. "Is that a carriage I can see approaching?"

CHAPTER 15

Vera couldn't help herself as she teased her brother for his empty promise, "A good spot where other folks won't bother us," she said, making fun of his words.

"Stop that. You're being childish!" Silas admonished her. "You are pushing your luck, sister. If I didn't love you so much, I'd tan your hide."

Vera was about to answer back when she noticed Oscar's half smile. "And I would help him," he chuckled, and then stood up to observe the carriage as it pulled up nearby their own.

"I am sure that I recognise that carriage but surely it cannot be?" Oscar mumbled to himself, looking more than a little annoyed. "It is...it's that dreadful woman again. Can I not escape her, even out here in the dunes?"

Vera pulled out an apron and tied it around her waist. She knew it would be better if she looked the part of a maid, whether Oscar liked it or not. She started to tidy up the food to make it look as if only one person was feasting from the picnic blanket.

Silas quickly followed her lead, "I'll go and get the tables and chairs. I doubt we'll get rid of them," he told Vera as he headed towards their own carriage.

Vera growled to herself, wishing her brother had not packed the picnic table and chairs, then the women might have left. But she knew better, it wasn't his fault. They must set up the scene for a more luxurious picnic for His Grace. They didn't want the ladies suspecting that Oscar was picnicking with servants.

Through the corner of her eyes, Vera glanced over at the scene where Oscar had been forced to walk out to meet the visiting carriage. Her stomach felt heavy with disappointment at having their private time together ruined in such a way. Silas arrived back and unfolded the wooden table. She threw a tablecloth over it as Silas opened up three chairs.

Moving a plate of food from the blanket to the table, she also moved the half bottle of wine. The twins had set the scene to make it appear as if His Grace was to sit at the table. They would serve him from the feast spread out from the blanket on the ground. Once done, Vera and Silas stood and awaited the arrival of His Grace's guests, so they could serve them. But Vera was more than a bit fed up at having their day interrupted.

Oscar went to open the door to the carriage and reached his arm inside to help a lady step out of it. Sure enough, it was Lady Smith from Silsbury Manor. Vera almost giggled at the larger lady's enormous hat. At least the hat that the younger one wore was quite pretty. Their driver had gone to the other door to help the younger lady step out. Vera gasped at the blonde lady's beauty, it was Lady Brent, the widow of the late Earl of Gosmore. Vera felt a sudden sickness in the pit of her stomach. It was more than disappointment; it was utter despair.

Vera didn't always understand why she felt that way whenever she saw Oscar with another woman. She knew perfectly well that she and Oscar could never be together. Yet, seeing him another Lady always brought home the truth of their situation. No matter how hard Oscar tried to promote his friendship with them, they would always be his servants.

Even Silas looked troubled as he spoke, "Oscar is right about one thing," he said to his sister under his breath. "That woman is determined to grab him for her daughter."

Vera choked as she fought back tears. *What was I doing letting Oscar make me think everything was back to normal? I'm such a fool.*

She looked up, taking in a deep breath to control her emotions. This was not going to be easy, watching Oscar pamper the lady. After all, what she but a cook, a servant, not a lady. It was high time she accepted that. Readying herself for the extra guests, she looked over and observed Oscar raise his arm as he gestured for them to join him. The group started to walk towards the picnic table.

"Good job I brought three chairs," Silas murmured sounding annoyed. "Mind you, that woman might not fit in it, it's only a small chair."

Vera stifled a smile at his comment, she knew he wasn't being disrespectful on purpose, but only trying to cheer her up.

"My daughter finds great solace from walking along the shoreline," Lady Smith's words lingered in the air as the group approached. "She is such a gentle, romantic soul, and as her mother, I like to pamper her needs."

Oscar didn't reply to the lady's comment, instead, he put out his arm to once again offer up his table to them. Vera and Silas each took hold of the back of a chair in acceptance of their guests. By coincidence, Lady Brent accepted Vera's chair.

"I never imagined we would bump into another person whilst we rode along these dunes," Lady Brent commented. "Is this not a lonely place for you to be all by yourself, Your Grace?"

"Not at all. I too find solace in being by the seashore," he answered, taking the only vacant seat as he glanced at Lady Smith struggling to get into her chair.

For a moment, Vera thought he looked like he was going to

offer her some assistance, but then he seemed to stop himself. It was as if he had thought better of it. Vera was pleased that he hadn't, the less he indulged the woman the better.

Lady Brent put her gloved hand to her mouth as she gasped, and they all looked her way. "My apologies, Your Grace. It was insensitive of me to assume that you did not wish to be alone. Are you sure we are not intruding on your mournful grief?"

"Do not distress yourself, Lady Brent," Oscar replied as he glanced over at Vera. She was serving out plates on the table, with her famous fruit cake and a wedge of cheese. "I woke up this very morning to embrace the turn of events in my life. I felt a trip out here, with the soothing sounds of the ocean, might help me to think. Your company is a most welcome break from my deliberations."

Vera watched Lady Brent look genuinely relieved. Was she being a little hard on the lady? She did not seem at all false, as did her mother. Though she did wish that Oscar would tell them that he preferred to be alone in his grief. Maybe then they'd take the hint and leave, allowing their private party to continue. But as she listened to their conversation develop, she knew their private time together was over.

She and her brother stood at a distance, once she had served the cake and Silas had poured the wine. As expected, he had topped the wine glasses up with a little water too. Vera wished he had forgotten that part. If Lady Smith had too much wine, she might have begun to tire and left. But no such luck.

Glancing back at Lady Brent, a little guilt swelled up in Vera's mind. The lady was very attractive, and she too had gone through grief, at the loss of her husband.

Vera knew all too well what it was like to be in love, most especially with a man who she could never share her life with.

"You have much in common, my daughter and you, Your Grace," Lady Smith said, her voice echoing out in a loud monotonous tone. Vera thought she must talk that loud all the time as she seemed so at ease with making herself the centre of attention. "Olive has come through her grieving and is ready to face the world. You know what that means for a lady, do you not?"

Vera noted that Lady Brent's face flushed as she glared at her mother.

"Mother, please, can we not enjoy our time by the sea instead of discussing such matters?" Lady Brent said, looking a little annoyed with her mother.

"We are on a picnic, my dear," Lady Smith responded to her daughter as she tucked into the fruit cake and homemade cheese. "What better time for conversation, I say. Well... Your Grace, I will tell you it means as I know you are a little out of touch in your grief. My daughter is ready to seek out a suitor so that she can produce grandchildren for her mother. She knows how much I yearn for the patter of tiny feet."

Again, Lady Brent looked embarrassed as she turned to Oscar. "My apologies, Your Grace, Mother forgets her manners. I am in no rush to re-marry."

"Do not feel the need to explain to me, Lady Brent," Oscar said to her, in a soft tone. "I do understand the pressures that society can put upon us. I too have demands from close relatives, and friends of my family. It can become tedious, but I am sure they all mean well."

"You see, Daughter, His Grace is most understanding," Lady Smith asserted.

"Oscar has just given Lady Smith permission to go on and on with her matchmaking, what is he thinking?" Vera whispered to her brother.

"Well, it is true, Sister," Silas whispered. "He does need to find a suitable wife, otherwise the Bodmin Estate will suffer without an heir."

Vera gave him a light nudge with her elbow, she was annoyed at him for more or less agreeing that Oscar had to marry. Of course, she knew that was the truth, but she didn't want her own brother rubbing her face in it.

"Yes, but he does not have to marry the first lady that comes along," she told him. Her voice came out louder than she had intended, causing all three to look her way. She prayed they had not heard her words.

Oscar gave Vera a resigned look, showing her that he too was feeling dispirited. In her view, it seemed that he regretted the interruption. Other than sending the ladies away, which would cause Lady Smith to gossip terribly, the situation was beyond his control. But that wasn't Vera's main worry. As she listened to the developing conversation and observed Oscar, it seemed clear to her that Oscar was quite taken by Lady Brent. *Is she the future Duchess of Cornwall?* Vera wondered.

She wanted to feign illness so that she could get out of watching the scene before her, though she knew it would be frowned upon. Knowing that she had no choice but to watch as her dreams of Oscar and her together were being shattered before her very eyes. She had always known, with a deep certainty, that was all it would ever be, a dream.

CHAPTER 16

At last, someone hinted that it was becoming a little chilly. Did this mean that the women would depart? Though, it had surprised Vera that it was Lady Brent who mentioned it. Vera would put up with being frozen anytime if meant being with Oscar.

"Hmph! If she thought anything of Oscar, she'd put up with being a little chilly!" Vera mumbled to herself as she started to pack up the food.

"What was that?" Silas asked as he collected the skittles together. "I left the skittles out in case the ladies wished to have some fun and play a game. Instead, poor Oscar has put up with an hour of Lady Smith wittering on and on. Mind you, don't think I haven't noticed that Oscar and the younger lady keep smiling at one another. Anyway, did you say to me?"

"Nothing for your ears," Vera snapped back, reaching down to pick up the blanket and give it a good shake. She shook the blanket vigorously, taking her temper out on it to calm her inner rage.

"I see that jealousy thing is raising its ugly head again," Silas leaned in to whisper in her ear. He didn't stay around for an answer as he went to put the skittles into the storage area.

"I'll give you jealousy..." Vera continued her mumblings, now folding up the picnic blanket to put it away in the large wicker basket, along with the food. "Thank goodness they're starting to make a move," she said to Silas as he returned to carry the basket back into the carriage.

Silas and Vera remained standing by the carriage as Oscar waved the ladies off. He was all smiles and grace, at least until they were out of sight and then his face changed to thunder.

"That woman even managed to bring the rain with her," Oscar said as he came to stand by Vera. "Why are standing out here?" he asked as he put out his hand to help her into the carriage. "Put the roof up, Silas. You'll need the blanket over your knees, Vera, it's going to be a chilly ride home."

Vera didn't bother with the blanket, but as they sat side by side Oscar placed it over her knees. Neither spoke to the other on the ride back, and Vera thought the chilly air was appropriate to everyone's mood. She knew that if she said anything, she would only say something wicked about the ladies who had interrupted their perfect afternoon. Although she was grateful that Oscar had covered her legs with the blanket, as she was now shivering.

Silas called back to Oscar, who seemed to have drifted into thoughts of his own. "You do know that Lady Smith is playing at matchmaking for her daughter?"

"I know she is. Though Lady Brent hardly needs her mother's assistance, she is a fine lady in her own rights," Oscar called up to Silas.

Her brother was seated on the higher driver's seat up front. Vera knew that sitting separately would not stop Silas from having a conversation with them. Even if it means having to talk out loud for them to hear each other.

Oscar spoke again, continuing his reply, "She at least understands my grief, unlike her mother. I swear, that woman seems to care about nothing but marrying her daughter off."

Vera remained silent as she listened to their conversation. It was clear to her that Oscar did not dislike Lady Brent, and that in itself was enough to confuse her emotions even further. He did not care for Lady Smith, so why would he want anything to do with her daughter? Imagine, if he were to marry Lady Brent, then Lady Smith would live at Welwick Hall too. That was not a pretty thought, but neither was losing Oscar.

"Anyone who's undergone grief deserves some happiness, don't you agree?" Oscar asked Vera, though it didn't seem as if he was expecting an answer as he muttered the rest of his words to himself. "The lady is very pleasing to the eye too."

Vera couldn't believe that he had said those words, though she knew she was not meant to have heard his mumblings. Now Oscar had forced her hand and she couldn't keep from asking, "Does that mean you will be considering her for your wife?" A part of her wished she hadn't opened her mouth because she was dreading his answer.

Oscar didn't answer straight away, and she wasn't sure that he had heard her. Then, he turned to look at her, as if her words had just reached his ears, and he smiled.

"Slow down there, Vera," he said, looking at her as if she had said something unexpected. She looked back at him in surprise. "I am not yet ready to make such an important decision as that one."

Vera wanted to feel relieved at his answer. Yet she was more upset he hadn't told her outright that he had no intention of marrying Lady Brent, or anyone else for that matter. She could see that Oscar had drifted off into deep thoughts once again, and she left him to it. How she wanted to throw herself at him and tell him of her love. The scene played out in her mind and no matter how she imagined it, there was no happy ending to that story.

Silas shouted something else back to Oscar and the two of them continued to have a conversation about how the weather had turned. That led to how the waves had picked up, so there must be a storm out at sea.

Vera could not join in the general chit-chat because she was seething inside. Her emotions played havoc with her head and her heart, causing her almost to the point of tears. And all the while, all her brother and best friend could talk about was the weather.

She could not believe it when her brother brought up Lady Brent once again, saying that it was a miracle how the dour Lady Smith had such a pretty daughter. The worst of it was that Oscar agreed, which meant that he thought the lady was pretty too. Vera looked at her hands, covered in burns and hard skin from all her labours in the kitchen.

She recalled the pretty outfit that Lady Brent had worn, in comparison to her drab, dark blue dress. *And what about that dainty hat upon her beautiful blonde locks?* she thought, reminding herself how dark her hair was in comparison. *Lady Brent is a typical fair-haired lady of the gentry, with the perfect manners, and the beautiful clothes that go with that. While all I am is a servant and a commoner. I'm clumsy and ugly, while Lady Brent is graceful and dainty, with the prettiest face for miles around.*

"Do you not agree, Vera?" Oscar's voice came to her as she became aware that he was asking her something.

"I suppose so," Vera answered, with no idea what she was agreeing to.

"See, even Vera agrees," Oscar called back to Silas, and they were both laughing at something.

"Well, you can tell him then, Sister," Silas called back to her.

"Tell who, what?" she asked, feeling flummoxed at whatever she had agreed to.

"You can be the one to inform Barker that we've found him a suitable wife," Oscar said to her, now looking at her puzzled.

"Have we? And who might that be?" she asked, looking equally puzzled.

"I thought you agreed?" Oscar asked. "You do not agree, do you? In fact, you have not been listening to us, have you?"

"I... I was contemplating over food preparation in the kitchen," she lied, not wanting him to question what she had been daydreaming over.

"We agreed that Barker and Lady Smith would be suitable for one another, and I thought you agreed with us?" Oscar said, looking incredulous at her blank face.

"But he is a servant, and she is a lady?" she questioned, not quite understanding the humour.

"Yes, that's the whole joke, don't you see?" Silas called back trying to help Oscar out as his sister was acting so stubborn. "Whoa, there!" he called out to the horses as he pulled the carriage up outside the main doors of Welwick Hall.

Vera had not realised that they were home. At least now she did not have to put up with their nonsense, and she wasted no time in jumping up and getting out of the carriage.

How dare they joke around while I'm suffering a broken heart? she deliberated. If only she could tell them that, but she could never admit the truth to Oscar. All that was left was for her to find employment elsewhere. *I'll have to leave because I cannot bear to see him happy with another woman. I hate my life and I hate my brother too.*

As she hurried away, she did not even thank Oscar for the trip, nor did she say goodbye to him. All she could think was that she had to get away from him.

Before she arrived at the servant's entrance near the kitchen, Silas grabbed her arm. "Slow down, sis," he called out, panting from dashing after her. "You got a bee in your bonnet over something?"

"I'm a servant, Silas," she snapped, and it hurt her to see the worried look on her brother's face. "That means that I must get to my duties and stop imagining things above my station. You can tell Oscar that these trips must stop, do you hear me?"

"What the? What's brought this on?" he asked, and she knew by his eyes that he was confused. "All we did was make fun at Barker's expense. Why are you so mad at that?"

"I don't have time for idle chatter," she replied, scowling back at him.

Shaking her arm from his grasp, she turned towards the servant's door. "I am sorry, brother, but can you not see that I'm upset? The entire day was ruined, all because of some pretty lady."

Leaving those words lingering, she pushed open the door, ready to do her duties in the kitchen. What had she been thinking? As if she didn't have enough on her plate without allowing Oscar to give her hope. "Hope that can never, ever show itself again," she cried out to herself, bracing herself before entering the busy, noisy kitchen.

CHAPTER 17

Olive had felt uncomfortable at disturbing the Duke of Cornwall on his picnic in the dunes. When her mother had called out excitedly that she'd spotted another carriage, Olive had been quite surprised. It wasn't an area where one would expect to bump into anyone else. It seemed an odd coincidence that it turned out to be the Duke of Cornwall, but at first, she had thought nothing of it.

She had relented and agreed to pull up as it was so much easier to give in to her mother's demands than to argue with her. At least her mother told the truth when she said that Olive liked to take the carriage for a drive by the seashore. There was something very special about the ocean waves that she enjoyed. They represented certain freedom that she didn't have. They could crash around in any direction they liked, smashing against the cliffs and rocks. Whereas she had to move wherever society dictated, and more so where her mother decreed.

She was thankful that the Duke hadn't seemed too annoyed at their disturbing him, so she was thankful for that at least. Today though, they had been invited to a soiree at a country mansion known as Heligan House. It was home to Lord Granville, the Baron of Levan. Her mother had gone out of her way to get an invitation because the Granville's had older sons, and they were all seeking wives.

Olive was expecting the whole affair to be a bore as she followed her mother around dutifully. Shortly after arriving, they soon found themselves sitting in a parlour with a group of chattering ladies. What had happened next though, caused her to wish she had never agreed to attend the soiree. Her mother was boasting, with much exaggeration, that their relationship with the Duke of Cornwall was more than it really was.

"The Duke of Cornwall is fast becoming a close acquaintance of ours," her mother announced as Olive cringed. "He has taken a shine to my daughter, and who can blame him? She has all the right breeding and etiquette to become the next Duchess. I am sure that is what he was hinting at on our recent trip with him to the beach."

Olive had purposely not taken a seat by her mother's side, so she would not be forced into any conversations. Now she wished she had sat with her so that she could shut her up.

"Do tell us all about it, Lady Smith," Lady Montgomery encouraged her mother. "I am most intrigued to hear everything about the new Duke."

"We accompanied him on a beachside picnic only yesterday," her mother replied.

"Goodness, I have been trying to get an invite to Welwick Hall for a while now," Lady Montgomery remarked. "My husband tells me that they are not to be holding any balls or public events anytime in the near future."

"It is a great pity if you ask me. Especially when you consider how much Lady Sarah Wold loved to host balls in the winter months," another female voice chimed up. "The new duke must be missing the guiding hands of his parents."

Olive glanced over to see who was speaking and recognised

Lady Gregory, a woman with many daughters. No doubt she was here for the same reason as her mother, seeking suitors for her daughters.

"That is why he needs to take a wife," Lady Montgomery suggested. "A wife can bring a steady hand to someone who bears great responsibilities."

"None more so than my daughter," her mother's voice quickly replied. "Being the late wife of an earl, she has much to offer in the way of guidance and support."

"Oh, how is your dear daughter, Lady Audrey?" Lady Adam's voice came to Olive's ears.

Was the woman blind? Could she not see her seated among them?

But her mother did not supply this information, instead, she continued joining in with the idle gossip. Half an hour later, her mother stood up and glanced her way, indicating that she was to follow her. As she did so, one of the hostess's sons approached, asking if she cared to dance, to which she agreed. Anything would be a light relief to get away from her mother.

"I hear tell that the new Duke of Cornwall has you in his sights," her partner said as he stood awaiting their turn in the steps of the dancing group.

"No, My Lord, I do not know him well at all," Olive replied, determined to undo her mother's gossip.

"How odd," Lord Granville said, looking puzzled for a moment. "I could have sworn Lady Gregory informed me that you are the Duke's first choice as a wife and that he is not looking elsewhere. You seem to be the envy of all the young ladies."

"You should not listen to the idle gossip of ladies, My Lord," Olive said with a smirk that she hid from him. "I am currently not looking to marry anyone."

She knew it was most likely too late to put a stop to her mother's rumours, nonetheless, she refused to go along with them.

When the dance ended, Lord Granville, the eldest of the hostess's sons, thanked her and apologised for his misinformation. As he was leaving, her mother approached her.

"Oh, my dear girl, there is a joyous buzz around the room, have you not heard it?" her mother asked, looking a little giddy.

"I have, Mother, and I am not at all pleased about it," Olive replied with a sternness in her tone. "Your information is based on exaggerations and lies, Mother. I demand that you stop discussing me where it concerns the Duke of Cornwall."

"Whatever do you mean?" Her mother asked as she raised her fan to her face.

"You know exactly what I mean, Mother," Olive accused. "I do not like it, so please stop doing it. You are far too bold. I would also like to know how we coincidentally bumped into him at the beach dunes yesterday because I now believe that you were behind it."

"Well... I...may have been speaking with his butler, who I assure you is an honest man," her mother replied, looking not the least bit guilty.

"I cannot believe it," Olive shook her head. "Well, actually, I can." Olive huffed.

"It wasn't my fault, I bumped into the man in the market square in my morning visit to the tea rooms," her mother admitted. "He happened to mention that His Grace was going out for a picnic by the sea. When I enquired where that might be, he told me that he had a good idea because he knew that he wanted to be alone."

"Are you and this butler trying to matchmake together?" Olive asked, unable to comprehend that her mother had an ally, or rather a spy within Welwick Hall.

"Well, I understand that he wants what is best for the Duke, and I want the best for my daughter, where is the harm in that?" her mother asserted. "Anyway, who told you of the rumour, you have hardly spoken to a soul?"

"I have ears, Mother, and you have contradicted yourself in your little plot," Olive said, walking away.

"Come here, Daughter," her mother called to her, and when she ignored her, she promptly followed in her wake. "I say, do tell me what you mean by such a harsh statement. Everything I do is for you, my dear."

Olive stopped and turned around to confront her mother, "No, Mother, it is for you. And now you have put off every other eligible bachelor in Cornwall by announcing I am to marry the Duke. When, in truth, I am to marry no one."

"But it is all for you, Olive," her mother wittered, unwilling to give up the fight. "The Duke is very interested in you, that much is obvious, and why shouldn't he be?"

"Oh, I don't know, Mother," Olive said as she leaned close to her mother to speak in a hushed tone. "Perhaps because I give him no cause to be interested in me. I do not wish to marry, remember?"

By now their raised voices were beginning to attract the attention of other guests, and many stared their way. Olive guessed that everyone by now knew she had fallen out with her mother, but she didn't care a jot. Still ignoring her, she headed for the door to go outside. Her mother hated the cold, and today was a particularly chilly day in more ways than one.

Once outside, she decided to stroll around the garden area that was close to the house. It might help clear her head a little. She knew that her mother would never stop, not until the day she was re-married.

I do like the Duke, but unless he is willing to undergo a very long courtship, I am in no hurry to be wed, she mused. *What he is going to think should these rumours get back to him, I hate to think. Mother does more harm for her cause than she does good.*

"Ah, Lady Brent," a familiar male called out. "How lovely to bump into you again."

It was Lord Granville again, of whom she had danced with earlier. And now she felt a little uneasy at being alone with him in the garden. Perhaps it might be better if she went along with her mother's lies after all, and then other men would stay away from her.

"Along the lines of our earlier conversation," he said to her. "You may not know it, but I too am seeking a wife."

"I am sorry, Lord Granville, but I must turn in another direction. I do not wish to be seen alone with any gentleman," she told him, which was the truth as it might cause yet another wave of gossip.

"I realise this, and I will not keep you, but I want to ask—"

Olive cut him off, for she could not bear to speak with him alone. "I suppose you know by now that the rumours over myself and the Duke of Cornwall are true?" she said, hoping this might stop him from pursuing her around the garden unaccompanied. Her mother would have a fit if she knew she was alone with him.

"Oh, I see," he said, looking astounded at her admittance. "Then I will leave you to your peaceful walk," he said, bowing slightly and heading off in a different direction.

"My apologies, my Lord," Olive said with a mischievous smile as she watched him leave. *Well, it seems my mother's wild imagination has its uses after all. If it keeps away possible suitors, then I am all for it,* she concurred, smiling wickedly to herself at her cleverness.

Hopefully, the Duke of Cornwall would be far too busy to ever know of the gossip circulating about the two of them. Meanwhile, she might as well use it to her advantage.

CHAPTER 18

Vera had done all she could to avoid both Oscar and her brother. Ever since their beach trip a few days ago, she had started to accept defeat. She knew that if she couldn't fight her feelings for the Duke, then she would have to leave her childhood home. It was the only way. But worse, Silas had told her that he would go with her, and that would mean ruining his life too. She was not willing to do that.

She had gone about her normal business in the kitchen, but her thoughts had got the better of her. At every turn, the image of Oscar and Lady Brent together played out in her head. She had tried to reason how right it would be but was finding it so difficult to accept.

How can I leave someone who I've loved for as long as I can remember? she churned over in her mind. *I don't want to be the one who forces such changes in my brother's life. Yet I can't stay here and watch Oscar wed. I cannot do it.*

For now, she had decided that the best way to make her decision, was to avoid Oscar altogether. Then she would get a feel of what it would be like without him in her life. Yet her heart pined, and she felt so empty inside. Unable to control her moods, she had been cranky towards the kitchen maids at every possible moment, and she was aware that they were now trying to avoid her.

For this reason, she spent a lot of time in her tiny office, catching up with the catering accounts. It should certainly please the housekeeper, Mary. She was forever complaining to Vera for not doing the catering paperwork. Now she would shine in Mary's eyes, while the rest of the world avoided her moody outbursts.

Even Barker had stayed out of the kitchen when she was around, and he was never one to be afraid of her. She knew that her moods were affecting everyone who loved her, but her life was so miserable that she didn't care.

A knock on the door brought Frances wavering at her door. *The poor girl must have drawn the short straw into being forced to approach me,* Vera mulled over as she waited for her to speak.

"I...I...need t-...to tell you—"

"Spit it out, girl!" Vera snapped, regretting it immediately when the girl faltered even more with her message.

"The butcher's here," she spat the words out at speed so that she could leave.

"I'm on my way," Vera said, flaring her nostrils as she acknowledged that it was a task only for her and no one else.

After Frances left, Vera spent a few moments pulling herself together. Folding her arms around her body for warmth, she knew it was getting harder to deal with people face to face. Her emotions were spiralling out of control, and she must get a grip on herself.

Taking a deep breath, she forced herself to leave her little bolt-hole and was soon walking through the kitchen. The familiar sights and smells comforted her somewhat, as steam rose from the pans and the smell of gravy and roasting meats permeated the air.

"I hope someone is keeping their eyes on those roasting chickens," she called out as a reminder. "If they burn, there will be hell to pay."

She entered the outer room where Jeffrey, the local butcher, was spreading his wares out, on a large wooden table, for her inspection.

"Ahhh, Jeffrey, those rabbits had better be fresh!" she instructed because he had already skinned them, making it harder to tell.

"Shot only yesterday, Vera, you know my reputation, I only sell the freshest of goods?" the large man replied with a sure voice.

His ruddy cheeks gave him a healthy shine, but it wasn't that he was a fit and well man. It was more that he worked in the cold all the time, and his cheeks were always red and shiny. Or maybe it was the gin he drank to warm himself up in his slaughtering yard.

"Hmmm, I hope so for your sake," she tutted back at him, not in any mood for his cheeky demeanour.

"I'm surprised you ain't ordered any celebration meats yet. I have some fine venison hanging out the back, or a whole pig for the roasting," he suggested, grinning as he shook a head adorned with a flat cap. "Happen ye want it reserved, do ye?"

"I don't see why we should want that," she replied, wrinkling her nose as she looked annoyed at him rather than puzzled.

"The whole household must be lookin' forward to the celebrations then?" he asked, this time laughing so hard he was showing all his teeth, and they were not a pretty sight.

"Why are you acting so odd today, Jeffrey?" Vera asked. "Have too many flies got into your ears, and now they're buzzing around inside your head?"

"No, Vera, I don't allow flies in my place, I does not," he remarked, looking insulted as he tugged at his ear lobe.

"Hmm, I doubt that to be true," she noted, watching him squirm. "I would have thought it unavoidable when you're slaughtering animals all day long."

"I thought you'd be in a better mood given all the good news that's spread around town," he said, looking defeated by her mood.

"What is it that you rant on about, Jeffrey?" she asked, now intrigued by his ramblings. "I have heard no good news to cheer my thoughts, so you had better share yours I suppose."

"The Duke," he revealed, looking pleased to be conveying such news to her. "He be gettin' wed, that's what they be sayin' anyways."

"What?" she asked, staring at him with frozen eyes. "Where did you hear such nonsense?"

"It's the talk of the ton, it is. It be so important it's now made its way down to all the servants," he told her with a mighty grin on his red face. "They all be sayin' how there be a romance goin' on between the Duke and Lady Brent."

Vera was motionless for but a few seconds, but she soon came to her senses. "I'm surprised at you, Jeffrey Parkins, that you give weight to such gossip," she snapped back at him. "It is only Lady Smith who thinks such thoughts, and I bet you a shilling that she is the instigator of this untruth."

"Don't know about any in..instig...giting," Jeffrey stuttered back at her as he fumbled with his words. "But Lady Brent is a pretty sight for any man's eyes, that be fer sure."

"Well, I'll now give you another rumour to spread around. Lady Smith, her mother, is so desperate to marry off her daughter that she's spreading lies like a runny butter!" Vera yelled. "That is all it is, after all, an old woman telling exaggerated lies. It's a disgrace if you ask me."

"I'll not be sayin' that to anyone, Vera, 'cos it be true," Jeffrey insisted, even at the risk of Vera's wrath. "Ye must be burryin' yer head in the muck if ye don't know what be goin' on."

Vera was about to give the butcher another lashing of her tongue when she stopped herself. *What's the point of arguing with a simpleton? It's likely half true anyway.*

"You are quite right, Jeffrey," she said, shaking her head and submitting to him. "Lady Brent is a very attractive lady with a sweet nature. It's no wonder that the Duke of Cornwall has an interest in her."

"I suppose we'll all know the better of it in due course," Jeffrey said, cheering up because Vera had stopped snarling at him. "Mind you, ye right about that old mother of hers. Lady Smith is a well-known gossipmonger. I tell ye somethin' else fer free, she's a fussy customer too."

Vera allowed herself a small laugh as she accepted the bill for the delivery. She said not another word so that he would not be delayed any further. She'd be glad to see the back end of the butcher and his idle gossip. *Poor Jeffrey,* she pondered as she became conscious that she was tapping her foot. *He's a good enough man, always giving us good cuts, but I'm not on the mood for his wagging tongue.* Sure enough, he turned and left, leaving her to her thoughts. Taking a moment to straighten herself, she held onto the paper bill with a vacant expression in her unseeing eyes.

Walking back through the kitchen, she called out for someone to put the delivery into the storage. Though she gave no instructions to anyone in particular, she knew the job would be done. Not waiting around to see if they complied with her instructions, she headed straight back to her lonely, little office room.

Once there, she sat down fidgeting with the butcher's paper bill in her trembling fingers. "How dare that swag-bellied old woman spread such lies?" she growled between clenched teeth. "I hope that Oscar puts a stop to it all when he hears about it."

But then what's the point of that? Her thoughts bounced around her head. *He's going to marry some lady or other, and Lady Brent has a kindness about her that will be good for Oscar. I've got to let him go. He won't be wanting childhood friendships once he has a new woman in his life.*

In her heart, she knew that it was time. It was time to accept the inevitable and begin to look elsewhere. She must learn to move on and live her life in another place. If she kept her intentions from Silas, then he wouldn't need to upend his life all because of her.

"That's what I must do," she mumbled, her shoulders slumped

in defeat. "I must start looking for a position with a household that is a long, long way from Cornwall."

CHAPTER 19

"I don't have time for this, Mary," Vera complained to the housekeeper as she met her on her walk to the big hall for a gathering. "Do you have any idea what this nonsense is all about?"

"Barker instructed me to gather all the housemaids in the big hall. And then to inform you and your maids too, to come to the hall for a meeting," Mary shrugged as they walked along a corridor together. "That's all I know."

"No doubt it's Barker's way of reminding us all that he's in charge, don't you think?" Vera responded, annoyed at being called away from their duties at such short notice.

"I doubt even Barker would dare to disturb the running of Welwick Hall for no good reason," Mary pointed out.

Vera had reached a point where she had lost all interest in the running of Welwick Hall. Not that it mattered because her kitchen ran like a well well-oiled machine. Menus were put together well in advance, and everyone knew their part well. That had always been one of her skills; organising. Her brother and Oscar had often teased her about it when they were younger. Her fussiness had even got her into trouble with Oscar's father once. The memory made her shudder as it came to mind; He'd found her putting books into alphabetical order by the authors' surnames in the library. Then, he'd made her put them all back on the shelves they originally came from. She'd gone to bed in tears that night because she felt that the library was in chaos.

As she and Mary entered the large dancing hall, she could see that Oscar was there. Upon seeing him she felt a thumping sensation in her chest. A hot flush burst out around her face, so she stayed at the back of the gathering crowd of servants. She and Mary separated as the housekeeper made her way to the front. It was Mary and Barker's place to be at the front as they were the head servants. Vera should be joining them too, but she had no desire to be so close to Oscar.

"Alright everyone, calm your noise down," Barker announced as he raised his arms to hush the chatter. "This will not take you from your duties for long, so I expect you all to return to them once His Grace has spoken with you. And do so in an orderly manner, this is not a school room full of children, even though it sounds like it."

Vera rolled her eyes at Barker's comments. She heard a murmur run through the gathered servants as their curiosity got the better of them. Asking all the servants to gather this way was something new, so even she was a little curious. She just wished they'd get on with it so she could get away from Oscar.

After making her decision to leave Welwick Hall, she'd also decided to avoid Oscar and her brother as much as possible. They knew her too well and would guess she was up to something. If her brother asked her what ailed her, he would no doubt guess what she was up to.

But seeing Oscar only served to bring home how much she pined to be with him. And that was a feeling that she knew she had to put a stop to; even at the price of losing her brother.

The buzz in the room was reaching a crescendo as Barker raised his arm again. "Hush your voices!" he yelled, and it seemed to Vera that he was enjoying this whole moment of exercising his power over the staff. "His Grace wishes to say a few words now that we are all here."

That did the trick, and everyone stopped whispering among themselves, all eyes now on the master of the house.

Oscar stepped forward, his handsome form teasing at her brain. He gave his entire a gentle smile and began. "I know this is an unusual way to go about things," he said, raising his voice for all to hear him. "But I wanted to tell each of you about my plans over Christmastide because the success of those plans depends on every one of you. You are the ones who hold Welwick Hall together, you are its backbone, and I am merely its puppet. That is what gave me an idea."

Again, the servants whispered, marvelling at their master's words of praise. Even Vera wondered what Oscar was up to and she looked around for her brother. She could not see him anywhere, which could only mean that he already knew of Oscar's plans. Yet neither of them had sought out her counsel, and this bothered her more than usual. She tapped her foot to the ground, wishing Oscar would hurry and get this affair over with.

"I am planning to host a masquerade ball on a very special day," Oscar said, grinning at his audience as if he was pleased to be delivering his words. "I have always been a fan of the Shakespearian plays, and none more so than Twelfth Night, so we will hold our ball on the twelfth day of Christmastide."

The younger maids clapped their hands together in delight and Vera wondered why. It wasn't as if they would be dressing up to go to the ball, and she doubted they even knew anything about the works of Shakespeare. A glimmer of a memory came to mind. One of being excited as a young girl, at seeing all the ladies and lords dressed up for the many balls hosted by Lady Wold in the past. It helped her understand, that for the younger servants it would be a thrilling moment to experience. A time when they would imagine themselves among the very guests they would be serving. A young girl's dream...

"I don't know if you all know what a masquerade ball entails, but for the guests, it will be most amusing," Oscar continued. Vera could see that he too was excited at the prospect of his special idea. "They will all wear exquisite masks of some sort or other, making the ball more fun and informal. I don't wish to host a dreary ball. Instead, I am aiming to make the twelfth day of Christmastide into a very special day."

Oscar paused for a moment, allowing the servants to chatter in their excitement. All it meant to Vera was extra work for the kitchen maids, yet there they all were, jumping up and down in glee.

"We will deck the halls with colourful decorations," Oscar went on, looking happier than he had in a while. "We will invite the village into our home and send them packing with baskets of food. Where is Cook, where's Vera?" he asked, glancing around to look for her.

Hearing her name caused her to cringe. She did not want to be the centre of attention, but everyone turned around in her direction to show their master where she was hiding.

"Vera, we will have much to discuss," he called over to her. "I plan a whole season of merriment for all, nobles and commoners alike and you will be a part of it."

Vera smiled at him, and that seemed to satisfy him. She was in no mood to join in there and then, and who knows, she might even have left by Christmastide.

"And on the Feast of the Epiphany, the twelfth day, we will end the celebrations with our masquerade ball," he called out to a sea of smiling faces.

Vera half felt like standing up to ask them why they were all so happy. This celebration that the Duke had planned, would only mean they would be working longer and harder over Christmastide. Were they all so stupid not to realise that?

"We will all have a slice of twelfth night cake, guests, and servants alike. And in it, we will put the traditional dried pea and dried bean. Whoever finds them in their slice of cake, will be crowned the king and queen of the Welwick hall, for the night," Oscar told them.

This caused a murmur of excitement around the hall, but not for Vera. "That's going to be a lot of cakes for me to make then," she mumbled to herself, for it was her responsibility to come up with all this food.

"We will burn yule logs. The children will play games at the daytime feast, like the bobbing of apples," Oscar seemed as if he did want to stop with his grand news. She could see he was feeling excited with the prospect of an extra special Christmastide. "It was a game I loved as a child. And on the fifth day of January, we will give out presents to all our guests. So, I ask you, my partners, who wants to come a wassailing with me?"

The servants were all caught up in their master's enthusiasm, and Vera wondered what had occurred to make him so happy. "Happen he's found himself a wife," she mumbled under her breath as she turned to leave the hall.

The meeting had come to an end and the original buzz of curiosity had now developed into an atmosphere of joy. Even Barker looked pleased as he chatted with Mary. They were no doubt planning far too much work for the kitchen maids.

Once Vera was back in her kitchen, she set about her daily tasks. She wanted to work hard to take her mind away from her turmoil. It looked like she might need to postpone her departure, but then again why should she? No doubt Lady Brent would be at the ball flaunting her beauty and enticing Oscar with her charms.

"Grrr!" Vera growled to herself as she went about making soup in a huge pot.

She would get one of the kitchen maids to stir it over the open fire range once she'd added all the ingredients, but for now, it wasn't ready to hand over. The forced calling of a servant's meeting had put her schedule behind. Vera worried that the soup might not be ready for the midday meal that she had planned. *Damn Christmastide, and damn Welwick Hall.*

"Sister, Sister," Silas's voice rang out as he hunted her down in the kitchen.

"I don't have time to stop for idle gossip, Brother," she snapped at him without even looking up. "Whatever it is that you want, be quick about it."

"Are you not in the least bit excited at the Duke's idea of a masquerade ball?" he asked, looking at her in surprise.

"No, it only means double the workload in the kitchen," she grumbled back at him.

"But could you not see the reference to the Twelfth Night?" he asked, following her around as she went to gather more ingredients.

"Oh, grow up, Silas," she barked at him. "We will all of us be working extra hard. There'll be no time to enjoy a moment's peace over Christmastide. That's what we are, servants, and don't you forget your place. The ball is not for you or the likes of me to have fun. It's for the gentry is all."

"No, Oscar specifically chose the Twelfth Night to celebrate the tidings with his friends. That's you and me, Vera," Silas insisted. "Whatever has got into you?"

"Get out of my kitchen," she snapped, unwilling to give in to his giddiness. But she soon felt remorseful as she noticed the shocked look on his face. Before she could apologise, he had already turned to march out of the kitchen.

Vera knew she had gone too far. Deep in her heart, she knew that Oscar had chosen the theme of the Twelfth Night in memory of their friendship. But she was unwilling to get carried away with the sentiment.

As she looked up, she noticed the kitchen maids all suddenly look away from her. She felt a pang in her heart as more regret flooded her emotions. How she was behaving was out of character, and the kitchen maids didn't deserve to be living in fear of her moods. But her future was not with these people anymore. As soon as Christmastide was over, she would set her plans in motion. That way, Oscar would be free to marry a lady fitting his status, and not put up with her a moment longer than needed.

CHAPTER 20

Olive had awoken to a chilly morning. As she climbed out of the warmth of her bed, she walked over to the window. Opening the drapes, she looked out with sleepy eyes at the rich oranges and reds upon the trees. Summer was fast turning into autumn, and a sudden thought came to her mind. Perhaps it was time for her to make some changes too, just like the seasons. The idea of doing something different appealed. It would be nice to have a break from her domineering mother, whose only concern seemed to be marrying her off as soon as possible.

She shivered the cold and wrapped one of her cashmere shawls around her slender shoulders. It seemed that lately, she was always reaching for a shawl, to fight off the cold. Most especially at breakfast, which was where she was heading now, to speak with her mother.

"We must get the maids up earlier, to stoke up these fires," her mother complained, the moment she stepped into the dining room.

"I would not wish to disturb their sleep, Mother," Olive replied, taking her seat at the large table. "They go to bed late as it is and I am loathed to wake them even earlier than they already rise. You have plenty of shawls to keep you warm first thing, do you not?"

"They have a roof over their heads, do they not?" her mother called out and tutted. "You are far too easy on the commoners. They are here to work, not to rest all day long."

Olive felt uncomfortable, but the maid serving breakfast showed no signs of unease at the words that were being spoken.

"Mother, please," Olive tried. "We shall discuss this matter in private."

Her mother looked over at the maid, giving her an annoyed stare, but said nothing more.

"Besides, I have something else I wish to discuss with you this morning," Olive changed the topic, leading up to the news of her decision. "I intend to take a trip to Scotland soon."

"What nonsense is this?" her mother declared as she shot a look of horror her daughter's way. "We cannot be making such a treacherous journey at this time of year."

"Not we, Mother, it is only me," Olive said, buttering a piece of bread as she avoided her mother's withering gaze. "It has been far too long since I have seen Father's sister, and I am fond of my aunt. You, on the other hand, never liked her."

"Well, I wouldn't go all that way to see that woman anyway, but I would like to know what has got into you?" her mother asked, looking flustered. "What's more, I will not allow you to make such a journey, not at the onset of inclement weather."

"Mother, I hardly need your permission," Olive remarked, now looking her mother straight in the face. "I am no longer a child and I do believe that you forget that sometimes."

"There is no need to take that tone with me," her mother barked, looking quite lost for words.

They finished their breakfast in silence. Before Olive left the room, she turned to her mother and asked, "Would you like to take a turn in the garden with me, now that the sun has broken through?"

"I would like to talk some sense into you," her mother replied as she remained seated at the dining room table. "Yes, we will wrap up warm and walk together. The air will do you some good and make you see what a foolish idea you have concocted."

"Good, and we will take the dogs too," Olive added. They will enjoy a run in the garden with us. I will go and find a suitable pair of shoes; shall we meet in half an hour?"

"Yes, yes, I will be ready," her mother snapped, and it was clear that she really didn't want to go out in the cold.

Olive had guessed this all along, but she decided it was time to turn the tables a little on her mother. She was so domineering at times, but Olive was determined she would no longer follow along in her shadow. It's time her mother understood that this was her house. A house that *her* husband had left to *her* when he died. It was time to become the real Lady of the house and she should have done it sooner before her mother assumed she could still rule *her* life. Marriage, if it was to happen at all, would be on her terms and not her mother's.

Olive sincerely loved her mother, but there were times she could be overbearing and even overprotective. She had been like that ever since her father passed away; always trying to better their position in life. What her mother needed to realise was that she did not need any protection. They had enough money to live on, thanks to her previous marriage. Well, it was enough for her, but it seemed not to be for her mother. She had become accustomed to some of the better things in life and strived to return to that status.

Olive sat in the parlour at the agreed time, but there was no sign of her mother. Almost an hour later, she was still waiting, adorned in all her outdoor clothing. As she sighed at the wait, the door opened, but it was one of the maids that crept into the room.

"My Lady," she said as she half curtsied. "There be a letter arrived for you," she announced, holding out the small silver tray used for such purposes.

The maid approached her and Olive took the letter from the tray. "Thank you, Perkins," Olive smiled at the maid who promptly left with the empty tray.

Unfolding the letter, she was surprised to see the letter heading of Welwick Hall. Although it wasn't a personal letter, it was in the form of an invitation. The Duke of Cornwall was inviting them to a Christmastide Masquerade Ball, that he was calling The Twelfth Night Ball.

"Oh, Lord, this is all I need. I can't let Mother see this," she mumbled to herself. "I'll never get away to Scotland if she knows about it."

For a few moments, she mulled over what to do, and soon after she began to tear up the invitation. "Sorry Mother," she spoke to herself as she stood up and threw the pieces of torn paper into the blazing fireplace. "But I'm not ready to be pushed into the Duke's arms yet. I have other ideas for my life."

Olive decided to wait no longer for her mother, so she took it upon herself to find her. Making her way to look into the larger drawing room, there was no sign of her there. Passing the dining room, she peeked in there too. Her mother was nowhere to be seen, so she climbed the stairs and went to knock on her mother's bedroom chamber. Sure enough, her mother was in there as she called out for her to enter.

"Are you ready yet, Mother?" Olive asked, wondering if there had been two invitations to the Duke's ball. That could be why her mother had been delayed. She prayed that she was wrong.

"Very well, if you insist," her mother said, ringing the rope for the maid to come and get her shoes and coat. "I warn you now, we are discussing this silly idea of yours."

The dogs were already in with her mother as they spent most of their time in her bedroom chamber. She doted on them like they were her spoilt little children. No doubt because they were more inclined to behave themselves, whereas Olive was starting to rebel on the odd occasion.

The little dogs yapped their way all down the stairway, once her mother was ready. They sensed that something exciting was about to happen. They were normally walked daily by the maids, but today they would be walked by their mistress. This was making them giddy, and they were most enthusiastic to get outdoors.

Olive laughed at their antics as they scratched at the door to escape. She opened it up and they pounded outside, yapping none stop. As Olive glanced at her mother, she noted that she at least looked content as she watched the little dogs running around.

What Olive found even more relieving, was the fact that her mother had not mentioned anything about the invitation. That must mean that only one invitation had been sent to the household. Olive had no intention of being the one to divulge that information to her mother, who adored balls.

"Why can you not wait until the summer months when the journey is safer?" her mother asked her. "I do not want you to find a husband while you are there, do you hear me? We will not be having any Scottish Lairds for they may not be peers."

Olive had no opportunity to answer either question as her mother rambled on and on to herself. "I do wish you would take it more seriously, this search for a new husband. I want to be sure you will be well looked after I am gone."

"What is this nonsense, Mother?" Olive finally responded, and maybe a little too forcefully. "You are going nowhere, and we are quite comfortable as we are."

"But a lady needs ballgowns and jewels, my dear. Have you not noticed that you have worn all your gowns many times over?" her mother asked as they walked at a slow pace around the falling, brown leaves. "People will begin to notice, mark my words. The ladies of the ton have a different dress for every occasion."

"I am loving my walk around the garden with you, Mother," Olive said in reply. "But I do not wish to discuss husbands or gowns."

"Will you discuss the treacherous journey you are considering then?" her mother stopped in her tracks and asked. She had a look about her that caused concern for Olive. "For I may lose my daughter to a broken wheel from a speeding coach, or a wicked highway robber. You vex me, Daughter, have you considered my position if something were to happen to you, I would be all alone."

"Mother, I have not yet decided if or when I will make the journey. When I do, you will be the first to know," Olive told her, hoping that would stop her from worrying so much. "Now let us meander down to the stream. The sound of running water might help to relax you, and dogs will love it."

"It will be the maids who can dry them," her mother complained. "I refuse to have them in my chamber if they are smelling of dirty water."

Olive took no notice and she continued to head towards the small stream that passed through their land. She was enjoying the little warmth that the sun had to offer as it occasionally popped out from behind the grey clouds. The weather was quickly changing, and if she was to make the long journey to Scotland, she would need to set off soon.

CHAPTER 21

"I will not have the workers in the tin mines treated ruthlessly, Henry," Oscar stressed to the family solicitor who often visited to advise him. They were now meeting in his study. "What if we suggest searching for copper? Some mines have been successful with it."

"All the landowners that had copper have no more left. They're shutting down the smaller mines and that's the end of it, Oscar. Your father knew this day was coming years ago and he accepted it, and so should you," Henry advised.

"I recall what happened in one of the smaller villages when I was a boy," Oscar said. And well he remembered how his father often took him along on business trips. "Their local mine had closed, and so the villagers were taken on by another mine, another landowner. But they were treated like slaves. Many of them starved and the children were dying from malnutrition. Father arranged for the men to be taught new trades. Some took to fishing, others to farm labouring. He saved that village from the brink of collapse. I won't have anything like that happen again while I am the Duke of Cornwall."

"Yes, I understand how you feel, Oscar, but smuggling is fast becoming a problem. As the Duke of Cornwall, you must act, the law demands it," Henry stressed to him. "I'm afraid you can't save these smaller mines. You must accept the financial reality and send out the order to close them down because they are becoming so unsafe. The landowners are wreaking havoc as they blow up more tunnels underground."

"I will meet with some of them to discuss it. Can you organise the meetings?" Oscar asked his family friend who he trusted implicitly.

"Of course, I can, but don't delay the matter much longer," Henry warned.

"You know that we'll lose many of the smaller villages," Oscar mumbled, but more to himself. The consequences of closing so many smaller mines would have a terrible effect on the poor. "What will the people do?"

"As your father showed, they will need to turn their trades to farming and fishing," Henry said. He began to gather the documents together, that he'd used to show the evidence of the problem.

"Yes, but for many of them that will mean abandoning their homes. It saddens me greatly to think of that," Oscar sighed as he tried to accept the reality of what he had to do.

"Mining is a treacherous business, Oscar. The sooner the people of Cornwall stop depending on it, the better, if you ask me," Henry pointed out his opinion.

"I won't be surprised if we do not see an increase in more illicit trade," Oscar remarked as he tapped his fingers on the desk before him. "While ever the rich are willing to pay for their brandy and tea on the cheap, smuggling will be tenfold."

"Well, we can only deal with one problem at a time," Henry said, standing up as he readied to leave. "I will arrange a meeting for you with the local Judge Hanson, that will be the best start. The local landowners think highly of him. He's a man you want on your side."

Oscar stood up and shook Henry's hand, "Thank you for your time today, Henry. This is all so new to me. I mean, the troubles are not new, but my being the one to oversee the decisions on Cornwall's prospects is quite daunting."

"That's why it's better that you start to introduce yourself around and I will guide you to your father's friends," Henry assured him. "Oh, and don't forget my advice on taking a wife. Someone who can assist with the running of the Bodmin Estate, then you can concentrate on the broader social issues."

"As always, you are a treasure to my family, Henry," Oscar said as he walked with the family solicitor to the front doors.

"Your family owns around ten percent of Cornwall's lands, Oscar, and that's a great responsibility to take on," Henry reminded him. "Your father should have started to teach you sooner but knowing him as I did, he would have been trying to protect you from the burden."

"Oh, before you go, can you arrange for extra grain to be delivered to the affected villagers?" Oscar added. "Particularly to those mines with no copper. I will fund it."

Oscar was about to walk outside with his family friend when Barker approached him and coughed to get his attention.

"It seems I am needed elsewhere, Henry, but let's keep these meetings going now that we have started them," Oscar suggested.

"Indeed, Your Grace," Henry said, reverting to Oscar's official title now that they were in public. "I will arrange the extra grain, but you know all too well that's not the long-term solution."

"I know, but it will alleviate some of their worries," Oscar said, smiling. "Goodbye old friend, I will see you next week at the same time."

As he watched the solicitor pass through the main door of Welwick Hall, Oscar turned to his butler, "What is it, Barker?"

"While you were in your business meeting, Lady Smith

arrived," Barker replied, looking a little defeated. "She insists on awaiting an audience with Your Grace."

"Does she indeed. You must be getting soft in your old age, Barker," Oscar said with a slight sternness to his voice. "In your heyday, even I could not get past you, not even if I wished an audience with my father on his busy days."

"My apologies, Your Grace," Barker bowed his head in defeat. "But she was most...erm—"

"Insistent?" Oscar finished the sentence for him, raising his brow at the old man.

"Precisely that, Your Grace," Barker nodded. "She is in the blue parlour room, drinking tea."

Oscar made his way to the small parlour, wondering why this woman haunted him day in, and day out. *What must I do to be rid of her?*

"Lady Smith, what an honour it is to see you," he lied as he greeted her and took a seat in a chair that left some distance between them. "What can I do for you?" He asked as he watched her face burst into a huge grin.

"I wanted to ask if you had a pleasant time in my daughter's company on your beach picnic, Your Grace?" she asked.

Oscar smiled as he pondered on the rather random question.

"Lady Brent was a most gracious and charming, if not rather unexpected guest," he replied in short, wondering what was coming next.

"Then I have another question that I must put to you, Your Grace," she said, jutting out her chin in defence of something or other.

"Please feel free to speak, Lady Smith," he said to her, wishing he could say the complete opposite and turf her out of his home.

"I hear you are to host a very special Christmas Masquerade Ball that you are calling the Twelfth Night?" she asked, leaving the question lingering.

As Oscar realised that she was to say no more, he replied, "That is correct."

"So, if you enjoyed my daughter's company, then it vexes me as to why you would not invite her and myself to your ball?" She spat out the words. "Your Mother always invited us to her many wonderful balls."

"But you have been invited," he countered, looking puzzled at the accusations. "I oversaw the invitations myself, and there was most certainly one for Silsbury Manor."

"You see, Your Grace, my daughter is in great need of some kind of distraction," Lady Smith continued, ignoring what he had said and the fact that he looked somewhat surprised. "It turns out that she is planning a treacherous journey to Scotland, would you believe? I must have something to talk her out of it."

"But the invitations have gone out an—" he tried again, frustrated that he couldn't seem to get her to listen to him.

"We are eminent members of the local elite and attend every ball that is arranged in Cornwall," she droned on. "Why we would not receive an invitation from Welwick Hall is an absolute mystery to me."

"One has been sent to Silsbury Manor, I assure you, Lady Smith." He tried once again to interrupt the conversation that she appeared to be having with herself.

"Oh, I see," she gulped and blinked her eyes rapidly in surprise. "So, where is it?"

"Now that I cannot answer," he said, giving her a friendly smile as he could see this conversation could turn one or the other. "It must have been misplaced among the many that I sent out."

"Well, we have not received one, but I thought as much," she said, raising her hand to pat her high head of grey hair. "It is fortunate that I have not informed my daughter of this incident. She would be most upset, I am sure, thinking that you had forgotten her."

"I have forgotten no one," Oscar said, keeping his face friendly, even though it was an effort because quite frankly, he'd had enough of the woman. Nonetheless, he chose his words carefully, as he didn't want her getting the wrong message. "Here is what I shall do to rectify the matter. I will send my personal valet along with a replacement invitation. It is what I do for anyone who's invitation had gone missing. Will that be acceptable for you, Lady Smith?"

"Quite so. But you know what the best thing for my daughter is, do you not? While she is so young and attractive, it would do her good to marry once again," Lady Smith announced. How quickly she seemed to forget about the missing invitation.

"That is a splendid idea. Perhaps she will meet a fine suitor at the Welwick Hall ball," he suggested putting on his best smile.

His words seemed to placate his visitor and she was soon readying to leave. "I will make haste and inform my daughter of what you have said," she said to him, now looking a little excited.

Oscar let out a sigh of relief when she finally stepped through the front door to make her exit. Returning to his study to write up the invitation, he didn't want to forget it and have her return.

God forbid that woman finding another excuse to bother me again.

Once completed, he sent word for Silas to come to his study, and he arrived within moments.

"I have a special job for you Silas," Oscar said as he motioned for his valet to take a seat.

At that moment the open door was pushed a little bit wider as Vera's head popped around the opening.

"I have a list of suggested menu items for the ball, Your Grace," she said in a quiet voice as she also looked over at her brother.

"Thank you, Vera," he said, motioning for her to enter his study. "Please, take a seat so we can discuss it."

Vera looked unsure as she once again looked over at her brother.

"Silas can look at the menu too, we can decide on it together,"

Oscar suggested. "I could do with all the help I can get. Already I am burdened with problems regarding this ball."

"I am sorry to hear that, Your Grace," Vera said, her eyes down and her demeanour rather odd.

"How can there be problems when we've only sent the invitations out a couple of days ago?" Silas questioned.

"It appears that Lady Smith, of Silsbury Manor, has not received hers," Oscar told them. "And so, I was privileged to a visit from her this very afternoon. I assured her that you would take this invitation directly to her door, Silas," Oscar said, pointing to the invitation on his desk.

"Of course, so long as she doesn't eat me when I deliver it," Silas said in jest.

"Having the invitation delivered personally should put her in a good mood, so you will be quite safe," Oscar assured his friend. "For now, let's look at this menu Vera has put together for us."

For the next half hour, they discussed the menu, or rather, it seemed to Oscar, that only he and Silas deliberated on it. Vera was unusually quiet, which confused him. Even more so when Silas mentioned an ongoing romance that he was having with one of the upstairs maids. Oscar pulled his leg about it, and even then, Vera said nothing. It seemed that her thoughts were very distant.

Quite unexpectedly, Vera stood up and announced that she needed to return to her duties as she had much to do in advance of the ball. Whilst it concerned Oscar, Silas was so intent on discussing his latest romance that he took no notice of his sister's dour face. Silas stayed on after his sister left, he was so animated that Oscar enjoyed his company a little longer.

"This is what you could do with, Oscar," Silas said as he finished telling the tale of his romance. "A beautiful lady to come into your life and sweep you off your feet. I feel like I'm walking on air ever since Lucy agreed to walk with me."

"And your sister, does she approve? Oscar asked though he didn't wish to dampen Silas's enthusiasm.

"She's too busy planning your ball to notice what's going on around her," Silas replied as he too stood up to leave.

"Do you think she needs extra help in the kitchen then?" Oscar asked, the thought of her working so hard disturbed him.

"No. She wouldn't accept it even if offered," Silas assured him. "You know what she's like, she likes to feel in control. Anyway," I'll be off with that invitation then. The nights are drawing in much quicker now and I want to cuddle up to my Lucy to keep warm."

"You scoundrel," Oscar laughed as he handed over the invitation. "Be off with you and treat my maids with honour or I will be in need of a new valet."

"Have no fear master," Silas over-emphasised the *master* in jest. "I will treat Lucy with the highest of respect."

Oscar smiled at his friend's exaggerated deference, but he took it in the spirit it was intended. Silas's situation was not like his though, he had an ongoing pressure to find a wife. But for now, all he could think of was Vera, as he wondered what ailed her.

CHAPTER 22

Before Vera entered Oscar's study, she'd overheard him giving Silas instructions. He was asking her brother to deliver an invitation for the ball to Silsbury Manor. In her desperation and confusion, it gave her an idea. An idea that might at least stop Lady Smith from badgering Oscar to marry her daughter.

Vera felt certain that the woman was only interested in his title and wealth. While she liked the young Lady Brent, she wanted to do her best to make sure that Oscar had a wife who would make him happy. A wife who was seeking wealth would not do that, and she didn't want Oscar to be taken in by her beauty.

Since she'd arrived back in the kitchen, after dropping off the menu suggestions to Oscar, she'd headed for the herb garden. This was an intentional move because she would see her brother on his way to the stables from there.

She hadn't said much in the study, even though she was aware of Silas's dilly-dallying with Lucy, one of the upstairs maids. It was the latest chatter on all the maid's tongues because they all vied for his attention. But she had no time to ponder over such simple matters, she had more urgent things on her mind.

While she'd made up her mind to leave after the ball, she still wanted to make sure that if Oscar chose Lady Brent, it was for the right reasons. Hopefully, her plan should sort that problem out once and for all.

Rubbing at the purple lavender in the garden, she inhaled its perfume. At the same time, she spotted her brother taking his usual big strides toward the stable.

"Silas!" she called out and waved him to come over to speak with.

"Sister!" he said as he approached her. "I don't seem to have spoken with you in a while, how do you fair?" he asked with concern in his tone. He'd been wondering if she'd been avoiding him but could see no reason why, so brushed the feeling away.

"I'm well enough," she answered, not wishing to get into any long-drawn-out conversation. "I suppose you're on your way to Silsbury Manor?"

"That I am," he nodded. "Oscar's keen to get the invitation delivered this very day. I wish I could deliver it tomorrow though; you see I'm meeting Lucy later and I wanted to bathe," he explained, but his sullen face changed to a big grin when he mentioned Lucy's name.

"I can help you with that problem," she smiled back at him. "Why don't I take it for you? I could do with a ride out. You'll still go need to go and order the horse to be saddled up if you don't mind."

"Are you sure?" he asked, looking unsure. "You'd need to set off soon as the darkness is drawing in much earlier."

"I'm going to go and get an overcoat while you get the groom to ready a horse," she replied, making a turn to show she wanted to go and ready herself. "Can you do that for me?"

"Of course, I can," Silas replied, looking pleased with the prospect of not having to run the errand. "Thanks, Sis, I won't be stinking now when I meet Lucy. You're a star."

"Oh, and Silas, don't mention to the groom that the horse

isn't for you," Vera called after him. "You know what the head groom Williams can be like if he gets wind that servants are using the horses. He'll force me to get a note of permission from Oscar."

"Aye, that's true enough, but he'll see you when you go to collect it anyway," Silas pointed out.

"Yes, but at the last minute I can say that you've been called away on another errand," she explained. "He knows that you ordered the horse, so he's not likely to question me and accuse me of using the horses for my own purposes."

"You think of everything," he said, leaning in to embrace her. "Thanks, Vera, whatever did I do to deserve a wonderful sister like you? I'll be off then," Silas said as he turned to set off again. "And you go get yourself ready, I don't want you riding out too late in the day."

She watched Silas walk away as he went to do his part of the agreement. Part of her felt a little bad, that she was deceiving her brother. Then she convinced herself that what she was doing was for a good cause. Vera knew that she would not be around when Oscar finally chose his wife. In the meantime, though, she hoped to give him direction for his future happiness.

Finishing picking the herbs she wanted, she'd need to arrange to get them dried off for tomorrow's dishes. So she returned to the kitchen first. Dropping off the basket of herbs with the scullery maid, she said, "Can you put these out to dry, Frances, I want to use them tomorrow."

"Yes, Ma'am," Frances replied in her usual manner.

Before leaving, Vera checked that everything was as it should be as she left for the day. Every course for the evening meal was in the right hands and there should be no reason for her to be missed. Being the Head of the kitchen, she didn't need to tell anyone she was leaving early. Working long hours, it wasn't unusual for her to finish a little earlier than the others, so they'd assume she was in her room resting.

Going up to her room, she went to change into something more suitable for her errand.

Within the hour, she was entering the stables to collect the horse. There she was met by the head groom, Williams, who would have sanctioned the use of the horse for the errand. It wasn't unusual for Silas to ride the horses, so no questions were ever asked when he ordered one to be saddled up.

William nodded at her, and she returned the gesture. The air was chilly, and she kept her scarf over her face, yet still, her breath made steamy clouds in the freezing air.

"It's a good job you got your long coat buttoned up," Williams remarked. "There's a change in those skies, so you need to keep wrapped. We've draped a heavier blanket over the horse, in case you get caught out in any rain."

She nodded her head in approval but didn't say anything as she mounted the horse.

"How long ye gonna be?" he asked, holding the reigns while she mounted.

"I'll be back after dark," she replied in a muffled voice because of the scarf over her mouth.

"I shouldn't need to tell you to be careful. There could be ice in them muddy puddles so don't be galloping at speed," Williams warned, and she nodded her acceptance.

Setting off at a trot, she was soon well away from the sight of Williams, and she breathed a sigh of relief. He hadn't suspected that it wasn't Silas riding the horse, so she hadn't needed to explain anything to him. With an inward laugh, she patted the horse's head and set it into a canter.

Besides teaching her and Silas to read and write, Oscar had also taught them how to ride a horse too. It was something she'd loved to do as a young lady with the boys, though she rode as a man and not side straddle as a real lady would. They'd often sneaked the horses out of the stables and then rode off together for a day's adventures. When they returned to the stables, she and

Silas would be punished, usually with a few hours labour cleaning out the stables. Despite that, they still managed to do it time and again.

Vera took a longer route because it allowed her to ride along the clifftops that overlooked the ocean. Her scarf blew to its full length, causing Vera's dark hair to fly with the breeze. A chilly wind blew fresh on her face, and she loved it. How she wished she could ride horses more often; it was a most invigorating experience and one she adored.

Reaching the top of the cliffs, she slowed the horse down and dismounted, allowing it to graze on the luscious grass. Taking time to look out at the dark grey ocean, she breathed in the salty sea air. The wind was bracing but that made her secret mission all the more enjoyable. There was nothing as good as the smell of sea air.

The light wasn't too good, and she could see mist coming in from the sea, but it wasn't dark yet. The sky overhead was looking a little yellow, causing her to suspect a storm was brewing. Not that it bothered her being out in a storm. If anything, it made her journey more interesting, and she smiled to herself.

"All grown up and still a mischief-maker," she said out loud as she looked over the ocean. At the sound of her voice, the horse looked up and stopped its grazing, walking over to her.

Stroking the horse's soft fur on its neck, she looked over the cliffs and noted the tide was in. It was causing the waves to crash with loud banging noises against the cliff walls. Vera could have stayed there much longer, enjoying the sounds and the smells of the wild, but she knew she must get on with her mission. Sea birds flew overhead and out to sea, their haunting cries carried in the wind. She smiled at how good it felt to get away from that steaming hot kitchen.

"A life of servitude, that's my lot," she mumbled to the horse. "And soon I'll be living a lonely life without my brother or Oscar."

Oh, Oscar, we can never be together you and I. Her mind churned over with mixed thoughts as she gasped at the wind blowing hard against her body.

The wind was no doubt picking up, so she knew she'd best be on her way. Yet the wild wind and the power of the crashing waves all felt a part of her troubled soul. But it wasn't fair on the horse to keep it up on the freezing cliff tops.

Soon, she was mounting the horse once again and heading toward Silsbury Manor to carry out her secret intentions. She knew it was unwise to ride at speed, and so they took their time to return to the path that would lead them to their destination. Down the edge of farmer's fields, they took a turn and entered a dense woodland area. All the while she was conscious of the horse's footing, making sure it had time to tread with care.

"I could just keep riding and never return," she said to herself. Her thoughts once again on her departure from the home she had lived in since her childhood.

Vera didn't want to leave Welwick Hall, nor leave her brother behind, but she knew she couldn't stay. *Seeing you with another woman in your arms will be unbearable, my love*, she pondered, Oscar always in the forefront of her mind.

Arriving at Silsbury Manor she stopped momentarily to wrap her scarf back around her face and neck. It felt comforting and warm as the wool fabric touched her cold skin. It was now semi-dark, and the weather was definitely turning stormy. Staring at the manor house, she wondered where she might end up living. Not many of the larger estates took on female cooks. The latest fashion was to bring in male French cooks, and she couldn't compete with them.

"Shall we get this out of the way?" she said, patting her horse's head again. "I bet you want to get back to your nice warm stable, don't you? Me too, I'll be glad to be wrapped up in my bed tonight, after we've finished here. C'mon then, girl, let's get you into this stable here, while I go and speak with the residents."

She turned the reigns to lead the horse towards Silsbury Manor stables. There, she found the stable master who greeted her with a warm enough welcome. He took the horse indoors, leaving Vera standing alone as he shut the stable doors.

Time to go and carry out my plan, she told herself as she set off to knock on the front door of Silsbury Manor.

CHAPTER 23

"I was looking for you earlier, Mother, but Perkins informed me that you had taken out the carriage," Olive queried as they settled down for the evening.

Her mother didn't reply but Olive didn't mind. She was too busy enjoying the heat of the orange flames in the hearth of the parlour. This room was much warmer than the chilly dining room they had just come from, after their evening meal.

"She said that you looked as if you were in a hurry to go somewhere," Olive added, wondering what her mother was up to now. "Was there an emergency somewhere, that you have kept from me?"

Still, her mother remained silent, which indicated that she must have been up to some mischief or other.

"You look flushed, Mother, are you well?" Olive asked, continuing to push her mother into submission. This was her new persona, and she was determined to be more forthright with her mother from hereon.

"I... I was visiting a friend who has taken ill," her mother replied, not looking up from her sewing.

What made Olive suspicious was how her mother did not elaborate more on her supposed mission of mercy. It was unusual for her not to brag and want to talk about it in much more detail. Her mother never did anything unless there was a motive behind it, but Olive let the matter drop. Whatever she was doing, it would most likely not be very interesting anyway. Instead, she took out some embroidery that she'd been working on, making a show that she wasn't interested in her mother's actions.

"My dear, you have such a skill with your embroidery work. Why don't you make a gift for the Duke of Cornwall," her mother suggested, as she finally looked over at her.

"Why should I wish to do that, Mother?" Olive asked, smirking but not looking up.

"If you were to embroider his initials on a gentleman's handkerchief, you could present it to him for Christmastide," her mother proposed. "Can you imagine his surprise that you had paid him so much attention?"

Olive put down her work and looked over at her mother. "But I do not wish to give him such a surprise Mother. You, on the other hand, might be the one to do such a thing."

Olive returned to her work, hoping to herself that she would not be around at Christmastide. She'd already penned a letter to her aunt in Scotland, to ask her advice about the journey, and she hoped for a quick reply.

Unexpectedly, her mother rose from her chair, but Olive ignored her, feigning indifference. Though it wasn't difficult to ignore her mother these days, as she had very little interest in what she was up to.

Her mother walked over to pull the rope that would bring one of the maids into the room, but still Olive remained silent. Her mother remained standing as she waited for the maid's arrival. It was as if she was willing Olive to speak to her and ask if she needed help. But Olive would not be her puppet a moment longer, and she continued her embroidery work, ignoring her mother's silent plea.

The door opened and Perkins entered the room, "I be at your service, Ma'am," she said with a small curtsey.

"Yes, yes, don't dawdle around and put some more coal on this fire will you girl," her mother ordered, taking her frustrations out on poor Perkins.

"Yes, Ma'am. There be talk of snow so you must keep warm," Perkins said with a cheery voice. Though it annoyed Olive a little that her mother couldn't have put more coal on the fire herself.

She hid her annoyance and continued a conversation with the maid. "Surely not?" Olive declared. "It is only November."

"It be all the talk on the farmlands, Lady Olive," Perkins said as she poked at the fire and popped more coals onto it.

Olive could smell the earthy smell of burning coals, and she shuddered at the thought of early snow. She smiled at Perkins for calling her *Lady Olive*, as she had instructed all the servants to do so. Unlike her mother, who disliked the servants behaving so informally.

"It may only settle on the high hills, Lady Olive, but who knows," Perkins chirped on. "Best to stay indoors and keep warm as toast."

Her mother sat back down again, huffing at the conversation. Perkins looked her way and asked, "Shall I put a blanket over your knees, Lady Smith?"

Whilst her mother didn't bother to reply, Perkins did it anyway, making sure it was tucked in so there were no drafts. With a smile, the girl turned to leave the room.

"Thank you, Perkins," Olive called out before the maid left the room. Her mother never thanked anyone for anything, but she refused to be so unfriendly towards their own servants. They worked hard to care for them, and she for one appreciated that.

The room lit up as the new coals took flame, and Olive decided to put down her embroidery work and picked up her latest novel instead. She was in no mood to concentrate because all she could think about was planning her journey to Scotland. Her aunt lived in a mountainous region, so it would be a hard track, especially if winter came early. Then again, winter always came early in the far Northern regions, and she hoped she had not left it too late.

She'd considered doing part of the journey by sea, to avoid the highways which could be treacherous with mud and water, and maybe even icy. Without realising, she drifted off into deep contemplations when someone shook her shoulder.

"Did you hear me, Daughter?" her mother's voice came to her. "I am taking to my bed early as I cannot seem to feel the warmth this evening. "I do hope I have not picked up any illness from some unhealthy servant," she remarked with a scowl.

Olive said goodnight and did not bother to query her mother's supposed ill health. Of course, it was unlikely that she'd picked any potential illness up from the servants. It was more likely that it was due to her gallivanting around in the carriage on cold days. She couldn't help but wonder if her mother was being truthful about her trip. Or was she up to something to stop her intended journey to Scotland? Then again, if she had visited an ill friend, that could be the answer.

A few moments after her mother had left the room, the door opened again. Olive assumed that her mother had forgotten something, but it was Perkins who entered and approached her to speak.

"Lady Olive, there be a young man at your front door. He be making a nuisance of himself by insisting on speaking with you," Perkins said. She looked a little flustered at the news she was giving to her mistress. "I tells him that cannot be, not on such a cold night, but he don't listen. If you likes, my Lady, I can get Jenkins from the stable to see him off, if you wishes it so?"

"How peculiar at this time of day," Olive said, but she was too intrigued to refuse. Removing the blanket from her legs, she got up and led the way to the front door, Perkins on her heels.

"I mades him stay outdoors, my Lady," Perkins explained tutting and looking pleased with herself that she had been brave enough to protect her mistress such an intruder. "And then I shuts the door on him."

"Well done, Perkins, but I do not think that we need to fear a caller on such a cold night, do you?" Olive remarked as she allowed Perkins to open the front door.

There, on their porchway, was indeed a young man in a long, heavy coat. A chill blew through the open doorway, causing Olive to speak to him, "Do come inside, please, if you will."

The young man stepped inside and once in the hallway; he then proceeded to unbutton his coat so that he could take out a letter. Olive could see that the man was dressed as a valet.

"Would you care for a hot drink in the kitchen?" she asked him.

"No, Lady Brent," he said in a gruff voice, no doubt frozen from the chill outside. "I've been entrusted to deliver this to you, and only you, Lady Brent," he told her as he held out a folded piece of paper for her to take.

As she accepted it, she happened to look into his face and smile at him. His eyes were watery with the cold wind, and for a moment she thought she recognised him.

"What is your name, young sir?" she asked.

"I must be going now, Lady Brent," he replied to her, not returning her smile, or answering her question.

She supposed he would be in rush to get back to his home, with the unsettled weather as it was.

"You may shelter in the stables and see if the storm subsides," she offered, feeling sorry for him at having to do errands in such bleak weather.

"Thank you, Lady Brent," he said, redoing the buttons on his heavy coat. "Please, read your letter straight away, as I understand there is some urgency to it."

With that, he turned and opened the front door to leave. A brisk wind blew in and Perkins stepped forward to close the door behind him.

Olive's first reaction was to look up the stairs and make sure her mother wasn't standing there. She didn't wish her to be aware of their visitor until she'd read the contents of the letter. At the moment, she had no idea who it was from.

Returning to the warmth of the parlour hearth, she went to unravel the letter and noticed that the seal was broken. Recognising the seal as Welwick Hall's, she pondered on why it was broken. Not thinking much of it, she assumed it must have been the haste in which the valet had been forced to get here. But then, that thought confused her further...

Why would the Duke need to contact me so urgently?

She decided to wait before opening the letter and hid it underneath the book on her knee. If her mother had heard the caller, she would soon come down to investigate. It was so unlike her not to notice when something was amiss, and she half expected her to enter the room any moment. Olive wanted to make up an excuse if she did, rather than show her the letter, and she pondered on what she would say.

"I will say it was a beggar wanting to take refuge in our stable for the night," she whispered to herself. "She will believe that, I am certain of it."

While she was keen to open the letter, still she held off. Patience was needed and she listened out for any creaks or squeaks of doors or floorboards, that would indicate her mother was on the prowl. Closing her eyes, she would feign sleep should her mother enter. That way it would appear as if nothing untoward had taken place.

The house was silent, and all Olive could hear was the coal crackling on the burning fire. She concluded that her mother must have been very tired not to have heard the commotion in the hallway. As she started to trust that no one would enter the room, she decided the time was right to read the letter and unravel this peculiar mystery.

CHAPTER 24

Olive felt a little apprehension as she looked at the letter. It felt as if, for some reason, she was dreading its contents. She paused before taking the letter out from underneath her book. As she sat still, she once again listened out for any signs that her mother was up and about, but all was quiet. Until she knew what it contained, she did not wish to share the letter with her mother yet, if ever.

She glanced around the room with tired eyes, catching the flickering flames in the hearth. For a moment she was mesmerised by the dancing flares and sparks.

I suppose it is time to unravel this mystery, she thought, reluctantly pulling her eyes away from the fire's warm glow.

Staring at the letter with its broken seal, still she delayed taking out the written parchment. Instead, she stood up and reached over for the blanket that she had crocheted in all her favourite colours. Sitting back down again, she covered her knees. The cold air that had entered through the open front door had chilled her through to her bones.

Briefly, she pondered the attractive face of the young man who had delivered the mysterious letter. She wished he'd agreed to stay in the stable because the storm could only get worse. The roads would be dangerous with ice, and that would make his return trip hazardous.

Shaking such thoughts of him from her mind, she finally unfolded the letter. As she did so, a smaller piece of paper fell onto her lap. It was a scruffy-looking folded note, appearing as if it had been torn from a larger leaf of paper. But before she unravelled that one, she noticed that the main letter was a repeat invitation to the Duke of Cornwall's ball.

"Why would he send a second invitation?" she whispered. "He cannot know that I destroyed the first one. And what is this other—"

Without warning, the door opened and her mother entered the room, "I have been informed that we have had a visitor?" she questioned. "Perkins brought me the warm drink I requested and told me of such."

Olive was disappointed that the maid had revealed all, but she did not blame Perkins. She'd not informed her that the strange visitor was to be kept secret so how was she to know?

Her mother went to sit in her chair, moving it as closer to the fire as she could. She pulled the mohair shawl on her shoulders even tighter around her body, as if that might keep out the chill. "Are you going to share with me what that letter is on your lap?"

"Yes, Mother, of course," Olive smiled in reply. There would be no getting out of the ball, not now that her mother was about to become aware of it. "It is an invitation to a Christmastide Ball," she started to explain as she looked down at the larger letter. Though she continued to hide the smaller one underneath her blanket. "And I note that the Duke has written an apology that we did not receive the original invitation. But I wonder how he would be aware of that?"

Olive looked over at her mother, starting to suspect something was amiss. "I do not recall informing Welwick Hall that we had not received an invitation, do you?"

"May I read the letter?" her mother asked, not volunteering any explanation.

Olive reached out to pass the letter over, careful not to let her blanket slip to reveal the smaller piece of paper. She watched her mother's expression as she scanned the words on the invitation. As she did so, she couldn't help but notice a certain smugness as the corners of her mother's lips became upturned.

"Did you know of this ball, Mother?" Olive asked, not taking her eyes away from her so that she could see her reaction.

"I may have heard about the ball whilst chatting with other ladies in the tearoom," her mother replied.

"You must have craved an invitation," Olive said with bitterness in her tone.

"Very well, I will explain," her mother looked resigned as she held the letter in her hand. "We have always been invited to every ball at Welwick Hall. Not once did the Duchess, Lady Sarah Wold, forget our invitation. As I was listening to how the ladies had all received their invitations, I could not help but wonder why we had been forgotten on this occasion."

"You never miss a trick, do you, Mother?" Olive said, her tone still hostile.

"I cannot think what you mean by such a remark. It is only in your interest that I went to visit the Duke," her mother admitted, turning her eyes to the letter in order to avoid looking at her daughter.

"And you could not have spoken with me first before you took it upon yourself to make such a decision?" Olive asked, unable to keep her annoyance at bay.

"There was no need to bother you with such silly details," her mother brushed off her daughter's hostility. "As it happened, the

Duke had already sent us an invitation. He saw me immediately and informed me that he had sent out so many, that ours must have somehow become mislaid."

"How inconvenient," Olive sighed, knowing her mother had bested her yet again.

"He promised me that he would have a new invitation delivered by hand, and here it is, this very same day," her mother declared, holding up the letter in triumph.

"Yes, here it is," Olive repeated her words in frustration. This invitation would change everything she had planned for her escape.

"Is it not good news, my dear? That the Duke is willing to go out of his way for us," her mother pointed out.

"Not for the poor messenger who had to deliver it in the darkness of a stormy night, no," Olive said with venom in her tone. She couldn't help it; her mother's behaviour had annoyed her to the point of boiling.

"I don't see why the messenger is any concern of ours, my dear," her mother replied, showing no remorse for the inconvenience she had caused. "Now then, we have a very special ball to plan. You must look so stunning that the Duke will not be able to resist dancing with you all night long."

"Mother, that would be scandalous and set all the tongues wagging," Olive replied, shocked at such a notion.

"Good, that is what we want," her mother grinned, and Olive could see that she was busy hatching all the ways that she could pair her off with the Duke of Cornwall.

"You waste your efforts, Mother, I am not yet ready to marry, how many more times must I tell you this?" Olive tried, but she knew it would have little effect.

"Then we will seek a long courtship, and then a long engagement," her mother replied haughtily. "Once we have the marriage secured, there will be no need to rush."

"Mother, I do not have feelings for the Duke, nor him for me," she stressed, unable to stop herself from pleading with her mother.

"That does not matter at this point in time," her mother assured her, now looking wide awake as if she would never return to her bed. "Love can come later, along with your children."

"What do you know of children, Mother?" Olive snapped. "You only see them as an extension of yourself, and there to jump at your every whim."

"We will need to visit the best dressmaker we know. You will require a new ballgown fitting. That one in Falmouth will do," her mother said, ignoring her daughter's sarcasm. "It is where all the ladies of good standing go, and they will hear of your very expensive ballgown"

Olive stood up, dropping the blanket to the ground, "Why do you never listen to me Mother? We cannot afford new ballgowns and I have plenty in my wardrobe," she called out. She raised both arms in confusion, but then remembered the smaller letter underneath her blanket

"Must you be so over dramatic, my dear?" her mother replied, disregarding her daughter's words. "We are only having you fit for a new ballgown, nothing more."

Olive could take no more and she sat back down in her chair exasperated. As she brought the cover over her knees, she felt for the small note. Annoyed with herself, she knew that she was allowing her mother to take over her life again. It was so much easier to give in to her than pull all the effort into fighting against her. If she had managed the trip to her aunt's, she might have been able to save herself.

"We shall make the trip to Falmouth after the snow has passed," her mother wittered on.

"Snow, you say?" Olive asked.

"Yes dear, I saw it through the window," her mother replied. "I know it is disappointing not to be going to choose fabrics and discuss the ball with all the other ladies, but it can wait a few days."

Olive didn't have the energy to reply, but she knew that the only one disappointed was her mother. Her concern was for the handsome young messenger who would be caught out in the snow. She prayed that he would manage to return home safely before the snow started to settle.

Her mother stood up, causing Olive to flinch in surprise as she looked up at her.

"As you are paying me no attention, I will return to my bed," she barked at Olive. "We can both sleep on it and discuss the ball in further detail tomorrow. One would have hoped that you might be more excited, my dear. From what I hear, this is going to be a very special ball."

"And why is that?" Olive asked, even though she had no interest.

"Because when I spoke with His Grace, he mentioned how you may find a good suitor at his ball. Now that I think on his words, I do believe that he was hinting at himself," her mother informed her.

"Did he say that he meant himself?" Olive asked, with a renewed thumping in her chest.

"As good as, I do believe. But I am off to my sleep. There is going to be much to do over the next few months," her mother announced as she walked towards the door with a renewed spring in her step. "It would be good to be out of this drafty house for the following Christmastide, do you not agree?"

"I like this house, Mother, you know that," Olive said, but not feeling in any mood to rise to her mother's caustic remarks.

"You will like Welwick Hall much better," she proclaimed as if she had won the biggest prize of all and was now rubbing it into Olive's face.

With that last statement, her mother finally left her alone and in peace. The silence fell on her ears, and it was bliss. Leaning her head back in the chair she rubbed at her eyes. Her new resolve was fading fast. If she did not travel to Scotland, she knew that she would be trapped forever with her mother ruling every part of her life. Scotland had been her freedom, but now her mother would never let her out of her sight.

CHAPTER 25

Olive looked at the piece of paper and wondered why anyone would be so wasteful. Paper was an expensive commodity and should not be wasted in such a way. She closed her eyes and waited another ten minutes to make sure she had no more surprise visits from her mother. But the time had come to read the smaller letter. Opening it, she read the words.

A friend would like to seek a private audience to speak with you. It is of an urgent nature, and you have my assurance that my request is very genuine. I will await your arrival in the stables this very night. Please come at your first convenience, and rest assured that you have my word no harm will come to you. I also ask that you keep this meeting a secret so that the gossipmongers among us are unaware.

In anticipation, from a friend in need

Olive gulped as she finished reading it, shocked at who it could be. She could think of no reason why any mysterious person should seek to speak with her in private. Should she go to the stable and resolve this mystery? Then again, if she was seen, word would undoubtedly get back to her mother and she'd never hear the end of it.

VERA AT THE BALLROOM

Olive got up to ring the bell for Perkins to come into the room. Soon, the door opened, and her maid entered as expected.

"My Lady?" she questioned, bowing her head a little as she awaited her instructions.

"I am to turn in early this evening, Perkins, and you should too," Olive said. She wanted no one hanging around downstairs if she was to go outside.

"But I have not yet finished my duties and—"

Olive raised her arm to stop her maid mid-sentence, "Sometimes things are best left until tomorrow. Whatever tasks you have not completed can wait, can they not?"

"Yes, my Lady, of course," Perkins replied, looking a little surprised.

"You work long hours, and you work very hard," Olive added. "Winter is around the corner, and we must all take care of ourselves, that includes you, Perkins. I know that I felt the chill from that open doorway earlier this evening. That is why I go to my bed now. It must have chilled you to the bones too. Have you looked through the window?"

"Aye, my Lady, I have that. The snow has settled all over the courtyard," Perkins answered.

"All over the lands more like," Olive smiled. "Off to your bed, do you hear?"

"I could do with an early night, My Lady, I'll not be denying that," Perkins said, looking pleased to be finishing her duties early. "I'll be up earlier to make up for it."

"Nonsense. Lady Smith does not rise early, and most especially in the cold," Olive pointed out. "So long as she has a fire burning for when she arises later, or we will never hear the end of it."

"Very well, my Lady, but if I don't clean out all the hearths this very night, then I will need to get up earlier to brush out the ashes," Perkins argued.

"Leave all the fires burning for the night, it will help keep the chill out of the rooms," Olive said. "I for one will not complain if there is no fire burning first thing. Now off you go. Get wrapped up in your warm blankets and get some sleep. Make sure the scullery maid has extra blankets too."

"Thank you, my Lady, it's much appreciated," Perkins said as she bowed her head to leave.

For a brief moment, Olive felt bad for deceiving her maid over her real intentions of sending her off to bed early. She decided that she would look at giving Perkins a half day off soon, even though her mother would complain incessantly about it.

Olive retired to her bedchamber as normal, she didn't wish to arouse any suspicions. Listening out for any noises, she paced her room as she tried to decide whether to go and meet the mysterious writer of the note. Whoever had put the note inside the letter, must have been the one to break the Duke's seal. Yet who would dare to do such a thing?

The drapes in her bedchamber had already been closed by Perkins, so she moved one aside to look out into the blackness of the night. It was surprisingly bright with the snow reflecting what little light there was. Olive wondered if the messenger had known the seal was broken on the Duke's letter. If he had, then he most likely knew who the second note was from too. If only she'd noticed the broken seal then, she could have questioned him over it.

Shivering, she took out a heavy, woollen shawl to put over her shoulders. The fire in the hearth of her bedroom had been lit earlier in the night, but the embers were now dying down and the air was starting to chill a little.

"I cannot go outside in this snow?" she said to herself, still debating on what to do. "But the writer said they were a friend, out of respect I should go," she mumbled in a hushed voice.

Unsure of the right decision, she paced her bedroom floor. *Was the note from the Duke himself?* She wondered. *But he would not need to hang around in my stables to speak to me.* Thinking of the Duke brought back memories of her short marriage to the late Earl of Gosmore.

She had married at an older age than most. Even then, it had been a marriage of convenience. Not only had the poor Earl needed someone to tend to him in the later stages of his life, but she and her mother needed help too. Not that Olive minded caring for the ailing Earl, he was a kindly man and left her quite comfortably off in his will.

And then there was the incident that had happened during her short marriage. Something she had never divulged to anyone, neither the Earl nor her mother. It was partly why she was in no rush to experience a loveless marriage ever again.

Even though the Earl was old and ill, they had consummated their marriage almost immediately. She recalled the memory of what had happened in only the second month of her marriage. It was then that she missed one of her 'courses', and soon began to suspect that she might be with child. It was a time of mixed emotions for her. A part of her was happy that she might be bringing new life into the world. She was also saddened that the child would have parents who cared little for each other.

Whatever her feelings, it didn't matter in the end. A month later she fell ill and had great pain and turmoil for two whole days. Olive confined herself to her room, claiming an ailment of the stomach. When she had awoken on one of the mornings, with excruciating pains in her midriff, her sheets were soaked in blood. At first, she had assumed that her course had come very late.

She had never known the real cause of what had happened to her during that night, it was more of an instinctual guess that perhaps she had been with child. Not that she knew much of such things, but she had called for Perkins to come to her aid. Perkins had been an upstairs maid in the Earl's household, and Olive had always preferred her to the other servants. It was she who had confirmed what could have been the cause of her illness. And it was a secret she swore to keep and had indeed kept it well.

Unable to share the loss with any but Perkins, she had become even fonder of the maid. That was why she had insisted on taking her with her when she left the household. But the whole experience had shaken her. She had unwilling to share her worries with her husband as she hardly even knew him. And she had not wanted to discuss the event with her mother either.

Perhaps she was being unfair to assume the Duke of Cornwall would be anything but kind to her, but her first marriage had felt so empty. If she was to take another husband, she wanted it to be for love. But her mother's point had been a valid one when she had suggested a long courtship. That would give them time to get to know one another. If the Duke was willing to prolong any talk of marriage, then she could be persuaded to consider a relationship with him.

Opening her bedchamber door, a little, she listened out for movement. With no sign of life, she opened it some more and peeked her head down the hallway. All was quiet, if she was going to do this then now was a good moment to go.

Shuffling down the darkened hallway, she'd decided against a candle lamp in case her mother saw the light. Olive tread with care to avoid the areas of the floor where she knew there were creaks. Making her way down the stairway, she thought she heard a noise and froze. Staying deathly quiet, she regretted sneaking around in the darkness of the night. But it was the only way that she would resolve this mystery, so she decided it was best to continue. Once she was sure that no one stirred, she set off once again, taking each step slowly.

Olive had already decided that the outside door in the boot room would be the best way to leave the house, and she headed in that direction. Had she gone through the kitchen door, she would have disturbed Evans, the scullery maid who slept on a cot in one of the pantries. The fewer who knew of her secret assignation, the better.

Turning the large metal key in the lock, she pushed down the heavy door handle to pull the heavy door towards her. A flurry of snow gushed through the open gap and hit her in the face. It was so cold that she put her head down and pulled her shawl even tighter.

This is not a good idea, she reminded herself, wondering again if it would be better to ignore the letter and go back to her warm bed *But I've come this far so I'm not stopping now.*

Closing the boot room door, she left it unlocked for her return to the house. Olive followed a dirt path at the side of the house, that would lead her to the stable. She hoped that the stable worker who slept in the hayloft would not be awake, otherwise all her sneaking around would be for naught.

At least the snow has stopped, she thought as she continued. *I do wish I had worn an outdoor coat. The breeze that is blowing around these buildings is freezing. What am I thinking?* She stopped to ponder. *I have no idea who this person is or what they are about. I cannot see it being the Duke, he has no reason to sneak around in the middle of a storm.*

As her teeth began to chatter with the cold, she moved in the direction of the smaller door that led into the stables. Opening that one would make less of a noise than the bigger double doors. Soon, she found herself standing inside the stable, where at least it felt a little warmer. The smell of damp hay and musky horse assailed her nostrils, but all was quiet, even the horse. It seemed to her that whoever had sent the note must have given up and gone to their bed if they had any sense because there was no one around.

Closing the small door to stop any drafts, she waited, deciding that she would warm up a little before heading outdoors and back to the house. In a sense she was relieved that the writer of the note had gone, but then again, would they try again on another night? No, it would have been better to get this over with, whatever 'this' was.

CHAPTER 26

That night, Oscar readied himself for bed without the assistance of his valet, Silas. He had sent him to Bilberry Manor to deliver the replacement invitation for the Christmastide Ball. Glancing through the window as he drew his drapes closed, he wished he had not sent him out on this night. The snow was beginning to settle, and the roads would be difficult for horses and riders alike. He knew that Silas was an experienced rider, as indeed was Vera because he had taught them both himself.

Pushing aside his concerns, he climbed into bed and reached out for the open book on the bedside table. There, he awaited his nightly visit from Vera. She had begun to bring him a warm, milky drink last thing at night. And then she stopped doing it without any explanation. He should have told her that he looked forward to her nightly visits. It helped him to relax, knowing that he would get a brief conversation with her before he went to sleep. It was Vera's way of helping him through his grieving period, and it had been working well until she stopped without warning. Every night, he hoped she start it up again.

But the hour was late, and still, she hadn't turned up. It could be she was running late every evening now, what with all the extra baking for the Christmastide Ball. He chided himself and decided he would ask her tomorrow if she needed some extra hands in the kitchen, at least until the ball was over.

He read another chapter of Robinson Crusoe, though he had hoped to read the book with Vera. He'd be happy to re-read it with her if she arrived, but again, it didn't look like he was coming. Perhaps the arrival of an early winter storm had kept her busier than usual, but he couldn't see why. Had the water frozen over in the new iron pipes they'd had fitted into the kitchen? Oscar pondered on whether he should get dressed and make a visit to the kitchen and check out if Vera was having problems down there.

For the first time, he realised that he had come to rely on Vera's nightly visits, and he had to ask her why she had stopped them. Jumping out of bed, he went to glance out of the window again. The snow was much thicker than when he had looked earlier, less than an hour ago. Deciding that he didn't want to interfere in the running of the kitchen, he returned to his bed. He tried reading again, but he couldn't concentrate. Instead, he lay there staring at the door, willing it to open. He so much wanted Vera to walk into his bedchamber with her usual warm and beautiful smile.

It was no good, he was agitated and would never be able to settle for the night, not knowing why Vera had stopped her visits before she turned in. Oscar left his bed and dressed in a thick dressing gown to keep out the chill. He was far too unsettled to be able to sleep, though he knew that he risked a scolding from Vera. At least it would ease his worries once he saw her so he would accept her reproach.

Making his way towards the kitchen, he had half expected things to be noisy with much activity going on. What met him though was a deep silence, and he was somewhat surprised, and a little perturbed. There was no sign of Vera and her maids. He even tried the pump in the kitchen to check that the water in the metal pipes hadn't stopped running with the snow, but all was well.

Where could she be? He wondered, starting to assume that she must believe he no longer needed her help. With nothing left for him to do, he made his way back to bed, determined to speak with her in the morning the next day.

As he walked through the kitchen, a banging noise caught his attention. It was coming from the room they used for deliveries, and as he entered, he felt a draft blowing through an open door. Assuming the kitchen maids had forgotten to lock it, he closed the door and set the bolts to secure it for the night. It surprised him that Barker hadn't noticed as he was in the habit of checking all the doors and windows on a night.

Without another thought, he passed back through the kitchen. It felt warm now that he had felt the outside air. He could see that the heat was escaping from the overnight bread oven. Holding his hands over the dim light around the oven door, he warmed himself as he pondered whether to go and knock at Vera's door.

He was aware that Silas and Vera lived in a small wing that extended from the kitchen, and he looked over at the door that led off toward those rooms. Should he go check if Silas had returned home yet? And indeed, was Vera in her room? But he was loathed to disturb them when they both worked so hard during the daylight hours.

He had another of his many moments when he wished his best friends were not servants. His thoughts swirled as he enjoyed the heat from the bread oven, and he deliberated on how he was now the Duke of Cornwall, Heir to the Bodmin Estate. That meant that he was able to make any changes that he wished. He would speak with them both and look at making them guests as opposed to servants.

But in his heart, he knew they would not accept his offer. Both had grown up as working people and constantly had their position in life made very clear to them. Not only by his father and the butler but by society itself. All he knew was that he missed being friends with Vera and Silas. Their closeness helped him through what had been a very difficult year. But if he were to tell them that, they would likely admonish him. It seemed that he too had his place, and there would be repercussions for him if he was to change the status quo.

There was nothing for it, he must accept Vera would no longer bring him his night time drink. Not only would he miss her, but he was well aware that he could not tell her that. She would only admonish him for not adhering to the rules. The thought of Vera lecturing him on societal rules caused him a half-smile. Vera was such a well organised young lady, that he wondered why she had not left the employ of Welwick Hall to go and work in the Royal Palace itself.

That thought caused his smile to change to a frown. What if she was ever to leave him? He could not stop her, but nor could he imagine his life without Vera in it. No, he would see to it that it never happened, he would be lost without either of the twins.

With so many confusing thoughts rolling around his head, he made his way back to his bedchamber in the dark. He didn't need a candle to light his way, he knew the house like the back of his hand. He and the twins had often sneaked around it in the dark hours as children. That memory caused him to chuckle to himself.

His night time excursion had left him fully awake, so instead of going straight back to his bed, he headed for his study. Still in the darkness, he poured himself a sizeable measure of brandy and carried it to his bedchamber. Climbing into bed, he sipped at the amber liquid, enjoying the warm glow it gave him.

Settling back into the warmth of his blankets, he looked longingly at his open book. Novels always reminded him of Vera. Her passion for reading far outpaced his own interest in books. She even wrote poetry when she had time, and that reminded him that he must ask if he could read any of her latest writings.

The fact that he'd missed her so much caused him to consider his relationship with Vera.

Is it that you I could not live without you in my life, my sweet Vera?

He wasn't sure of the answer to that question because he didn't know what such a notion meant. *Certainly, I miss you when I do not see or speak with you on any given day. Silas is in my life every day, in his capacity as my valet, but you seem to avoid me lately. Or is that my imagination?*

Oscar took another sip of brandy, waiting for the liquid to burn his throat and heat his body again. Enjoying the warming sensation, he then downed the rest of the glass to dull his mind of the conflict he felt over Vera.

I cannot expect you to run around after me all of my life, can I? he thought, wishing she had simply come to say goodnight to him so that he would not doubt himself so much. *What do I do when you are not around? This night has proved that I pine for your company. But I cannot understand why this is so. Have we both not moved on now that we are older?*

Unable to come to any sensible answer, he blew out the candlelight and closed his eyes. Sleep came all too soon, thanks to the brandy.

He soon found himself in a dream where he was racing a horse with Vera.

She was beating him, her horse in front, but only because he allowed her to be. He had always wanted her to win any competition because he didn't like to see the disappointment on her pretty face.

She kept turning around to laugh at him as she raced. He adored her laughter, and her loose hair blew around in the wind. The sun shone above them, yet a chilly wind was blowing in. It brought with it some dark grey clouds which began to block out the sun. He shouted to her, telling her to stop the race, but she seemed oblivious to the darkness that was surrounding them. Vera turned her back on him and upped her speed. He couldn't catch up with her and called her name over and over. She was getting further and further away from him until she and her horse disappeared over the edge of a cliff.

He jarred awake, shivering at the scene that had unfolded in his dream. As he came to his senses, he replaced his warm blankets over his cold but sweaty body, shaking off the nightmare and thinking no more of it.

Soon, he was dreaming of Lady Smith, of all people. She was chasing him down, in a fast-moving carriage. He was on horseback and attempting to get away from her. Her head stuck out of the carriage window, and she shouted after him that he had to get rid of his servants. He knew that she spoke the truth and a scene played out whereby all his servants were jumping over a cliff edge.

Again, he awoke with a jolt, his covers had fallen to the floor, he must have been restless in his sleep. This time, he relit the candle lamp. Waiting until the effects of the nightmare had passed him by, he decided not to go back to sleep yet. Picking up his open book, he read another chapter of Daniel Defoe's travelogue about living on a lonely island after being shipwrecked.

A thought came to his mind; *I wish something like that might have happened to my parents. Perhaps they didn't drown in the shipwreck and managed to save themselves. What if they found themselves on a desolate island and they're still alive? How will I ever have any way of knowing? Damn my bad dreams, they're affecting my sleepy mind.*

It was the lack of Vera's visits that had set his mind in motion with turmoil. Tomorrow, he would seek her out and speak with her.

Am I not within my rights to demand that you bring me a warm drink every night? If that is the only way to make you do it, then...

He closed his book and slammed it down on the side table in frustration.

It would be unfair to force you to do that, what am I thinking? He berated himself. *I am going to tell you how much I miss your company. And then you might agree to come and say goodnight to me at the end of your day. But is it fair to ask that of a servant? But then, you're not a servant, not in my eyes anyway. You are my most important woman that I have ever met.*

With that revelation in his mind, he sat up to consider what it all meant. Why he felt that way about Vera, he wasn't sure. *Do you mean more to me than I had ever realised?*

Annoyed with himself for his confusing thought, he decided it was something he could ponder over another day. For now, he blew out his candle and attempted to sleep once again. Knowing that Vera was not far away from him, would have to be comfort enough. At least she was in the same house, and he had to make sure things stayed that way. He was soon to drift off again, this time into a dreamless, but restless sleep.

CHAPTER 27

When Vera returned to the stable of Silsbury Manor, the stable hand had already gone, most likely to his bed. Opening a smaller door at the side of the building, she was most careful not to awaken the sleeping groom. There was one other horse in the stable along with hers, so she approached it to make sure it became familiar with her scent. Once the friendship was formed, all be it brief, she went to her own horse to reassure her that she hadn't forgotten about her.

With both horses settled, she peeked through the wooden slats in the smaller door, to see if there was any sign of Lady Brent's arrival. This whole escapade had been fraught with risks. Dressing up as her brother might not have been a good idea, but at least it got her here. The breaking of the seal on Oscar's letter to place her own note inside had been very disrespectful, but it was a necessary evil. They all felt like good ideas at the time, but now, standing in the cold dark stables, she wasn't so sure. It could be that Lady Brent will choose to ignore her note. Especially if she thought that meeting a stranger in her stable, in the dead of night, was a little too risky.

Vera had tried to stress her reassurances in the note that no harm would come to her. Not that it meant the Lady of the house would believe her words at face value. Then there was the possibility of Lady Brent informing her mother of the note's message. That was half the reason Vera was on high alert; in case Lady Smith was to come charging into the stable, ready to discover who the writer of the note really was.

As time passed by, and with no sign of the mad old woman, Vera guessed that Lady Brent had at least kept the note to herself. Peeking through the slats of the door again, she watched the snowflakes flurrying to the ground and settling down into piles. It didn't bode well for her journey home, but she would worry about that when it was time to return. For now, she had other worries on her mind. Would Lady Brent come to the stable? If she did, should she reveal her true identity, or continue pretending to be her brother?

She wished that Lady Brent would hurry so that she could get this over with. The more she waited, the more deceitful she felt, but it was necessary for the sake of Oscar. A man she loved with all her heart, but a man that she could never be with. If Lady Brent were to marry him, then Vera wanted to make sure that she was the right choice for him. Then again, what right did she have to interfere in Oscar's life?

With doubt settling into her mind, she returned to the horses. Stroking the hair on their gentle heads was more for her comfort than anything else. This whole affair was all very vexing, and she wished she was home in her cosy, warm bed.

"We'll soon have you home too, and in your own, comfy stable," she whispered to her horse, careful not to raise her voice.

She'd heard the sounds of low snoring coming from the hayloft, and assumed it was the stable worker dreaming of warmer days. If When Lady Brent turned up, if she did, she must remember to warn her to keep her voice down. Vera doubted the lady would want her stable hand aware of her secret meeting with a stranger.

While continuing to stroke her horse, she heard a slight squeaky sound. She knew it to be the smaller door that she had entered the stable by. Someone had opened it, before quickly closing it again. Olive was certain that it must be Lady Brent, if it were Lady Smith, there would be much more commotion. Nonetheless, she remained perfectly still, keeping her breathing low. A dark shadow appeared to be moving around, but Vera had no way of knowing if it was Lady Brent.

Observing the silhouette, she waited in silence in the background, until she could be sure who it was. As the figure went to peek through the slats in the door, the same way that she had done, she could see enough. Lady Brent removed a part of her woollen shawl from her head, showing a glimpse of golden-blonde hair.

Vera stepped out of her hiding place and stood in a sliver of moonlight so that the Lady could see her. She kept her disguise intact for now and smiled over at Lady Brent to reassure her that she was safe. Holding her finger up to her lips, Vera pointed to the hay loft to remind the lady of her servant who slept in the stable. To her surprise, Lady Brent moved closer to her.

"It is most improper to expect a lady to meet with a man all alone," Lady Brent whispered. "There had better be a very good reason for this, young man."

Vera heeded the warning and took the lady by the hand to lead her to the farthest point of the stable where they could speak a little louder. She was a little surprised that Lady Brent allowed her to do this, but she didn't hesitate to indicate that they needed to move.

Once they were better positioned to talk, Vera looked at Lady Brent, "My humble apologies, my Lady, for bringing you outside when it is so cold. I can assure you that I've taken every precaution for secrecy so that you will not be compromised."

"Well, it is not every day that a handsome, young valet seeks an audience with me," Lady Brent gave Vera a friendly smile to show her compliance. "But I would appreciate speed with your message, so I can return to my warm bed."

"I do understand," Vera replied, pleased that the lady still believed her to be a man and a handsome one at that. "However, you are not as exposed to scandal as you believe, because you see, I am not a man."

With those words, Vera took off her hat and allowed her long, dark hair to fall over her shoulders. She also used her own pitch of voice, which was much higher than she had been using for her disguise.

"My goodness, what is this?" Lady Brent exclaimed, bringing her hand over her mouth to dull her gasp. "I know you, do I not?"

"Indeed, you do, Lady Brent," Vera replied with an exaggerated bow, as a man would do, or a performer on a stage. "I am Vera Atkins, the Duke of Cornwall's cook at Welwick Hall. But please, I beg of you to hear me out," Vera added as she raised her hands in submission.

"I do not see what a cook could possibly want of me?" Lady Brent interjected, doing her best to keep her voice low at the shock that had just been exposed to her.

"My apologies, once again, Your Ladyship, for bringing you out into the darkness of a chilly winter's evening," Vera continued. "But I had to speak with you without others knowing, and this was the only way I could think of to do so."

"Very well, I will accept your ploy, for now," Lady Brent said, though, from the tone of her voice, Vera knew that she was not pleased. "What is it you want of me?"

"First, I wish to tell you of the deep devotion that every member of the household of Welwick Hall has for the Duke," Vera began in earnest. "We all know our places, but the Duke treats us as if we were his friends. That has led to a tight-knit group of servants, loyal through and through."

"I am pleased for the Duke, it is a virtue to treat one's servants well, and a merit to his character," Lady Brent said. "But still, that is nothing to do with me."

"I ask for your patience, my Lady, as I try to explain myself," Vera attempted to explain her purpose. "Since the deaths of the Duke's parents, we have all been most aware of his sensitive side. It has made the Duke very vulnerable, though he would never admit it. Not only are his servants concerned for his welfare now, but also in the future, which would include any wife that he takes."

"I still do not follow why this involves me?" Lady Brent stressed as she rubbed at her arms to keep any body heat on the move.

"Please forgive my forwardness, my Lady, but if you do not see then you must be blind," Vera warned. She was starting to wonder whether Lady Brent was playing games with her. "The Duke of Cornwall is fast becoming fond of you, my Lady. I beg only that if you agree to marry him, it is for love and not his title."

Vera put her head down in shame as she finished her words. Did she really have any right to question Lady Brent's motives? Most likely not, but it was all she could do to ensure Oscar's happiness.

"I see," Lady Brent sighed. "Are you sure that you are here on a mission for the household? It seems to me that it could be a more personal reason. I would even go as far as saying that you, Vera Atkins, are the one who is in love with your master."

Vera became disconcerted at this comment, her lips trembling in fear that she had been found out. "I... I...no, that is not true. It's not why I'm here," she tried, but in her heart she knew that the truth had been discovered.

"It is a very bold move you make, Vera, for a servant," Lady Brent inferred.

The tables had been turned, and it was now Vera's turn to look shocked. "I... I must be leaving now, my Lady," she stuttered, making her way over to her horse. "I have said all that I have to say.

Only that you consider Oscar... I mean His Lordship's heart, should he ask you to marry him."

With those final words, Vera was coming to the realisation of what she had done. She had no right to speak on behalf of the other servants, let alone for Oscar. Shame wracked her body, and all she wanted now was a way out. She took little notice of what the lady was doing and went to lead her horse by its reins to the larger stable door. Opening it, she quickly mounted and shook the reins to set her horse into an immediate gallop.

Of course, her horse obeyed, even in the settled snow she galloped according to the orders of her rider. Vera was oblivious to the cold and the snow, for she carried such a heavy weight on her shoulders.

What was I thinking? She questioned herself as tears escaped the corners of her eyes. The biting wind swept over her face, bringing her to her senses, at least for the sake of her horse, and she slowed the horse to a canter. It would not do to injure the poor beast with her own shameful behaviour.

Taking the main track back to Welwick Hall, Vera remained insensible to her journey. She felt none of the cold, or wetness that soaked through to her skin. Her mind concentrated on a safe journey for her horse. Focusing on that alone was enough to keep them both safe, but all the while, she could not stop the shame that dug deep into her soul.

"Why did I do that?" she cried into the howling wind. "I am such a fool, a simpleton even. Why would I assume that the Lady would even care for my opinion?"

Lady Brent is sure to mention this to Oscar, she thought as they passed through the woodlands. *He will be so ashamed of me. Have I just jeopardised Oscar's marriage to a most beautiful lady of standing? He will never, ever forgive me if I have.*

Finally, the gates to her home were in view, but it was hard to see with the heavy snowfall that was restricting her vision. Lucky for Vera, her horse knew its way home and it stopped at the stable door. There seemed to be no one around, so she dismounted and opened the closed stable door. A young stable boy came to her aid, taking the horse to dry it out and bed it down for the night. She was grateful that the boy had the common sense not to say a word to her.

Leaving the stable behind, only now was she becoming aware of the bitter cold. Her body shivered uncontrollably, yet, shame was overriding all other senses and she ignored the cold.

"It's so unfair!" she cried up to the dark, night sky.

Vera walked from the stable to the kitchen entrance that she had left open. As she arrived to push the door open, it would not move. Someone must have noticed, and they had locked it. No doubt it would have been that interfering Morris Barker. But then she knew it was his job to check all the doors were locked at night.

Leaning on the door, it afforded her a little shelter in a small porchway. There, she quietly sobbed as her emotions finally overcame her.

"What have I done?" she questioned herself, over and over. "I've ruined everything, all with my own stupidity," she gasped, unable to control her tears. *How will you ever forgive me, Oscar? That I dared to interfere in your life.*

After a while, Vera's sobbing slowed a little. It was enough for her to realise she was still outside in the cold. With her teeth now chattering from the cold, she knew what must be done.

CHAPTER 28

Lying awake, in bed, Silas mused over his wonderful night with the beautiful Lucy. They had been unable to walk on the grounds of Welwick Hall because the weather had taken such a drastic turn. Instead, they sneaked into one of the gardener's outer sheds. There they held hands as they took cover from the wet snow. Chatting and laughing all night long, they got to know one another better. Lucy had even afforded him a goodnight kiss, that had been everything he dreamed it would be.

He couldn't wait to tell his sister that at long last, her brother might be in love. Real love at that. The kind of love that involved being with that one person as much as possible, alone, and together. The kind of love that might even end with a marriage. Silas hoped his news might give his sister some cause for cheer, for she had been so miserable of late. Which reminded him of the task he had passed on to her that very night.

He frowned at the thought of her out in such poor conditions, but he knew she was a strong rider and would not have found the errand too taxing. Still, she should have been back hours ago, and all tucked up in her room, fast asleep. Should he have checked on her to see if all went well? Knowing his sister, she'd only chastise him if he did so. Closing his eyes, he pulled one of his blankets over his head to warm up his cold ears. The snow had brought in a biting chill and even indoors it was hard to get warm. Tomorrow, he would visit the stores and get some extra blankets for his bed.

Only a few moments after he'd closed his eyes and forced himself to stop thinking about the new love in his life, there was a faint tap at his window. At first, he assumed he had imagined it in a half-sleepy haze. But as he turned over in his bed, it happened again, only this time it was louder and had a defined rhythm to it.

It caused him to jump out of his bed. Could it be Lucy, who had come to his room because she couldn't sleep without him? Shaking his head at such a thought, he knew that was his imagination playing tricks with him.

For a brief moment, he stood staring at the curtains that covered the glass. He hesitated before opening them, apprehensive about who, exactly, was out there.

The tapping happened again, only this time it was louder and sounded out with urgency. Without any further hesitation, Silas opened the corner of one of his curtains, only to see his sister standing there.

"What?" He called out as he opened his window. Now that he could see her clearly, her teeth were chattering together as she held her arms tightly around her snow-covered body. Even with a thick overcoat on, she looked soaked to the skin with white snowflakes all over her dark hair. "Go to the delivery room, I'll come and open up the door," he instructed, deciding to save the questioning until she was inside and warmed up. He needed to get her indoors before she died of a terrible chill.

Silas ran to the delivery room, being careful not to wake the whole household. All the bolts were set, and it seemed to take an age to unlock them. They had stiffened in the cold, and his fingers shook as he tried to open the door as quickly as he could. He wanted to get his sister inside before she caught her death with the cold. So many things flitted through his mind as to why she was out so late. He was a fool not to have checked in on her, and now she was in serious trouble.

Swinging the door open, Vera fell straight into his arms. Her body shivered uncontrollably, and her teeth continued to chatter. Scooping her up, he carried her to the large, wooden delivery table. It was empty of any stores, and he carefully laid her down on it, before turning back to re-lock the door.

When he returned to her, he could see she was no better and so he picked her up again to carry her to her room.

Peeling off the soddened, heavy overcoat, he laid her on her bed, pulling up the blankets to help warm her body. Then he laid on the edge of her bed and pulled up more blankets, rubbing at her body to get her warmed up. He hoped that his body heat might help her to thaw out, but what had happened to make her so late?

"I'm here, Sister," he whispered, holding her tight to lend her some warmth and comfort. "You're safe now, you're home. Though goodness knows what's happened to you."

She tried to say something to him, but the words were unrecognisable with her still rattling teeth. He hushed her, stroking her soddened hair, and then used the edge of a blanket to try and dry it. But Vera would not stop trying to speak, it seemed that even in such an appalling state, she had plenty to say.

"Ssshhh… Sister, you must rest now that you're safe," he spoke to her in hushed tones, hoping it might soothe her mind. Had someone attacked her and that was why she was so shocked? But she showed no sign of injuries so neither had she fallen from her horse.

Looking down at her face, he could see tears on her cheeks, she was crying!

"What is it, Vera?" he asked. "What has happened to you out there? I was a fool to let you go. I will never forgive myself for whatever it is that has befallen you on that road."

"N…no…it…wasn't…you," she managed to form some small

words on her lips, and he was relieved that her body was beginning to warm up.

"It jolly well was me. I was foolish enough to let you go off on my errand," he replied. "I knew all too well that you wouldn't return until darkness had fallen."

He felt her shake her head, and then she spoke against his chest. "I... I've d...done a terrible th...thing," she sobbed out.

"You, my sister, are not capable of doing anything terrible," Silas replied, not accepting her confession.

Yet still, she insisted on repeating the same words as tears continued to stain her cheeks. She was becoming almost hysterical, determined to have her say, but he would have none of it. He held her tight, pleased to see that the frightful shivering had subsided, and made sure she was well wrapped in the blankets. His main concern now was keeping her warm, whatever she had to say would wait until later.

"I must leave Welwick Hall!" She called out as she tried to pull away from him. "I... I can't stay here."

"What are you saying, Sister?" he asked, concerned that she might be having a feverish conversation. He had heard that people who had fevers could see things that others could not. Was she seeing something that frightened her?

"Oscar, he...he is going to know soon enough what I've done," she would not stop her unrelenting moans. "Silas, he'll never forgive me, I have been such a fool."

"What talk is this? There's nothing that Oscar wouldn't forgive you for," he insisted. "You're talking in riddles, Vera, likely because of a fever. Give yourself time to warm up and things will become much clearer, I promise you."

Vera began to shake her head from side to side in response to his words. Soon, she found the strength to sit up, and said, "I can't bear what I've done, Silas. You must help me get away so that Oscar need never look upon my ugly face ever again."

Silas stood up and placed his hands on Vera's shoulders, attempting to push her back down into her bed again.

"Whatever has happened, Vera, it must wait until the morning," he told her with a firmness in his tone so she would listen to him.

She started to sob again, and her body shook. Whether it was from her sobbing or the cold chill, Silas did not know. All he knew was that he had to comfort her, so he lay by her side, and on top of her blankets. Leaning over, he embraced his sister's prone form close to him for his body heat and hummed a tune. As he hummed, he rocked her, hoping the sensation would soothe her tormented soul. Whatever she had done, surely it could not be all that bad?

Soon, her sobbing subsided and her breathing had a relaxed rhythm to it. Risking a glance at her face, he was pleased to see her eyes were closed. Why was she calling herself ugly when she was so very pretty? Especially when her face wore such a relaxed expression, and he guessed that at last, she had fallen asleep. Although he'd managed to remove her wet overcoat, the clothes that she still wore underneath the blankets were still wet. He knew that he needed to get help to care for her.

Her forehead felt tacky and feverish, and her cheeks were flushed. Feeling at her neck, he knew that his sister was indeed suffering from a fever. As he felt her clammy skin, he noticed for the first time her strange attire of a stiff white collar. That was not something she normally wore. Peeling the blanket back from her neck, he could see that she was dressed in one of his valet uniforms.

"What's this?" he whispered, shocked to see his sister dressed as him again. "What in God's name are you doing dressed as a boy? Have you been to an inn and joined in a play? Is that why you are so late back?"

Though he knew there was no truth in his thoughts, he wrapped her back up again. Not wanting to wake her up for she needed rest, his questions would need to wait for another time.

Clearly, she had been up to something, but what it had been he had no notion of. With gentle, quiet steps, he left the room and closed the door behind him. He would go and get some help from the housekeeper; Mary would know what to do to help his sister's fever. She'd also help undress her from the sodden clothes that would be doing her no good.

As for his sister's mischief, that would have to wait, but he had no concept of what she could have done against Oscar. Vera would never do anything to hurt Oscar, but it was obvious she felt she had done something to cause their friend concern.

Not wanting to raise the alarm with Oscar yet, Silas sneaked through the house and up to the attic where the servants had their quarters. Soon, he was tapping on the housekeeper's door. It took only moments for Mary to answer, and he wondered if she had not even fallen asleep yet.

Holding out a lantern so that she could see who was at her door, she spoke up, "Silas, what on earth are you doing all the way up here?"

He could tell that knew something was wrong by the concerned look on her face.

"I need your help, Mary," he answered. "It's my sister, she has a fever."

"Gracious me, I wondered why had turned in early," Mary said as she went to get her heavy night coat.

"No, it's not that," Silas told her, dreading admitting that it was his fault. "She went on an errand for me. It was a horse ride away, and she should have returned hours ago. Yet, she's only just got back, and she's soaked right through to the bones."

The two of them made their way down all the stairways, through the kitchen, and into the extended wing where the twin's rooms were situated.

"She's still dressed in wet clothes," Silas, explained as they walked. "I managed to get the wet coat off her, but I didn't wish to go any further."

"It's a good job you came to me for help, Silas, well-done lad," Mary said as arrived in Vera's bedroom and saw the state that the girl was in. "You wait out here while I undress her and put her some clean clothes on."

Silas did as he was told but he paced the corridor as Mary aided his sister. Praying that his sister would pull through, he recalled how a servant not so long ago had died of pneumonia after almost drowning. Could his sister get that for being out in the wet snow? Never again would he allow her to do his bidding. If there was ever to be a never again. Silas fretted over his sister and made a pact to himself to stay by her side until she was well again.

Finally, the door to Vera's bedroom opened, and Mary stepped out with her later still lit.

"Have you been walking up down this corridor in the dark?" she asked him.

"I can't sleep until you tell me how she is," he replied, willing the housekeeper to tell him that all would be well.

"Go to your bed, for now, Silas. There is nothing more either of us can do for your sister," Mary informed him. "She is at the mercy of God now, let's hope she pulls through this terrible fever, as I fear she is quite ill."

"I can't sleep knowing my sister may not here when I wake up," he cried out, holding his hands up to his head.

"She will still be here tomorrow," Mary assured him. "It is how well she does over the next few days that will be important for her."

"Is she warmed through yet?" Silas questioned, his voice quivering with fear for his sister. "Her teeth were shaking and her whole body too. I should never have allowed her to be out so late at night."

"Hush now, Silas, your sister has a mind of her own, and don't think for a moment that she'd have done the errand unless she wanted to," Mary said in her attempt to calm him. "She must have had some kind of motive for doing your errand. Mark my words. Now off to your bed, so I can go to mine."

Whilst he went to his bed, Mary's words rattled around in his head. She was right, why had Vera wanted to do his errand, and even worse, why had she dressed up to make it look as though she was him?

Unable to settle, he took his blankets and entered Vera's room. Her breathing was raspy, so he went to get one of his pillows to prop it under her head. He dragged a chair to the side of her bed and covered himself in a blanket. This was the only way he would get any sleep this night, right by his sister's side.

CHAPTER 29

Oscar awoke with a start. As he lay in his bed, his body was soaked with sweat because somehow, he'd managed to wrap the blankets around himself too tight. He recalled shivering at some point in the night, but now he was far too hot. Not only that, but he had a dread in the pit of his stomach. Oscar assumed he'd had a nightmare. As his skin prickled, he knew that could be the only explanation for his feeling so wretched. For some reason, Vera was at the forefront of his mind. The more he thought of her, the more distant she seemed to get. He felt empty; as if she would never be in his life again.

He had felt that recently she was ignoring him, and he had no idea why she would do that. Which seemed off because if Vera was upset over something, she would tell him. That was how it had always been. She wasn't one to worry over airs and graces, she would seek him out and give him a piece of her mind. That was one of the things he loved about her.

The gnawing feeling wouldn't go away, as if he was sensing that something was amiss. His sensible side pushed away the anxious thoughts, it was most likely an after-effect of all that he had gone through that year. Losing his parents had certainly affected his emotions, causing him to feel vulnerable. Now, more than ever before, he wished his two friends were by his side all the time.

They had wanted to live their lives as was expected of them, and he had accepted that when his parents were alive. But now he was the Duke, and he had the power to put it to them to end their roles in his servitude. Pondering on how best to do this, he heard a light knock as the bedchamber door opened. In the back of his mind, he knew it would be Silas, and he felt very pleased to see him.

Silas did not even look his way as he went about his usual duties. His valet opened up the drapes to let daylight stream into the room. He then entered the wardrobe, coming out with suitable attire for Oscar's morning routine. They went through this same routine every time he had to change his attire throughout the day.

"Why can I not simply wear the same outfit all day?" he questioned his valet, at last gaining his attention.

Though Silas didn't even reply as he continued to lay out Oscar's outfit. If anything, his valet looked so preoccupied that Oscar wondered if he had even heard his question.

"Let me try this one then," Oscar said, climbing out of his bed. "Is your sister purposely ignoring me?"

Silas stopped in his tracks and looked over at Oscar, wearing a strange expression of worry on his face.

"Have I upset you, Silas?" Oscar asked, surprised at Silas's seriousness. "Is there something about Vera that I am unaware of?"

Oscar froze as he awaited an answer from his valet, and he knew in his bones that something was wrong.

"My sister is ill, Your Grace," Silas replied, and Oscar could see the worry in his friend's dull eyes.

"Vera ill?" Oscar repeated, as if it was the most ridiculous concept he had ever heard. "But she is as fit as a fiddle. Vera is never ill."

"She was caught out in the snow yesterday," Silas told him, the worry never leaving his stern expression.

"That must mean that she was out in the dark of night," Oscar surmised. "What would Vera be doing out at such a late hour?"

"Erm...you know my sister," Silas half laughed. "She...she was out covering some vegetables in her garden, fretting that they might get damaged in the frost."

"Yes, that does sound like something Vera would do," Oscar said. He smiled at the very thought of Vera attempting to wrap up her vegetables and herbs like a mother would her children. "I have heard from the head gardener that she's very protective over who tends her part of the garden."

Silas said nothing, he merely nodded his head in agreement and took on a solemn look again.

"Worry not Silas. Your sister is strong and will soon recover from a short spell of being out in the cold," Oscar said, going over to the dressing table that held a jug of water. He poured the water into a large porcelain bowl, proceeding to splash the sleep from his face. "Would you inform her that I would like to visit, and also read to her? That should keep her cheerful."

Silas said nothing in reply, causing Oscar to turn to look at him as he noticed him glaring out of the window.

"Did you hear me, Silas?" Oscar asked, rubbing his face with a thick towel. "Oh, and inform the kitchen maids that a cold dinner will suffice while ever Cook is ill." Silas nodded back at him, but still, he looked vexed. "I know you two are twins, but your sister's constitution is strong, and you know it. Stop all this fretting and let us get on with our day, shall we?"

"Of course, Your Grace," Silas said, still not breaking a smile.

"And stop calling me by that title," Oscar remarked. "When Vera is well again, there is something of great import I wish to discuss with you both."

Oscar looked over at Silas, hoping that his comment might have piqued his curiosity, but it was as if his valet had not heard anything he said today. Silas had returned to organising Oscar's wardrobe, going about his business as he did every day. Oscar decided that he'd leave his friend alone for now. He was obviously troubled over his sister's illness, and so he would say no more.

After breakfast, Oscar went straight to his study to sift through all the business papers and letters he was now receiving daily. He had never realised how much responsibility his father had undergone, at least not until those duties had become his to deal with. It was a royal pain, and that thought reminded him that he also had to arrange to seek an audience with the King at some point. It would be expected of him to report personally with an update on Cornwall's dealings.

That morning, he'd not gone rushing to Vera's room because he wanted to allow her some time to rest. It would not do to disturb her so early in the day. The more she slept, the sooner she would start to recover from whatever illness had befallen her. In turn, the sooner she'd get back to normal so that he could question her on why she was ignoring him.

When the afternoon arrived though, he was ready to stop his work and go to visit her. At midday, the kitchen maids had served him a delicious hot soup, and now he wondered if it might do the same for Vera. Soup was always a great healer, and with that in mind, he headed toward the kitchen.

As he entered the kitchen, the maids were in a flurry at his presence in their domain.

"My apologies ladies," he said graciously. "I wish to pick up a bowl of that delicious soup and deliver it to Cook's room," he explained as all faces were staring his way. "It is time I visited our patient," he added, hoping to snap them out of their fixation on him.

Lucky for him the housekeeper entered the kitchen, and she clapped her hands together to get their attention. "Everyone back to your duties, His Grace does not require you to stand around gawping at him." It seemed to do the trick and the kitchen, while still quiet of voices, soon became a hype of activity again.

"Thank you, Mary," Oscar said to her, grateful for her help. "I am here for a bowl of hot soup so that I may visit Cook."

"Of course, Your Grace, I will organise the tray immediately," Mary said with a bow of her head.

Soon, armed with a tray of steaming soup, Oscar set off toward Vera's room. He smiled to himself as he heard the kitchen maids once again chattering after he'd left. No doubt they'd be gossiping that their master was serving soup to a servant, but he had no time for their opinions and nor did he care. Knocking on Vera's door there was no reply, but he entered anyway. As he did so, Vera suddenly sat up and stared back at him in shock.

"Please, Vera, it is only me, Oscar. You need to lay back down again," he said in a soft tone. "I am sorry that I surprised you as I did, but I have brought you something to help keep you warm."

Shivering, she remained in her seated position, looking upset at seeing him. "How can you ever forgive me?" she said, staring at him as if he was a stranger.

"Come now," he said, putting the tray on a small table by the bedside. "There is nothing to forgive. You cannot help it if you are ill. Please let me help you sit up so you can eat. We need to rearrange your blankets to stop you from shivering. It is important that you keep your body warm."

"Oscar, I am so very sorry," she called out and looked as if she may burst out into tears. "I didn't mean for things to get so out of hand—"

Oscar raised the palm of his hand to hush her because she was looking so agitated about something. He assumed it was her fever talking, as he could think of no reason why she would need his forgiveness. Vera must have become confused as she lay in her sick bed, her illness making her seem so vulnerable. It wasn't something he was used to with Vera. She was always the strong one, a person to make decisions and see them through.

After helping her to position herself to be able to eat, he produced a book from the inside pocket of his jacket. He had brought it along in the hope that it might comfort her.

"And see, to stop you from becoming bored, I will read to you," he informed her as he placed the tray that held the soup onto her knee.

Although she began scooping the soup onto the spoon, she looked fearful as she ate it.

"Vera, stop your fretting," he attempted to reassure her as he sat in a chair by the bedside. "It gladdens me to see you idle for once. By the way, I have brought your favourite book, Twelfth Night," he announced, raising the book in the air for her to see.

"You can never read that book too many times, Your Grace," she said with a gravelly voice. "It is a wondrous tale."

"My thoughts exactly, see how we both think alike?" Oscar put the point to her. "But I can see that you still have a fever, so eat up and then lay back down so that I can tuck you into your blankets. Meanwhile, I shall enact all parts of the play and you can be entertained by my different take on the voices."

And that is exactly what he did, he spoke in a high-pitched tone when he read out the female lines. Going down to the baritone voice for the male parts. Noticing a small smile from Vera now that she was comfortably wrapped up, he continued to read the play.

"Now then, I have come to the part where a female plays a male, do you think I should use a high pitch, or a lower-pitched voice?" he asked her, knowing it should bring a smile.

Yet Vera was not herself and he could see that her smiles were strained.

"I tell you what, why don't you close your eyes as you listen?" Oscar suggested. "That way, you can rest too."

He continued reading the lines in the Shakespearean play. Glancing Vera's way, he soon noticed that she had drifted off to sleep, her skin still glistening from the sweat of her fever. Not wanting to leave her, he went to sit in the chair by her side, wishing for her to get better. For a quick visit into her garden to rescue her plants, it had taken a terrible toil on her health. It felt strange to see this strong young woman so struck down with weakness. Closing his own eyes, he found himself saying a prayer for his friend's speedy recovery.

As he finished his prayer, his mind wandered, and he recalled her asking for his forgiveness. Yet, there was nothing to forgive her for. Saving vegetables from a night time frost, hardly required a pardon of any kind.

Again, he assumed it was her fever confusing her mind. When she was well again, he would tell her how she fretted for forgiveness, and they would laugh over it. Following that, he intended on dismissing them as servants and welcoming them into his home as live-in companions. Later, he would arrange an income for them, so that they could both feel independent. No doubt they would argue against it, but on this occasion, he was going to be insistent. It was time for Vera to stop labouring in the kitchen, and somehow, he would ensure that she was by his side as an equal, of that he was determined.

CHAPTER 30

Through the misty haze of her fever, Vera had imagined Oscar's reaction once he'd discovered her betrayal. She had meant well. She had meant to make sure that Lady Brent would love him. Of course, not like she loved him, but at the very least she wanted to make sure that she would not marry him simply because of his title and wealth. Yet, all she had managed to achieve was to make things worse.

She could see Oscar's face, twisted in anger at her as he told her what he thought of her. *How dare you interfere with my prospective bride? You have never accepted your place as a servant, and now you have gone much too far by assuming that you can stand between and the lady I am to marry.*

Yes, his words would be harsh and cruel because she had done exactly that. Even to the point of fooling Lady Brent into believing she was a man. Her deception shamed her, it would be her undoing.

He will ask me to leave. I know it because I've made him look so bad in Lady Brent's eyes. She dwelled on all the bad things that were to happen to her. *I'll have no references, so I'll never get another job.*

Leaving was my plan anyway, but not to live in poverty. Oh, Oscar, you'll be so ashamed of me for interfering in your life, and I don't know how I'll ever forgive myself. I am but a woman in love, and I thought I could help with your happiness.

She didn't know what it was that she had thought. Her only intention was to make sure that Lady Brent would return his love. If he was to have a loveless marriage, he would be so unhappy. Confusing thoughts continued to tumble around in her mind as went in and out of consciousness. One time she woke with a cold, freezing shiver, and the next she felt as if her skin was melting, she was so hot.

My illness is my punishment for interfering in Oscar's life. Who did I think I was that I could even dare to question Lady Brent? Oh, Oscar... I am so very, very sorry...

When he entered her room, she had panicked that he had come to throw her off his lands in her delirium. Assuming he already knew of her secret assignation, he'd come to berate her foolishness and disrespect. But no, she caught his smile, and he had come bearing gifts. Vera didn't want to look at him in case he saw the guilt in her eyes. Her head pounded but she managed to calm down her nerves as she watched him.

Was she being unfair to him? It wasn't his fault that she'd deceived him, that blame was all hers. He attempted to get her to sit up to eat, and she played along, avoiding his eyes as much as she could. Accepting the bowl of soup, she scooped a spoonful into her mouth, but her throat was too dry and swallowing too painful.

Through the corner of her eye, she watched his every movement. He seemed pleased with himself that he'd brought her favourite book along. If only he knew of how that book had now ruined her life. Once he found out that she'd taken an idea from its pages to dress up as her brother, he would never want to look upon that book ever again.

Showing his concern, he took back the bowl and leaned in to tuck her into the heavy blankets. She spoke but a few words to him before finding it too difficult to utter anymore. Unable to confess what she had done, for it would be better coming from her, but the words would not form. It was clear by his kindness that he hadn't heard from Lady Brent yet. When he did, then no doubt his kindness would soon change to anger.

As he read to her, he did so with his usual sense of humour. Vera was frustrated that she couldn't appreciate his gesture, but the fever was making her so lightheaded. Her whole being felt chilled to the bone, but she could feel the sweat on her brow. Again, she shivered uncontrollably, but her skin felt as if it was on fire. Would she die right in this very bed? If she did, then it would be a just punishment.

Tucked in the blankets, with the man she loved close by her side, her mind was in terrible turmoil. She'd tried to tell him that she was sorry, but he'd not accepted her apology because he didn't know of her selfish deed.

Struggling to keep her eyes open, she let them droop a little.

But then, she awoke with a start, discerning that she must have drifted off. With some relief, she gasped to see Oscar was still with her, sitting in a chair by her bed as he too had dozed off.

"Oscar," she croaked, trying to get his attention.

His eyes shot open, and she could see that for a moment he was confused.

"What?" he called out as his body jolted. "Oh...my dear, dear Vera, I cannot believe that I am here to care for you and fell asleep. How are you?" He asked as he looked down at her with clear concern in his eyes.

"I...I must speak..." she said to him, trying so hard to get the words out, but the pain in her throat and head rattled at her core.

He leaned onto the bed, his handsome face coming closer to hers.

"Ssshhh...you don't need to speak, there'll be time enough for your chatter later," he whispered to her in a lulling voice.

She managed to move her hand and touch his to get his attention. Although it was comforting as he returned the gesture, she didn't feel deserving of any kindness.

"I...I want to say goodbye, Oscar, I..." she could only manage a few words at a time, and she had so much to tell him. She wanted to admit to her selfish deed. And then she wanted to explain that he need not put up with her selfish ways a moment longer. Then she would explain that planned to leave so that he could marry whomever he pleased without her interference. Vera knew that she had so much to say if only she could speak. And if only she dared to tell him of her love...but she could never do that to her lifelong friend. Vera knew that the only way to resolve things was to leave. That would allow him to get on with his new life, but how could she tell him all of this when she couldn't speak?

"No, no, no," he replied, smiling down at her. "Hush now. I do not know what it is that you are trying to say, but I promise that you are going to be fine. Please, Vera, stop trying to speak because it is clear that it is too much for your weakened state."

"I must leave..." she murmured again, her vision a blur as she attempted to hold onto her consciousness.

"You are delirious with fever, Vera," his voice came to her as if it was an echo in her head.

But still, she tried, "I would rather die than hurt you, Oscar," she said, wanting so desperately to tell him of her love.

"Stop, Vera, don't speak such words," she heard him say. "You are not going to die, I will not allow it, do you hear me?"

Vera could hear panic in his voice, but she couldn't make out all of his words. Had she told him of what she had done? She wasn't sure, everything was such a blur. She felt his hand gripping hers and it was warm and strong. Wanting to move her fingers so she could get his attention, her whole body felt numb.

Where am I? Hold me tight, Oscar, I'm losing you...

"You're not losing me, Vera. I am here and I am going nowhere. I am holding you tight, I promise" his words echoed in her head.

She fought hard to overcome the dizziness and soon she felt

the closeness of his cheek as he held her close. Holding her in his arms, he moved his face away to smile down at her.

"I will not allow this illness to overcome you, Vera," and she heard the steely determination in his voice, but it did little to comfort her. Even worse, she could see his face and it was wrought with worry. "I will never allow anything or anyone to harm you, I promise you, Vera."

She hated to see him looking so vulnerable, but as his words began to fade, so too did his face.

"I...need...to...leave..." she whispered, but she wasn't sure if the words could be heard. "I've ruined everything for you," she added, unsure if her mouth was speaking, or if it was all in her mind.

Soon, after a feverish darkness had overtaken her, she awoke again, and there he was, still by her side. Was she drifting in and out of sleep she wondered?

"Ahh," he looked at her to speak. "I knew that reading this play would help you through."

At last, she could make out his words. He was still reading the Twelfth Night. It cheered her a little as he changed his voice to suit the characters, high pitched for female roles, while gruff and deep for the male ones.

As she listened, something was niggling in her mind. And then her mind was flooded with memories.

She, her brother, and Oscar were running through the house making their way to the library. it was her favourite place in the whole house. For some reason, they were then hiding under a table in the library. A huge dark figure burst through the library door, and she called out.

"No! No!" she said, wanting to protect her brother and Oscar from the bad man. "The fault is all mine," she tried to shout. "I must leave... I'm so sorry Oscar, for what I've done. I love you, and I'll love you forever, but I must leave for my shame..."

CHAPTER 31

Oscar listened to Vera's incoherent ramblings with a sense of shock, did she say that she loved him? It was difficult to say with any real certainty what she was meaning. Her declaration of love was tied with other outbursts of blaming herself for something she had done, but he had no idea what it was. Settling her back down in her blankets, it worried him that Vera was flitting in and out of consciousness. She was getting worse with the fever, not better.

Once she'd fallen asleep again, he left the room to ask one of the kitchen maids to find Silas. He'd visited her earlier in the day, and they'd agreed that Oscar would stay with her for the daylight, and Silas would sit with her in the darker hours. They'd both wanted to be with her all the time until she recovered, but not knowing how long that could take, they'd agreed to do it separately. That way one of them could be by her side all the time.

He'd also collected a bowl of cool water and a clean cloth from the kitchen so that he could pat her skin with a cool, damp cloth. As he did so, the door swung open, and a worried-looking Silas dashed into the room.

"What is it, Oscar?" Silas asked, staring at his master with wide-eyed worry. "What do you think's wrong with my sister?"

"I don't know, Silas, but I want you to stay with her while I go and fetch a doctor," Oscar said urgently, looking up at his valet from his chair.

"We should send someone else to bring the doctor, Oscar, you can't go out in that weather," Silas said. "Or let me go instead."

"No, I have made up my mind," Oscar said, standing up and handing the damp cloth to Silas. "One of us must be with her for when she awakens. I must warn you that your sister is talking in riddles that only we should hear. And only one of us can go for the doctor because I know that we will do so with the haste that is required."

"So let me go then," Silas insisted.

"No, my friend, this is something I wish to do," Oscar said. "I cannot sit around this room a moment longer while Vera gets worse. I know the doctor well; Biggins will come immediately for me, but he may delay if it's you."

Silas nodded his agreement as he looked down at his sister on the bed. Beads of sweat glistened on her forehead, causing her hair to stick to her skin. With a pounding heart, he sat by her side and cooled her skin with the damp cloth.

Oscar left him with Vera and move with speed out of the back door of the kitchen, heading straight to the stables. The snow had been falling for hours now and he thought it odd that it had come so early this year. Autumn usually brought blustery winds and hail, but very rarely snowstorms.

Once at the stable, he called out for a stable hand to attend to him.

"Ready me the fastest horse we have," he demanded of the groom. "I want one with stamina too."

As he waited, he grabbed for one of the grooms' heavy overcoats that hung up nearby; it was going to be a harsh, cold journey.

Setting off at a canter, he soon instructed his horse into a jog.

Oscar wanted to ride at full speed for at least a couple of miles, and then he'd let his horse slow down a little. They had around five miles to go, to get to the hamlet where Biggins resided, so he needed to pace the horse, especially in the icy snow.

It was hard going, even on the main road. Oscar worried for the horse in case it lost its footing in any of the deep potholes that were covered in snow. The falling snow was making visibility hard too, requiring all his concentration to keep his horse safe.

After two miles of top speed, it was time to turn off the main highway and take a dirt track road. He could feel the heat coming off the horse's back and slowed to a canter. The hamlet was about three miles up the dirt track and they'd need to pass through wooded lands. The uneven ground slowed them down even more, but Oscar and his horse trudged on and on.

All the while, thoughts of Vera invaded his mind.

What is it you have done, Vera, that you carry so much guilt? his mind was racing as he dodged thick tree trunks and fallen branches. *Please hang on. I will be back with help soon.*

His horse whinnied at the various obstacles they had to navigate by, nervous and unsure of his footing. Oscar patted the horse's neck hard to comfort him and remind him that he wasn't alone on this journey. It seemed to do the trick and the horse settled into a good pace once again.

Soon, Oscar could see lights in the distance as it shone through the trees. As they neared them, he could make out the dark shapes of the buildings. There were not many houses there, but he only wanted one of them, and he prayed that Biggins hadn't been called out anywhere else.

Jumping from his tired horse, Oscar banged on the door of the doctor, relieved that a light burned through the glass window. Biggins opened the door warily, but he soon recognised Oscar and smiled at him in greeting.

"Come in, come in, Your Grace," Biggins beckoned upon seeing the Lord at his door.

Oscar did as he was bid and entered the warmth of the house.

"Do you have a horse?" Oscar asked with urgency."

"I do. Why, is something wrong with yours?" Biggins asked, not quite understanding the meaning of the question.

"He's tired and needs to rest," Oscar said, keeping his overcoat fastened up as he dripped with melting snow. "I want to get you back to Welwick Hall at speed, Biggins, and we need a fresh horse for the journey."

"Goodness, I wasn't planning on going out in this storm, but if it's urgent then I'll get my coat and boots," Biggins grumbled but moved to ready for the storm. He wasn't a young man anymore and didn't go out at night, but he would not refuse the Duke of Cornwall anything.

"Is it a large beast?" Oscar asked, rushing the old man as he helped him get his overcoat on. "Will it carry us both easily enough?"

"Yes, yes, Mable is a Shire," Biggins replied, sitting on a chair to pull up his boots. "She's not young anymore either, but she gets me where I need to be in all weathers."

Biggins led Oscar to the stable, leaving the Duke's horse with the stable boy so he could rub the horse down and feed it the best hay they had. Once Oscar was satisfied his horse was well tended, he mounted the huge shire horse, helping the doctor to climb on and sit in front of him.

"Are you going to tell me who it is I am tending to, and what it is that ails them?" Biggins asked as the Duke led the horse out of the stables and into the cold blizzard

"We have a young woman with a high fever, she's falling in and out of consciousness and I am gravely worried for her," Oscar explained, spurring the horse on as they started the return journey. "She was out in this storm and has taken a turn for the worse." He shouted to make himself heard over the howling wind that had picked up. "We must go with speed."

"Goodness, yes, yes," Biggins said, clinging onto his black bag that held all his equipment and medicinal vials. "She must be very important to you, Your Grace. I am sure she will be well."

"There is no one of more importance to me," Oscar replied, realising the truth of the words as he spoke them. Of course, he was close to Silas too, but Vera was...well...his life would be empty without her in it.

The ride back to the Bodmin Estate was awkward and slow with two people on the horse's broad back, and the snow was not letting up. The wind was almost a gale now, swirling clouds of powdery snow up into the air. They had lost all daylight and much of the way through the trees had to be done from memory as the dirt track was completely covered.

Oscar made sure the old man seated in front of him was secure as he forced the horse to a gallop once they hit the main road. The icy air cut into his face as all around was layered in a ghostly white covering. The primal force of nature seemed to be fighting against them as they made slow headway in the thick snow. The white dunes were reaching even higher than when he'd passed them less than an hour ago. Oscar knew it wouldn't be long before the road would be completely impassable. An eerie light glowed all around them as the whiteness reflected what little moonlight was cutting through.

When finally, the gates of the Bodmin Estate were in view, Oscar pushed the horse harder, if it were possible. He had been gone too long already, he needed to get the doctor to Vera's side straight away. Her smiling face came to his mind, and he longed to see her beautiful smile once again. He wanted her well again, and not in the vulnerable, weak condition she suffered now. Oscar wasn't used to Vera being frail and feeble, she had always been a strong one, and now he didn't know what to do.

As soon as the horse arrived in the courtyard, a couple of grooms came running out to tend to their lord. Oscar allowed them to get Biggins from the horse first, and then he jumped down straight after.

"This way, Biggins," Oscar said, directing the doctor towards the back of the house where the kitchen entrance was situated.

"Is she a servant?" the doctor asked, obviously expecting to enter the house through the front door.

"Her room is off the kitchen," Oscar explained, unwilling to say anymore.

As they arrived in Vera's room, Oscar felt a sense of relief to be back with her again. Though she looked much the same.

"She hasn't awoken once since you left," Silas said, his features etched with worry.

"Very well, young man, I will take it from here," Biggins instructed with some command, now that he was in his domain of expertise. "Send me a maid to help fetch some boiling water, and I would like to clear this room of people if you please."

With those demands, Oscar glanced over at Vera, and it broke his heart to see her so vulnerable. Her silky skin was pale, almost grey, and her lips pallid. She did not look like the Vera that he knew and loved so very much.

"Can I not stay with her?" Oscar asked Biggins, desperate to touch and hold her hands.

"She will fair better if you let me get on with treating her, m'lord," Biggins said firmly, taking no nonsense, not even from a lord of the nobility. "Now, off with you, and send me the help that I've asked for."

Both Oscar and Silas reluctantly left the room, looking lost. Oscar didn't need to send for a maid as the housekeeper arrived in the kitchen, looking flustered.

"I've only just got word that you've been out to get a doctor, Your Grace," Mary said, anxiety lining her face. "I've been on another wing of the house all day, sorting things for the ball."

"You are here now, Mary," Oscar said with a soft voice, he didn't want to make a noise with Vera so ill. "Can you assist the doctor?"

"Of course, I will, Your Grace," Mary replied, her eyes watery and her hands shaking. "Forgive me, but I'm a little vexed that no one sought to inform me that Vera had taken a turn for the worse."

"It only happened in the last few hours," Oscar explained. "But I would be grateful for your help. Will you send someone for me in my study as soon as the doctor is done?"

Mary nodded in agreement and then headed toward Vera's room to assist the doctor. All Oscar could do was watch her go, feeling useless now that he had returned.

"Come, Silas," he turned and said to his friend, leading him away from the kitchen and toward his study. He could tell that Silas was reluctant to leave, but he forced him away with a gentle tug on his arm. "We can do no good here, we will only be in the way. I am frozen through and in dire need of a warming drink."

CHAPTER 32

Olive was pleased to see the thick snow drifts in the garden finally melting away. She'd taken herself to the library to find a new book and was soon browsing the extensive novel section. Usually, she favoured female authors, their thinking was more appropriate for women's reading material. Although she liked the odd adventure too, and her aunt had introduced her to the author Walter Scott when she last visited her.

Taking a French novelist from the shelf, she recalled when she had bought the book on a visit abroad. Before she had a chance to open it, her mother entered the library, looking out of breath and agitated.

"There you are," her mother managed to puff out as if she'd exerted herself somehow. "I have walked those stairs up and down searching for you," she said with an accusatory tone as she took a seat at the library table.

Opening out a fan, that she seemed to have with her all the time these days, she wafted herself with some cool air.

"What is it now, Mother?" Olive asked, tutting, as she too went to sit down.

"It will do you well to keep using your French," her mother said as she pointed at the book in her hand. "After all you did receive the best of education, and I am pleased to see you practicing your expensive language skills."

"I doubt that you have come flurrying into the library to lecture me on my education, Mother," Olive said impatiently. Though she had no intention of reading the French book in her hand because she was more in the mood for some poetry.

"I have come to share some urgent news with you," her mother said, looking rather thrilled with herself. "But first I want you to go and ready yourself for a trip to Odell. Now off you go, daughter, and no dawdling. I will go and order the stable hand to ready the carriage."

"I am in no mood for an outing, Mother, the roads will be terrible in this weather," Olive complained, not moving from her seat. "And why must I rush?"

"If you go and ready yourself, I will explain everything in the carriage," her mother replied. "And choose a suitable outdoor cloak. I like the deep red one with the fur edging on it, that should do the trick."

"You are not to choose my outfits, Mother," Olive replied in annoyance. "You have not yet divulged where we are going. Or why we are to dash at speed on the muddy highway."

"Very well, I will enlighten your curious nature, I suppose," her mother fussed. "I received word that a certain lord will be visiting the apothecary this very day. But I was only given a small window of time, so it is my hope that we will not need to linger any longer."

"What? You are dragging me out into the cold because you want me to meet with a gentleman!" Olive called out. "I cannot believe it of you, Mother. There is no man that is worthy of making me suffer the deprivations of a cold winter's day."

"Oh yes there is," her mother chuckled to herself. "It is the Duke of Cornwall no less."

"And why do I need to meet the Duke at the apothecary, pray do tell?" Olive asked, scowling at her mother.

"I am very pleased that you asked me that question, daughter," her mother retorted. "You are to bump into him, by pure coincidence of course. Then you will look at him in surprise and thank him personally for sending his valet to deliver our invitations for the Christmas ball."

"If every lady was to follow him around to thank him for their ball invitation, he would think the world had gone mad," Olive countered.

"Yes, but you are not just any lady, and he is a most important lord, one of whom we should go out of our way to impress upon," her mother finished.

"I will only go if I do not have to travel by carriage," Olive insisted. "It is truly treacherous on those muddy highways. I will do the deed alone and we will not risk the wheels of the carriage."

"Daughter! You cannot ride a horse in this weather!" her mother bellowed, shocked at the very thought.

"I can and I will, that is if you wish me to bump into the Duke of Cornwall," Olive said, smiling to herself with a sense of achievement. "It is astounding how you are privy to such information in the first place, but I must go and change if I am to do this, Mother."

"I have my sources and they are very reliable," her mother answered, looking away as if she was hiding some dirty secret.

"You mean the Duke's butler, don't you?" Olive said, not wanting to play games and so simply telling her mother that she already knew who it was. "It is not very agreeable, Mother, allowing a servant to swoon over you in this way."

Olive chose her words intentionally, to make her mother feel uncomfortable, and it worked a treat. With a sense of satisfaction, she went to change her outfit for a riding skirt. She also chose the thick cape that her mother had mentioned because it had a warm hood, which would stave off the wind as she rode.

Before long, Olive was guiding her horse carefully toward Odell. What her mother didn't know though, was that she had no intention of riding into town to meet with the Duke. Knowing that he was absent from Welwick Hall, that was where she was headed.

As she cantered her horse on the journey, riding side saddle at speed was not an easy feat, and so she slowed her horse down a little. Thinking on the delivery of the Duke's invitation, Olive had accepted that her Scottish Christmas trip idea was dwindling away fast. It was looking like she would not be able to get out of the Duke's Christmas Ball.

After taking a shortcut through a thick forest covered in fallen leaves, Olive came out of the trees to enter the gate of the Bodmin Estate. Not wanting to risk being seen, she took a roundabout way to get to the courtyard in front of Welwick Hall. Staying some distance away, she noticed a small carriage standing close to the front door. Halting her horse, she watched from behind a large birch tree as the Duke walked down the stone steps toward the carriage. Next to him, she recognised a familiar figure. As the carriage pulled away, the figure was left behind, so she came out of hiding and trotted her horse towards him.

He stopped in his tracks as he spotted her from a distance, and he awaited her arrival.

"My Lady, I am sorry to tell you, but you have missed the Duke, I'm afraid," the man said to her. "He is gone into town."

"Yes, I watched him leave," she told him, watching his features with great curiosity. The woman who'd dressed in his outfit looked very much like him. Confused, she asked, "I am sure we met at the beach picnic, but remind me, young sir, you are His Grace's valet, are you not?"

"At your service my Lady," he replied with a bow. "I am Silas Atkins, and the Duke will trust me to pass on a message if you wish."

"No, I do not wish that. Now that I have established who you are, I would request that you take a turn with me around the gardens," she demanded. "But first you will assist me in dismounting from my horse."

"You wish to take a turn in the Duke's gardens with me, my Lady?" the man asked her, making no move to assist her as he looked on incredulously.

"It is you whom I wish to speak with," she replied. "Are you afraid to walk alone with me?"

"No, my Lady, it is you who I must consider," he replied, still looking a little dazed at her request.

"I will ride my horse to the maze, and we stroll within its walls undisturbed," she suggested. "Do not worry, young man, I will deal with the consequences should there be any."

The young man bowed, but still, he looked worried.

"I have a quick errand to run in the house," he informed her. "I must check on someone first. Are you able to afford me the time to visit my ill sister?"

"Ah...I see, your sister is taken ill?" she asked, her brow raised in question.

"She is, my Lady. But she was sleeping when I last saw her and is likely to sleep all afternoon," he explained. "The doctor has left us laudanum to help her body rest while the fever runs its course. His Grace has gone into town to replenish the small bottle."

"Of course. But know that it is your sister who I need to discuss with you," she told him. She thought it better to be open and honest in case he assumed she was making a romantic advance on him.

"My sister?" he asked with a puzzled expression. "Do you know her?"

"Erm... I do know some things about her, but let us leave that until your return," Olive suggested, hoping that he'd agree.

"Would you like to visit with her?"

"No, it might be better not to mention my visit to your sister yet as it may alarm her. I would rather not disturb her while she is bedbound," Olive replied. "Perhaps you could help me first, as there are a few questions I would like to ask."

She wanted no further conversation in the courtyard, and so turned her horse to ride in the direction of the hedged maze. There she would await the valet's return. She knew of the extensive maze of hedges that had been grown on the grounds, they had quite a famous reputation in these parts. It would afford them plenty of privacy.

Silas soon returned, and it took but an hour to convey her story of how his sister had dressed as him, in order to seek an audience with her.

"I am surprised at this news, I had no idea," he said, and Olive was getting used to his face looking constantly shocked.

"Perhaps when she starts to recover, she will give her own version of events," Olive said. "I was worried for her because she ran out into the blizzard on her horse."

"I can give you no explanation why she came to you as she did," Silas told her, shrugging his shoulders as he looked back at her. "But I'll be speaking to her about it as soon as she's conscious and more coherent. Did she tell you what she was about?"

"We talked some, but I have ideas of my own. It is for your sister to share what's going on in her mind with you," she stressed. "I know a little of your history, you are the twins who played with the Duke when he was a boy. It cannot be an easy situation being the childhood friends of your master, but from what I understand the Duke is a decent man."

"He is indeed," Silas agreed, and we are still friends, but my sister–"

Olive raised her hand to stop him from speaking, "I am not angry at your sister, so please let her know that. If anything, I am worried for her. But let us not discuss this matter anymore. I have done what I set out to do. I wanted to speak with you as her brother, hoping that you could help to alleviate her worries and check that she was well."

"She's been acting odd of late, but I've was so wrapped up in my own romance, that I didn't spare her much time," Silas admitted.

"Twins are meant to be close if I understand, are they not?" she asked.

"Yes, but we can't read each other's minds," Silas said with a sigh. "Thank goodness, I would not want her reading my thoughts," he chuckled to himself.

"No, but you can get her to talk to you and uncover the real reasons for her unhappiness," Olive hinted.

"I can, and I will, but you don't know my sister. She's strong-willed and stubborn at best of times," Silas smiled as he said those words.

"Well, it would take a certain type of character to do what she did, and all for her master's happiness," Olive pointed out. "But now, I must leave, or my mother will send out a search party for me. And there you have another stubborn woman, only this one can be mean too."

"Lady Smith is certainly a forceful character," Silas agreed, but then his face changed, once again taking on a worried look that he'd said too much.

Olive laughed, "There was never a truer word spoken, Silas. My mother is a force of nature, so I must get on my way. Will you help me mount my horse?"

Silas helped Olive to mount the horse and then thanked her for going out of her way to speak with him. "No doubt my sister will worry over it all once she's herself again."

"I hope she makes a speedy recovery. The Duke must think much of her for him to travel to Odell for her medicine when he could have sent a servant. Tell her that, will you, it may cheer her when she awakens. Goodbye my new friend and take care of that sister of yours. Oh, and please, tell her not to steal your clothes anymore."

With a wave of her hand, Olive spurred her horse into a slow canter and headed for home. She had already decided that she would inform her mother that she missed the Duke. That he had come and gone by the time she arrived in town. Knowing her mother she'd soon forget all about it and start on her next scheme.

CHAPTER 33

Vera awoke with a heavy humming in her head. She was alone and, in her bedroom, with no memory of how she got there. Rubbing her eyes to better focus, she sat up and looked around her room. On the little table by her bed sat the book Twelfth Night and instantly she thought of Oscar. At that point, her head felt as if it was avalanching with memories as she recalled all that she had done.

"Heavens, I can't stay here," she said out loud, as shame began to weigh heavy on her mind. *How long have I been laying here? Long enough for Oscar to know that I tried to interfere in his courtship with Lady Brent.*

She hung her head with tiredness, scratching at her hair to try and clear her fuzzy mind. *I need to get out of here. I can't face... I can't answer their questions. They'll all be so annoyed with me, I have to pack... I'll pack and leave before anyone comes back.*

Vera tried to get out of bed, but her legs were too weak, her head spun, and she knew she was in no fit state to get away yet. Collapsing back onto her pillows, she felt frustrated that she would have to face Oscar and her brother. They would never understand why she'd gone to see Lady Brent. The shame of what she'd done was forcing her to try and push herself; she had to leave, and quickly.

That was when her bedroom door swung open, and Silas appeared in the doorway. From the look on his face, she knew that she was in trouble. Sinking back onto her pillow, she pulled up the blankets and turned her back on him.

"I'm in no mood to talk to you, Silas, go away," she told him, but it was an effort to speak, and her voice was gravelly.

"Oh, you will talk to me, Sister, and before Oscar returns too," he said, sounding angry with her.

He knows what I've done, but how could he? Confused thoughts reeled over and over in her head. "I'm not well enough yet to remember everything that I've done, so go away," she snapped, keeping her back to him so he might take the hint.

She heard the door close, but she was sure that she could still feel his presence. Vera didn't want to look around to see if he was still there. Remaining perfectly still, she hoped that if he was, he would think her asleep and leave her alone. Then she could set her plan in motion to run away.

"I've had a personal visit from Lady Brent, and she kindly informed me of why you were out in the blizzard," he said, and she heard him pull up a chair by her bed. "I need to know why you risked your life to go and see her, and why you even needed to see her in the first place. Speak to me Sister, I must know what's going on in that silly head of yours."

Vera continued to try and ignore him. In her head, she wondered how she was going to explain herself for her unacceptable actions. She was still working it all out in her own mind, so how did he expect her to tell him the reasons why?

"I'm not going away, Vera," he spoke in a calm even voice. "You've been very ill with a fever, and no one knew what you were really doing out in that storm. Even Oscar doesn't know the full truth of it yet. It'll be far better if you tell me. Let me help you through whatever it is that made you do such a thing."

She knew he was right; her brother only ever showed her love. She shouldn't take it out on him, whatever the result of all this was going to be. Turning around to face him, she sat up in her bed to try her best to explain recent events.

"I... I no longer have a girlish crush on Oscar," she began, coughing to try and clear the lump in her throat.

"I'm pleased to hear it because—"

Raising her hand, she stopped Silas from replying, "You see, I now love him as a woman, and have done for what feels like forever."

She looked over at Silas, his face wrought with surprise.

"Don't worry, Brother. I have no intention of dragging you into any of this," she tried to reassure him.

"I'm not sure what that can mean but I am a part of anything that you're involved in, Vera," he said as his face softened. "We're together in whatever either of us experiences in our lives. You in mine and me in yours."

"No, we are no longer children," she retorted, determined not to involve him in her mess. "This is not something you can help me resolve, Silas. It's my burden and mine alone. I plan to leave Welwick Hall so that Oscar doesn't become aware of my...of my situation."

"You're going nowhere without me by your side, and you know that," Silas said, firmly. "And you haven't yet told me why you dressed up as me, and why you insisted on an audience with Lady Brent. What was it all about, Vera, speak to me, please?"

"You must forgive me for pretending to be you," she began to recall the night that she'd knocked on the door of Silsbury Manor. "As you know, I delivered the invitation for the ball to Silsbury Manor. I didn't want to raise any suspicions in case Lady Smith answered." She paused to catch her breath and ponder on whether she was doing the right thing involving her brother.

"Keep going. You can tell me, Sister, you must tell me so that I can help," Silas insisted, his eyes imploring her to continue.

"I broke the seal on the invitation so that I could slip in a note for Lady Brent's attention," Vera admitted. The memory of her actions was returning as she explained why she had behaved that way. "I'd insisted on delivering the invitation to her personally so that my note would not fall into the wrong hands. All the while I was dressed as you, or rather as Oscar's valet. And then I went into the stable to wait and see if she would turn up as I'd requested of her in the note."

"But why?" was all Silas could ask her.

"Because I knew that Oscar was taken by her. I wanted to make sure that if she was to marry him, it would be out of love. I don't want him having a wife who marries him for his wealth and status," Vera said, her voice shaking as she was reliving her confession. "You know what Lady Smith's like. She's only interested in Oscar for her daughter because he's a wealthy duke. I couldn't bear the thought of Oscar marrying a woman who didn't love him or make him happy."

"The whole thing might be funny if you hadn't become so ill," Silas said, lightening the mood in the room. "How did you come up with such a ridiculous plan?"

Vera picked up Oscar's Shakespearian book and showed it to her brother. "Do you know which play this is?"

"No, I never was that much interested in books, you know that," he shook his head.

"It's the one where a woman disguises herself as a man, all in the name of love," she sighed.

"What?" Silas looked at her and laughed. "What if Lady Brent had fallen head over heels in love with you, dressed as a man? Or rather, she'd have fallen in love with me really because I'm the handsome male in all of this, after all."

"Oh, you…" Vera saw the humour in her brother's words, and she threw the book at him. "Somehow, you've turned all this around and managed to lighten my mood. I've no idea how you always manage to do that when I'm down."

"Well, I do speak the truth in that Lady Brent would desire me and not you," he said with all seriousness, but she knew he was teasing her.

"Are you not mad at me for pretending to be you?" she asked.

"Lady Brent came to me because it seems that you came clean with her and showed your true self," Silas explained. "She first wanted to know if you had returned safely because the storm was raging that night. And then she asked me to tell you that she would keep your secret. I didn't understand what she meant, but now that you've admitted your love for Oscar, I can only assume that she knew why you did what you did."

"Are you telling me that Oscar is not aware of any of this?" she asked in surprise. "Didn't he want to know why I was ill?"

"It seems that you were out in your stupid garden protecting your plants from the storm," Silas said, pleased to see a smile, at last, on his sister's face.

"Tell me, Brother, I know we look alike, and that the young ladies all think you a handsome catch, but where does that put me? Do you think me pretty?" she asked, praying he would be truthful.

"You, Sister, have grown into a beautiful young woman, and me a handsome young man, of course," he added. "But as a man, I can tell you that it's not about how a woman looks. A good man will see kindness in you, he will see how clever you are, and he will admire your loyalty and determination."

"You think me loyal when I betrayed Oscar by nearly ruining his chances with Lady Brent?" she asked, laying back on her pillow, now that her worries were eased and all thanks to her brother.

"Lady Brent has proven that she is worthy of Oscar. She is not seeking to embarrass you or even reveal what you've done. All she cared about was that you were well," Silas pointed out the good things in the lady.

"Yes, I too think she's worthy of Oscar. That also breaks my heart," she replied, realising it would still be hard for her, even if Oscar and his new wife were in love.

"You're not running away from this," Silas insisted. "We will work through it together. You're surrounded by people who love you, Vera, you wouldn't like being alone."

"But you know I will suffer once Oscar marries?" she admitted.

"Let's face each day as it comes," Silas suggested, and his common sense surprised her. "For now, you need to put your mind to your work. You have a lot of food to prepare for this Christmastide ball."

"Yes, I do feel like I'll enjoy that challenge better," she nodded her head, and she knew that Silas was right, for now at least.

Silas stood up and leaned in to hug his sister. "You're not quite yourself yet, so you still need to rest. And no more planning on leaving Welwick Hall. Think, instead, of keeping it going. What is a lord if he doesn't serve good food, eh?"

"Thank you, Silas, I do feel better," she said as he turned to leave the room. "But the problem will not go away. Oscar does need to find a wife; we can't deny that."

"As I said, we'll take each day at a time, and when it happens, I'll be there to see you through it," he promised.

Vera laid back, pulling her blankets up around her head. She felt exhausted, even at only having a conversation. At least her fever had broken, and she'd pulled through the worst. But her love for Oscar would never leave her. As her brother said though, that was a problem for another day.

CHAPTER 34
1 MONTH LATER...THE BALL

Over the next month, Olive reluctantly attended the dinners and soirees that her mother insisted she attended. These included several dinners at Welwick Hall, which she welcomed now that she was getting to know the Duke better.

Olive did nothing to dissuade her mother's belief that the Duke was becoming fond of her, but she knew differently. It was lucky that, for most of the time, her mother was busy with the build-up of excitement among her friends, over the upcoming ball. This at least meant that she left her daughter in peace. The Duke had also been kept busy, finding his feet in his new responsibilities as the Duke of Cornwall.

Olive had come across the handsome valet, Silas Atkins, many times on her visits to Welwick Hall. She'd decided to maintain a means of secrecy about her growing friendship with the twins, from both her mother and the Duke. What her mother did not know, could not harm her.

After the incident with Vera, Olive had made secret visits to Welwick Hall to meet with Silas, so that she could better understand his sister. When Silas informed her of Vera's intention to leave Welwick Hall, she wanted to do all she could to dissuade her. She had a growing fondness for the Duke, he was a decent and kind gentleman. But her friendship with his two favourite servants gave her much joy.

At first, her visits were intended to assure Vera that she held no malice towards her for trying to deceive her and warn her off the Duke. She liked the young woman very much, and it turned out that they had a shared interest in books. As their friendship grew, the two women often met in the bookshop at the local town, where they would discuss their favourites of the latest literary works. Though Olive only ever met with Silas when she visited the Duke.

It was there that she'd first come up with a bright idea, or so she thought it was. Although it hadn't come about until Vera had confided in her that she yearned to dance with the Duke, as if she was one of the ladies at a ball. As it turned out, Olive was glad that she hadn't gone to Scotland because she had a plan that she hoped to put in motion. A plan that might help Vera live her dream because Olive knew exactly how it could be achieved.

The day of the Christmas ball had finally arrived, and her mother was bouncing around with far too much energy and enthusiasm. They arrived in their small, humble carriage, much simpler than the carriages that were lining up in the driveway to bring in the other guest. It seemed to concern her mother, but Olive herself was unimpressed. The attendees of this ball would be the very cream of society, but that failed to affect Olive in any way whatsoever.

Stepping out of her carriage, the gardens were buzzing with the ladies and lords of high society. They dressed in their elaborate refinery, milling around to show off their riches, likened to peacocks. Everyone wore masks to cover half their face for the masquerade theme, but for the most part, Olive could tell who was who.

One of her mother's friends, Lady Gregson, approached to

greet them, and her mother walked with the lady toward the entrance of the hall. She overheard her mother boasting how she hoped that tonight the Duke would announce his engagement to her daughter. Whilst it annoyed Olive, she had become accustomed to her mother's fantasy that she and the Duke were more than just friends.

It was true that she had got to know the Duke better, but unlike her mother, she knew that the Duke was not considering her as his future wife. Though she did like him and enjoyed his company too, and in the unlikely event he was to ask her, she knew exactly what her answer would be.

Once in the ballroom, they mingled and were soon swallowed up in the crowds of tittering and merriment. It was fun working out everyone's disguises, adding a touch of intrigue to the ball. The Duke came over to request she put him on her dance card, and she noticed her mother's face light up with delight as if it was her that he'd asked. Olive was a little less of a drama queen than her mother and she politely accepted, writing his name on her card that was almost full already.

"So, you recognised me despite my baroque mask then, my Lord?" Olive chuckled at the Duke.

"Well, it was more a case that your mother is not wearing her mask at the moment. That is what gave you away," he replied, giving her that dimpled smile that she knew all the ladies found very attractive. "I will leave you to enjoy the ball, ladies," he said, giving them a respectful bow.

"Did you hear that, Judith?" Her mother wittered to her little group of friends. "The Duke has requested to dance with my daughter. I wonder how many dances he will insist upon?"

Olive rolled her eyeballs discretely at her mother's ramblings. After an hour of shadowing her mother around the hall, she finally made her excuse to leave her, saying that she needed to get some fresh air.

"Let me see your card, dear," her mother insisted. "I see that you had better not take too long. You are to dance with the Duke next."

"I am well aware of what is on my dance card, Mother," she responded sharply. "Seeing as I was the one to write upon it."

Before her mother could utter another word, Olive turned around and marched away. She felt very smug with herself, envisioning her mother's face at her reply. She had looked aghast and was unable to reprimand her in front of her friends. It had been most satisfying.

Her light blue ballgown had been designed with a train and it trailed behind her, so she was forced to slow down her pace. Normally, she wore last year's fashions without a care for whether the ladies liked it or not. But for this occasion, she'd chosen a most exquisite and expensive design for a specific reason, and she had to admit to herself that she did feel good in it.

Floating through the crowds, she was turning faces with her most exquisite and expensive design. She was glad it had short puffy sleeves to cool her down, and she slipped a matching long, lace glove off her arm as she arrived outside. Her dress was made of light lacey fabric, covered from top to bottom in small, hand-sewn delicate flower heads. The square neckline afforded a peek at her cleavage, as was fashionable for ladies at such balls.

Standing for a while, she breathed in the cooler air. Her mother came to mind and Olive knew that the time had come to finally put her mother in her place. She'd had enough of her arranging every small detail in her life, and now enough was enough. Knowing that she should have done it sooner didn't help, because the fact was that it wasn't in her character to put people down. Olive liked to help people, not upset them. And that was why she was about to do what she had planned for a while now, and it was to happen on this very night.

"Do you know where Lady Olive has got herself to?" the Duke asked Olive's mother as he was looking for her for the next dance.

"Heavens, Your Grace," Lady Smith replied, with a look of indignation. "My daughter is a fool if she misses dancing with you. I cannot know what she gets up to. She went for some air outside, and it has been quite some time now."

"Not to worry, Lady Smith, the music has not yet begun," he said. "There is time yet. Are you enjoying the Christmastide ball, I see you do not wear your mask?"

"Oh, this thing," she laughed with embarrassment. "I find it too small and too tight. It doesn't help that I cannot hold conversation with my friends if I wear it."

"Do you not approve of my theme?" he asked, more to make light conversation while he awaited the return of Olive.

"Everyone looks wonderful in their masks. But I do like to see people's faces better. Then, I can better judge them," she pointed out, not the least embarrassed with her reply. Although Oscar knew that she liked to be centre of attention, the complete opposite of her daughter. "Ah, here she comes now, Your Grace" Lady Smith pointed her fan at her daughter who was approaching. "We went to another town for the fitting of that dress, is it not the best gown of the ball? You should crown her the Bella of the Ball."

Oscar turned to greet Lady Olive, saying, "Yes, and the mask you wear, Lady Olive, does you justice," he said as he bent his arm for her to hook into it.

"I apologise if I am late," she replied, turning around to glance around the crowd. "Shall we?" She dared herself to hook her arm into his elbow to get away from her mother, and the Duke led her to the dance floor.

Taking their place for the Allemande, he chatted to her, but she was exceptionally quiet. The music began and they started the twirls expected of them. He was pleased to have chosen this particular dance with her because it involved a lot of contact. As they moved around the dance floor, he was most impressed with her dancing skills. In fact, there was something odd in her behaviour, and he found himself with feelings he'd never felt for her before.

Oscar decided that he must have drunk too much brandy and wine because he had never felt this way about Lady Olive before. They had become good friends, despite her annoying mother. But this was the first time that she'd stirred feelings in him of this nature.

"Your perfume is different, is it not?" He'd asked her at one point because it was a fragrance that he was familiar with but couldn't quite recall where from.

"Do you disapprove of it, Your Grace?" she asked, and her voice trembled with worry. Yet he knew that Lady Olive never worried over anything much.

"On the contrary," he replied as they came together again in the steps of the dance. "It is an aroma I am familiar with, but I cannot quite place it."

As the dance routine caused them to part again, he was fast becoming confused. Why was Olive seeming so different? Could it be that had changed her mind and was now wanting to become his prospective future wife after all? If that was the case, then he really had to talk with her. He took in a deep breath while he was away from her, and they were soon back together again.

Oscar took her smaller hand in his, attempting to hold a conversation with her as they moved along. Surprisingly, she was still unwilling to communicate with him, answering with various nods of her head. He'd never felt that their friendship was strained before, but he was struggling to understand why she was behaving so distant with him.

"Have I offended you in some way, Lady Olive?" he finally asked as their bodies touched.

"Most certainly not, Your Grace," she replied, and he noticed her eyes looked surprised behind her masquerade mask. Eyes that were ever more familiar, but not with Lady Olive. "I am relishing our time together," she added in a whisper.

Whatever is going on? He wondered as he was forced to part from her. *Is she telling me that she has feelings for me? I was not even aware I felt this way for her, I mean, I don't... I...*

In his confusion, he missed a step, but he was an experienced enough dancer to soon put it right. Again, they came together, and each leaned into the other.

"By Jove, that's it!" He said louder than he had meant to.

This time it was Olive who faltered, "Are you unwell, Your Grace" she whispered as they glanced at one another.

"I have never been better," he said, giving her a huge grin as the steps in the dance forced them to go different ways.

It was only mere seconds, but he couldn't wait to take hold of her hand again. He longed to speak with her and felt tempted to take her from the dance floor, but that would cause too much of a stir.

At last, they were coming together for the end of the dance, and he took her hand in his, pulling her closer to him again.

Yes, it is you, is it not?

He kept his thoughts to himself as he glanced at her sparkling eyes through the mask. He would know that scent of sweet cinnamon in her hair anywhere. The brandy must have dulled his senses for him not to have realised sooner. Being this close to her made him realise that this was a woman that he truly loved. Here was a woman that he never wanted to lose, and now it was time to make sure that never happened.

CHAPTER 35

Overwhelmed with emotions, Vera felt certain that her trickery had been uncovered. In the final steps of the dance, the Duke pulled her closer to him, staring into her eyes. It was at that moment that she was sure he knew his partner was not Lady Olive. Panic set into her mind, and she felt a hard and fast thudding sensation in her chest. Should she apologise so that he wouldn't expose her? Feeling sick to the stomach, she was unable to think fast enough on what she should do.

The music ended and time seemed to slow down in her mind. It had come as an utter shock when her brother had come to her with Lady Olive's idea. They'd all become good friends and she soon learned that Lady Olive was not looking to marry, despite her mother's constant attempts.

She'd also come to believe that Lady Olive would make the perfect wife for Oscar, she was kind and caring and would learn to love him one day. Yet here she stood, in Lady Olive's sensational fashionable dress, in the arms of the man who she truly loved. But she never believed for one moment that he'd discover it was her and not Lady Olive, if she had she would never have agreed to the deception. The party mask over her face was meant to disguise her well, but it seemed that it had failed her.

Ah well... I have had the most wonderful of times dancing with you, Oscar, she thought as she waited to see what his next move would be. The music had been enchanting, her gown was exquisite, and her dancing partner was perfect. Thanks to Lady Olive, one of her dreams had come true, to dance with Oscar at a ball.

When Oscar remained on the dance floor, staring at her, she thought that she should make good her escape. Perhaps he wouldn't expose her there and then, and find her later to ask what she'd been playing at, deceiving him by pretending to be a Lady. Not only did she need to get off the dance floor, but she also wanted to avoid Lady Adelia Smith, at all costs. Lady Olive's mother would know immediately that the woman in the light blue gown was not her daughter.

Vera knew that she had to pull away from Oscar, and it took all her willpower to allow this moment to end. Turning, she wanted to leave the dance floor with pride and not rush at it, that would only draw attention to herself. As she twisted around to do so, the Duke grabbed at her hand, interlacing his fingers with hers.

What is this? Why is he holding my hand so intimately? Her mind jolted in fear. *He's going to expose me, but why? I can't exactly ignore him; I must hope that he isn't aware of the truth.*

All around her, ladies were pointing their fingers at her and she could hear their gasps. Was Oscar going to make a spectacle of her? It wasn't like him to do such a thing, but perhaps she'd taken things a step too far. The hall had reached a crescendo of gasps and gossip, with all eyes now on the Duke. An eerie silence erupted and in Vera's view, it was deafening because she was now the centre of attention.

They hadn't agreed on a plan of action if their deception was discovered. When Vera had asked her about it, Lady Olive had told her that she must not overthink things. Vera had been so excited at the prospect of a real ballroom dance with Oscar that she hadn't objected. *And now look where it's got me.*

The Duke let go of her hand, allowing Vera to look all around. She wished she hadn't done so because the look of surprise on everyone's faces horrified her.

As she turned back around to beg the Duke to forgive her, he was on one knee in front of her.

Oh no! He believes me to be Lady Olive, what am I going to do?

"You are indeed a mysterious lady," he said out loud, as the entire room hushed into utter silence.

Vera had the eerie sensation that it was only she and Oscar in the room and everyone else had magically faded away. He was smiling at her, and she knew that she had to take off her mask before he proposed to her instead of Lady Olive.

Again, Vera came back to the reality of the ballroom. This time she looked around desperately for Lady Olive. At least she might save her with some kind of explanation, but instead, she spotted her mother, Lady Adelia Smith, wearing a huge grin. She still believed she was her daughter.

Heavens, I've made a terrible mistake, and all to steal a dance with the Duke. Oh dear, it's such a cost to Lady Olive because now they all believe I'm her. I can't possibly reveal myself—

To make things worse, she noticed Lady Olive standing behind her mother, wearing a huge smile on her face. She watched in horror as she tapped her mother on the shoulder. Everything seemed to slow down as Lady Smith turned around to look at her daughter in total disbelief. The horrified woman then turned back to look at the dance floor; wondering who was with the Duke. Vera watched on as Lady Smith all but fainted, the gentleman by her side reached out to stop her from falling.

Vera knew that she had to be honest with Oscar, and she turned back to face him so that she could reveal herself. But she found it so hard to do, she couldn't bear to see the disappointment on his face.

All around her were squeals and gasps as the scene unfolded. Olive could hear whispers as the onlookers wondered who was this mysterious woman. But Oscar did not wear a look of surprise, he looked up at her with his dimpled grin and then he spoke.

"I would like to ask the mysterious lady if she will be my wife?" he said, his eyes never leaving hers as he spoke.

Vera's lips moved to reply, but her voice had deserted her. She could say nothing, but she had to. Oscar thought he was asking Lady Olive to marry him, she had to let him know of her trickery.

He looked at her and she swore she could see amusement in his eyes. *What is he up to? Oh, my word, I think I'm going faint too, what am I to do?*

∼

Oscar was giving the lady in the mask one of his best smiles because he hoped it would put her at ease. Right now, she looked like a rabbit caught in the stare of a predating fox. It was time to move things on and put her out of her misery. He stood up and took one of her hands in his. It concerned him how much she was shaking; he'd never meant for her to become so alarmed. The sooner he ended this the better.

With his free hand, he reached over and pulled the mask from his mystery woman.

As he revealed her beautiful face, the entire room gasped all at once. Their gasps soon turned into gabbles of gossip as they stared at the Duke on the dance floor.

Knowing that revealing her identity would set her in a panic again, he spoke to her, "At least you are not disguised as a man this time."

Not waiting for an answer, he raised the hand that held her mask to quieten down the throng. "Quiet!" he called out, and that one word caused the entire crowd to hush.

"I want to announce that my future wife is now chosen," he

began, looking around at his guests with a smile on his lips. "Lords and ladies, please meet the new duchess-to-be. Her name is currently Miss Vera Atkins, but that is soon to change. Will you all bow to the soon-to-be Duchess of Cornwall. I present to you the soon-to-be Lady Vera Wald," he proclaimed.

Turning back to her, he paused for a moment to study her face. Still frozen in horror, he knew that she was now in shock, but at least it was a different kind of shock. She wouldn't be trying to escape the room; she would be trying to take in what had just happened to her.

To help her, he spoke again. "I wish to remind you all, Ladies and Lords of the ton, that this is the Twelfth Night of Christmastide. Do you know what means?" He asked of them in a mocking tone because he intended on putting each one of them in their place. "Let me remind you then; it marks the coming of the Epiphany. The Epiphany is the night that we can undo all the rules, or, as Sir William Shakespeare put it, it is a night of What You Will."

Oscar turned to his sweetheart, hoping that by now she might have calmed, but instead her face had changed into one of horror. "I do this for you, my love," he whispered so that only she could hear him.

Then he turned back to his audience to speak with them again because this time there had been no outbursts of gossip. Even they were in shock as the event unfolded.

"You were promised that this ball would be a night to remember," he called out for all to hear. "To encourage you all to return to your evening of joy and merriment, answer me, who is ready to begin a time of wassailing?"

As he said his final words, from every doorway of the hall stewards entered with wheeled trolleys. Each brought in huge bowls of wassail ale so that the gaiety might continue into the night.

To his relief, it seemed to do the trick. The stewards filled silver mugs with the spicy liquid and the guests took gulps and then passed it around as the tradition dictated.

Pleased to see the attention was now turned back to drinking, Oscar turned to Vera, and her look of fear was now replaced with surprise.

"You have always been the woman who I was going to choose for my wife," he explained. "That was why I held this ball. But I didn't know how I would pull it off. It seems that you resolved that issue for me."

He paused, remaining close to her, and hoping his presence might help her relax.

"Well, then, my love, what say you? Will you marry me?" he asked for a second time.

"If you are truly interested in my answer, Your Grace, I say yes."

With that, he held out both hands, and she took them as they stared at each other, their love obvious for all around them to see. He led her back into the crowd, who were now busy enjoying the celebrations.

"But Oscar," Vera whispered into his ear before they left the dance floor. "How did you know it was me?"

"I didn't at first," he replied. "But the cinnamon in your hair gave you away. The fact is, Vera, I was going to propose to you tonight anyway. But thanks to Lady Olive's craftiness, it has allowed me to make my proposal a public event. That is far better because they will all know now of our love for one another. We have gone public, Vera, and if you will have me, then we can be together for the rest of our lives."

He could see that Vera was happy and that gave him a sense of calm and joy too.

"All this time I have loved you" he shared with her. "I was not sure if, now that you are a grown woman, you loved me too. Tonight, I was to put that question to the test. If you refused, then I was going to ask you and Silas to become my companions instead of remaining as servants at Welwick Hall. I cannot live a moment longer with you both in servitude."

"Did my brother know of your feelings for me?" she asked.

"He did not. I could not risk your rejection too early and so I came up with the idea of this ball," he said, squeezing her hand firmly. "But we are to be together now as equals, and soon as man and wife. It took a while before I realised this is what I wanted, but once I did, I knew I had to make it happen."

"I have always loved you, Oscar, and I cannot believe that you feel the same, but it makes me happy to know you do," she said to him.

He opened his arms and she moved into them to accept his warm embrace. Surrounded by the ton, they were together at last. And that was something they had both ached for and finally achieved on the Twelfth Night of Christmastide.

EPILOGUE
FOUR WEEKS LATER...

Where had the time gone?
　　Vera had been swept off her feet ever since that most wonderful Twelfth Night ball. With Lady Olive now her confidante, they had turned out to be the best of friends. With their shared interest in books, they'd soon found they had many other shared interests too.

It was the morning of Vera's wedding, and she was feeling ill with excitement. She paced around the huge bedroom chamber that Oscar had insisted that she move into. Still, she missed her tiny, old bedroom, it had been cosier, while this one seemed large and empty to her.

Will I ever get used to living in the main part of Welwick Hall? She wondered as her thoughts jumped all over the place.

She felt a sense of relief as Lady Olive entered her room.

"Come along Vera, you look ill with worry. You simply must put your mind to better things." Lady Olive spoke with a firm voice, which was exactly what Vera needed to ground her wandering thoughts. "The modiste has arrived and is waiting in one of the parlours to dress you in your gown."

Vera followed her friend down the huge stairway, and it seemed to her that the entire house was abuzz with activity. Sweeping through all the activity, it unnerved her. She should be with the servants, readying Welwick Hall for the event. When she arrived in the parlour, not only was the modiste there but there were so many other assistants too. Everyone milled around her to do her dress and her hair, and goodness knows what else they were to put her through.

"Is all this fuss necessary?" she questioned Lady Olive as the modiste was dressing her.

"This is a very special wedding, and well you know it," Lady Olive reminded her.

The entire fitting seemed to take forever. Finally, someone took her arm and led her to stand in front of a long mirror, and she gasped with shock.

"Oh, Heavens!" she called out with her hand to her mouth. "This is far too luxurious for me. Can I not wear something a little simpler?"

The modiste looked aghast at her remark, but Lady Olive was quick to step in. "Miss Vera, I assure you that this is a simple gown, and you look stunning in it. I helped to design it, and with every fold and tuck, I envisaged you in mind."

Vera glanced at the modiste who looked relieved that someone else was taking responsibility for the dress she had made, but not designed.

"But it seems so fancy, with all its lace and layers and...what I mean is that it's beautiful, but—"

"The fabrics are of the finest silks with delicate laces of the best quality," Lady Olive told her. "You must dress as a duchess now, Miss Vera, because you are to be one by the end of this day."

"I know, and I do thank you, Lady Olive, for all that you do for me," Vera said shyly. "I suppose it is all so overwhelming and I will adjust...eventually."

"Come now, we must get ourselves to the ballroom, or there

will be no wedding without the bride present." Lady Olive took her by the arm and led her out of the parlour room.

"I can't believe that Oscar acquired a special licence to hold the wedding in the ballroom. It was so romantic of him," Vera remarked as was shuffled along.

It wasn't that Vera didn't know where the ballroom was, but she was so nervous that it pleased her that Lady Olive led the way.

"Well, it is the place where your whole life took a change for the better," Lady Olive replied. "It is like a fairy tale where you finally got the man you love," Lady Olive added, smiling as she stopped in the hallway to give Vera one final check over.

"Look at all the food in the dining room!" Vera exclaimed as they walked past the open doorway. "How did they manage it all without me?"

"Oh, my dear, dear Vera, you shall never cook again so you might as well get used to it," Lady Olive told her as they neared the ballroom. "You will have to trust in your new cook from this day forth."

From a distance, Vera could see that the tall double doors to the ballroom were open. Even though there were not to be many guests attending their wedding, Vera was still shaking with nerves. She spotted her brother and felt an instant calm as he approached her.

"You look very dashing," she said to him, looking at his top hat and tailcoat.

"You don't look so bad yourself, Sister," he replied with a look of pride shining in his eyes. Reaching out, he took her arm to hook it in his elbow. "Shall we?" he said, pointing to the open doorway.

Vera was aware that Lady Olive had organised everything for her wedding, and when she stopped shaking, she would thank her. For now, she hooked her arm into Silas's elbow. He led her down the centre of the rows of chairs where the guests were seated.

To the front of the hall, Lady Olive had arranged a special scene using stage props. A huge archway was threaded with bright yellow and pink blooms. Vera could smell the sweet scents and it helped to settle her nerves a little. Underneath the floral archway stood her love, Lord Oscar Wald, the Duke of Cornwall. As she spotted him, her knees wobbled as her handsome fiancé smiled back at her with his familiar dimple.

For the next hour, she repeated the words she was told to say, but Vera fell in a daze throughout the whole service. Before long, Oscar's warm lips brushed against hers, and she melted in his embrace. At last, all her nerves and fears evaporated as she was in the arms of the man she had always loved. Now she was safe and loved. And now, they were husband and wife; was it all true, or was it a dream?

Barker and the maids led them all to the dining room, but Vera was escorted by her new husband. Even better, she was delighted to be seated by his side.

She watched on as servants, of whom she knew them all, began to serve the late breakfast feast. Vera made an effort to smile at every one of them because they were all her friends too. It pleased her even more as each of them went out of their way to whisper their congratulations in her ear; she loved them for it. Some even told her that they'd known all along how much she loved the Duke. The revelation had surprised her, as she had always thought that she had hidden it well, but clearly not as well as she'd hoped.

Finally, Silas stood up to give his wedding speech, and as he did so, all the servants entered the room.

"In this room all the people who are important to my sister," he began as he held open his arms to include the servants who were standing at the back and now holding a glass of bubbly.

"For you, my dear sister, I knew that you would want to include your entire household under that title, and so I've invited them all to come and take a toast with us."

With those words Vera stood up began to applause, and everyone followed her lead. She stood up and mouthed the word *thank you* to the servants, before sitting down again.

Silas went on to congratulate His Grace for being so crafty in thinking up a way that he could propose to his sister. He then went on to tell the guests how he had helped too because he'd never have a moment's peace from his sister if she hadn't married the man of her dreams.

Applause rang out and laughter filled the air as they all raised their glass in a toast. She felt the warmth of Oscar's arm touching hers and it felt good. Looking at those around her, she was pleased to see that they were all people who she trusted. These were the people who would help her accept her new life, a life she had only dreamed of, and now her dream had come true.

THE END

Oscar and Vera lived happily ever after... But the Welwick Hall is full of secrets and the Twelfth Night's Annual Ball was meant to bring love for more than one couple... Lady Olive has her own chance at true love at her story "Olive At The Ballroom"

Read it now!

THANK YOU

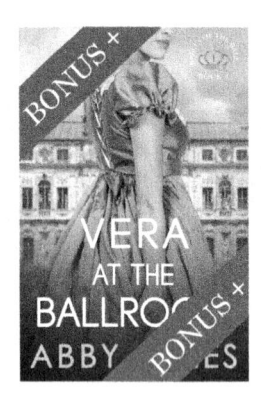

Thank you for reading "Vera At The Ballroom" and purchasing a book from me and Starfall Publications. It means a lot to us!

As a token of appreciation, we would like to offer you a Deleted Scene of this book and an exclusive free book available only for our VIP readers!

Type the following link on your browser:

https://abbyayles.com/aa-062-exep/

SCANDALS AND SEDUCTION IN REGENCY ENGLAND

ALSO IN THIS SERIES

Last Chance for the Charming Ladies
Redeeming Love for the Haunted Ladies
Broken Hearts and Doting Earls
The Keys to a Lockridge Heart
Regency Tales of Love and Mystery
Chronicles of Regency Love
Broken Dukes and Charming Ladies
The Ladies, The Dukes and Their Secrets
Regency Tales of Graceful Roses
The Secret to the Ladies' Hearts
The Return of the Courageous Ladies
Falling for the Hartfield Ladies
Extraordinary Tales of Regency Love
Dukes' Burning Hearts
Escaping a Scandal
Regency Loves of Secrecy and Redemption
Forbidden Loves and Dashing Lords
Fateful Romances in the Most Unexpected Places
The Mysteries of a Lady's Heart

Regency Widows Redemption
The Secrets of Their Heart
Lovely Dreams of Regency Ladies
Second Chances for Broken Hearts
Trapped Ladies
Light to the Marquesses' Hearts
Falling for the Mysterious Ladies
Tales of Secrecy and Enduring Love
Fateful Twists and Unexpected Loves
Regency Wallflowers
Regency Confessions
Ladies Laced with Grace
Journals of Regency Love
A Lady's Scarred Pride
How to Survive Love
Destined Hearts in Troubled Times
Ladies Loyal to their Hearts
The Mysteries of a Lady's Heart
Secrets and Scandals
A Lady's Secret Love
Falling for the Wrong Duke
Dukes and Duchesses of Love
Regency Rakes and Radiant Brides
Dukes' Bridal
Dukes Duchesses and Scandals
Dukes and Hidden Truths
Secrets Scandals and Society

ALSO BY ABBY AYLES

The Keys to a Lockridge Heart
Melting a Duke's Winter Heart
A Loving Duke for the Shy Duchess
Freed by the Love of an Earl
The Earl's Wager for a Lady's Heart
The Lady in the Gilded Cage
A Reluctant Bride for the Baron
A Christmas Worth Remembering
A Guiding Light for the Lost Earl
The Earl Behind the Mask

∽

Tales of Magnificent Ladies
The Odd Mystery of the Cursed Duke
A Second Chance for the Tormented Lady
Capturing the Viscount's Heart
The Lady's Patient
A Broken Heart's Redemption

ABBY AYLES

The Lady The Duke And the Gentleman
Desire and Fear
A Tale of Two Sisters
What the Governess is Hiding

∽

Betrayal and Redemption
Inconveniently Betrothed to an Earl
A Muse for the Lonely Marquess
Reforming the Rigid Duke
Stealing Away the Governess
A Healer for the Marquess's Heart
How to Train a Duke in the Ways of Love
Betrayal and Redemption
The Secret of a Lady's Heart
The Lady's Right Option

∽

Forbidden Loves and Dashing Lords
The Lady of the Lighthouse
A Forbidden Gamble for the Duke's Heart
A Forbidden Bid for a Lady's Heart
A Forbidden Love for the Rebellious Baron
Saving His Lady from Scandal
A Lady's Forgiveness
Viscount's Hidden Truths
A Poisonous Flower for the Lady

∽

Marriages by Mistake
The Lady's Gamble

VERA AT THE BALLROOM

Engaging Love
Caught in the Storm of a Duke's Heart
Marriage by Mistake
The Language of a Lady's Heart
The Governess and the Duke
Saving the Imprisoned Earl
Portrait of Love
From Denial to Desire
The Duke's Christmas Ball

~

The Dukes' Ladies
Entangled with the Duke
A Mysterious Governess for the Reluctant Earl
A Cinderella for the Duke
Falling for the Governess
Saving Lady Abigail
The Duke's Rebellious Daughter
The Duke's Juliet
Secret Dreams of a Fearless Governess
A Daring Captain for Her Loyal Heart
Loving A Lady
Unlocking the Secrets of a Duke's Heart

GET ABBY'S EXCLUSIVE MATERIAL

Building a relationship with my readers is the very best thing about writing.

Join my newsletter for information on new books and deals plus a few free books!

You can get your books by clicking or visiting the link below

https://BookHip.com/MDRMLCA

PS. Come join our Facebook Group if you want to interact with me and other authors from Starfall Publication on a daily basis, win FREE Giveaways and find out when new content is being released.

Join our Facebook Group

abbyayles.com/Facebook-Group

About Starfall Publications

Starfall Publications has helped me and so many others extend my passion from writing to you.

The prime focus of this company has been – and always will be – *quality* and I am honored to be able to publish my books under their name.

Having said that, I would like to officially thank Starfall Publications for offering me the opportunity to be part of such a wonderful, hard-working team!

Thanks to them, my dreams – and your dreams — have come true!

Visit their website starfallpublications.com and download their 100% FREE books!

A Message from Abby

Dear Reader,

Thank you for reading! I hope you enjoyed every page and I would love to hear your thoughts whether it be a review online or you contact me via my website. I am eternally grateful for you and none of this would be possible without our shared love of romance.

I pray that someday I will get to meet each of you and thank you in person, but in the meantime, all I can do is tell you how amazing you are.

As I prepare my next love story for you, keep believing in your dreams and know that mine would not be possible without you.

With Love, Abby Ayles

PS. Come join our Facebook Group if you want to interact with me and other authors from Starfall Publication on a daily basis, win FREE Giveaways and find out when new content is being released.

[Join our Facebook Group](#)

abbyayles.com/Facebook-Group

Join my newsletter for information on new books and deals plus a few free books!

A MESSAGE FROM ABBY

You can get your books by clicking or visiting the link below
https://BookHip.com/JBWAHR

ABOUT ABBY AYLES

Abby Ayles was born in the northern city of Manchester, England, but currently lives in Charleston, South Carolina, with her husband and their three cats. She holds a Master's degree in History and Arts and worked as a history teacher in middle school.

Her greatest interest lies in the era of Regency and Victorian England and Abby shares her love and knowledge of these periods with many readers in her newsletter.

In addition to this, she has also written her first romantic novel, *The Duke's Secrets*, which is set in the era and is available for free on her website. As one reader commented, *"Abby's writing makes you travel back in time!"*

When she has time to herself, Abby enjoys going to the theatre, reading, and watching documentaries about Regency and Victorian England.

Social Media

- Facebook
- Facebook Group

ABOUT ABBY AYLES

- Goodreads
- Amazon
- BookBub

Printed in Great Britain
by Amazon